This book should be returned to any branch of the
Lancashire County Library on or before the date shown

Lancashire County Library,
County Hall Complex,
1st floor Christ Church Precinct,
Preston, PR1 8XJ

Lancashire
County
Council

www.lancashire.gov.uk/libraries

LL1(A)

THORNFIELD HALL

Thornfield Hall, 1821. Alice Fairfax takes up her role as housekeeper of the estate. But when Mr Rochester presents her with a woman who is to be hidden on the third floor, she finds herself responsible for much more than the house.

This is the story Jane Eyre never knew — a narrative played out on the third floor and beneath the stairs, as the servants kept their master's secret safe and sound.

THORNFIELD HALL

JANE STUBBS

LARGE
PRINT

First published in Great Britain 2014
by
Corvus
an imprint of Atlantic Books Ltd.

First Isis Edition
published 2015
by arrangement with
Atlantic Books Ltd.

A catalogue record for this book is available
from the British Library.

ISBN 978–1–78541–054–3 (hb)
ISBN 978–1–78541–055–0 (pb)

Published by
F. A. Thorpe (Publishing)
Anstey, Leicestershire

Set by Words & Graphics Ltd.
Anstey, Leicestershire
Printed and bound in Great Britain by
T. J. International Ltd., Padstow, Cornwall

This book is printed on acid-free paper

To Alan who understood

Acknowledgements

Thanks are due to many people. Here are some of them:

First and foremost to Charlotte Brontë for writing a novel so full of vivid life that it is possible to walk about her creation and look behind the scenes.

To Teresa Chris for finding a publisher.

To Atlantic for bringing my infant to full term.

To the late Maggie Batteson, Pat Hadler, Mary Sharratt and Cath Staincliffe for their patient reading and helpful comments on my apprentice pieces.

Last but not least to A G de C Smale, she of the elegant initials who first introduced me to the glories of the English language and to all the others who followed in her footsteps.

My First Mr Rochester

1821

It was after I'd gone to my first Mr Rochester that my hair turned white. They do say it can happen overnight through disease or grief. In my case it was not so dramatic. Day by day the gold in my hair gently faded away until it was a pure snowy white. There I was, not yet forty and I had the hair of an old woman. I cannot blame illness for my transformation but I do think grief played its part. There had been many bereavements in my life, and in going to Thornfield Hall as housekeeper I said farewell to something that I had been raised from a child to regard as precious beyond rubies. According to my mother its preservation was as vital to an unmarried girl as her virginity. Like a maidenhead it was something to be treasured, not disposed of carelessly in an idle moment, for once lost it could never be recovered. I refer not to my virginity, which is long gone, but to my place in society. By being employed as a paid servant I was cast out from that privileged class of beings — the gentry.

My mother was gentry. As the daughter of a gentleman and the widow of a clergyman she claimed it as her birthright. She clung desperately to this status. It seemed to console her for the poverty and the meagreness of her life. Throughout my rather miserable childhood she drummed into me the importance of this mystical privilege that a gentlewoman must at all costs cherish and preserve. Never mind that we dined on crusts and scraps and had no fire before six o'clock of an evening; we were gentry and we had a servant to prove it, some poor unfortunate twelve-year-old village girl cozened into washing our dishes for a few pennies a week. If my mother ever discovered that I had swapped genteel poverty and semi-starvation for the good food and warmth enjoyed by the servants of a wealthy man she would turn in her grave.

For that is where she is. She left this world early but not before she contrived to see me suitably settled in life. Marriage was the only path open to me; my mother's constant lectures made that clear. I sleep-walked to my wedding. I woke one day to find I was married to the parson of the church in the village of Hay. Now a parson, no matter how poor he is, always counts as gentry. He will be invited to the big house for lunch during the week or supper on a Sunday. He will go to the front door and a servant will take his hat. The parson's wife, therefore, counts as gentry. And so my mother died happy that she had done right by me.

I was not with my parson for long. Just time enough to have and to lose one beautiful baby girl. Then the coughing sickness took my parson the next winter and by spring the new incumbent was knocking on the door of the parsonage. Mr Wood, the replacement for my

2

husband, had a pack of children and he was anxious to introduce them to their new home and to see the back of me. I was at a loss as to what to do.

My late husband was a sweet-tempered and mild-mannered man. He was very much a follower of the New Testament; he trusted in the Lord to provide. Consider the lilies of the field. Lay not treasures up for yourself on earth. That sort of thing. I am more of an Old Testament person myself. I like the drama of it: the feuds, the plots and the adultery. Perhaps that's why the Lord did not see fit to provide for me when I became a widow.

With no home and no income I became that most uncomfortable thing, a distant relative in need. My late husband was a Fairfax so I applied to his family. They sighed and held up their hands to show they were empty. They shuffled me about from house to house whenever there was extra work to be done. I sat up nights with the dying. I nursed the sick. While the family went away to the seaside I stayed to supervise the spring cleaning. They derived much satisfaction from being such exemplary Christians as to feed me and give me a roof over my head. They conveniently forgot that unlike a servant I received no wages.

It was an interesting if precarious life. A second cousin summoned me to help when her third baby was due. Her two lovely boys were soon joined by a baby girl. Such a pleasant time I had. I grew very fond of the children and began to hope I might make a real home with the family. One morning I was in the nursery supervising the children at their breakfast. The baby wriggled on my knee as I spooned porridge into her. Their mother arrived in her dressing gown with a letter in her hand. She waved it at me as she gave me the news. The wife of old Mr Rochester of Thornfield Hall had died; she too had been a Fairfax. To my second cousin the news was not all bad; she saw an opportunity to move me on.

"I'm sure Mr Rochester would be grateful for some help at this sad time, Alice. Especially from a female relation. Someone he could trust to deal with all those things his wife always dealt with. Men know nothing about running a house. You know what I mean: keep the housemaids in order, tell cook the soup was salty. I'll be sorry to see you go," she said, "but I won't need so much help soon. The boys will be away to school in the autumn."

I could see her mind working. She was thinking, Thornfield Hall is a large house. There must be a room somewhere that a parson's widow could occupy. She could do a little light needlework. She does not eat much. A bit of a fire in the winter. Old Mr Rochester is a man of property and wealth; he would not let a connection of his wife's starve. He would lend her back to me if, God forbid, I have another baby.

I was angry. And I was jealous. She had everything I had been denied. She had a husband with an income while I was a penniless widow. She had three healthy children while I had lain to rest my one baby girl who had scarcely drawn a breath. The rage churned about in my bosom all day. I hammered it down while I smiled and played with the boys and stroked the baby's soft hair. I knew I would be saying farewell to them soon.

My late husband always said his prayers before he lay down to sleep. In the morning he frequently claimed that his prayers had been answered. That night I berated God. I gave it to him hot and strong, told him that he had been unreasonably harsh in his dealings with me. I put it to him fair and square. I do not think my long and bitter diatribe could be regarded as a proper prayer but to my surprise I awoke with my mind clear and with a settled plan for determined action. You could say that my prayers had been answered.

I wrote to old Mr Rochester, with whom I was already acquainted. I reminded him that not only was I a Fairfax, I was also the widow of the parson at Hay whose church was close to the gates of Thornfield Hall. I included a suggestion that would have shocked my second cousin if I had been so foolish as to reveal it to her. I received an encouraging response. Some haggling followed but in the end I struck a bargain with the senior Mr Rochester that suited both of us. I knew how to run a house with economy and he could trust me not to steal the spoons. I became the paid housekeeper at Thornfield Hall.

Suddenly I wasn't gentry anymore. I was a servant, an upper servant to be sure, but a servant nonetheless. My second cousin went through a range of emotions. She was shocked that I had chosen to lose caste, angry that she could no longer call upon my unpaid services and finally relieved that the Fairfaxes could with clear consciences wash their hands of me. This they did with alacrity. I was on my own. It was frightening but also exhilarating. I squashed the flutterings of doubt that beat in my breast and set off to take up my new duties.

Mr Merryman, the butler, greeted me on my arrival at Thornfield Hall. I never saw anyone so unsuited to his name; his lugubrious face with its hanging jowls reminded me of the dogs they use for hunting hares and rabbits. Mr Merryman took it upon himself to ensure that I learnt how to do things properly. He would dine with me in the housekeeper's room. Our meals would be brought on a tray by one of the lower servants.

"We," he informed me, "are senior servants. Sometimes we are known as 'pugs' because we wear a serious expression with our mouths turned down like the pug dogs." He gestured to his own face with its drooping mouth. "Sometimes," he sighed, "I think it's permanent; I've done it for so long." As he showed me round the house Mr Merryman explained various other matters that he thought it important for me to know about my new position. As a mark of respect I would be called Mrs Fairfax by both the staff and the family, rather than just "Fairfax" as if I were a chambermaid.

Only two members of the family lived at the Hall. They were old Mr Rochester and his elder son Rowland. I remembered a younger son, Mr Edward, from my time at the parsonage in Hay. He was an open-faced friendly lad, usually whistling as he rode his horse about the countryside, but he had gone to live abroad somewhere.

6

As housekeeper I would wear my own clothes rather than a uniform. I promptly ordered a black silk dress to celebrate my new status as a woman who earned her own income. Mr Merryman explained to me that visitors sometimes came when the family was away. These callers might ask to be shown round the house. I was free to oblige them, as long as they were gentry of course. Mr Merryman tapped the side of his nose and for a moment his eyes twinkled in his sad face. "Tips!" He gave me a knowing look. "Good tips and all yours."

My bedroom was to be near the master's bedroom. As I was closely connected to the family it was thought more suitable. Mr Merryman had his own room on the next floor, close to where the servants slept. He liked to keep an eye on the young footmen, who could be quite frisky. All in all, Mr Merryman felt Thornfield Hall was a good house to work in. To be sure the wages were modest as old Mr Rochester was very near with his money, as we say in Yorkshire, but he kept a good table and there were enough staff to carry out the work of running a large house.

I soon got to know the staff. Leah, the under housemaid, quickly became a favourite of mine. There was Sam, officially a footman but really a Jack of all trades. He had been in the navy and had seen more of the world than any of us. There was a new footman, called John, though his given name was Timothy. It was the custom among the gentry to refer to footmen as John; it saved them having to remember their real names. The head coachman, who had been christened John, was usually called Old John to distinguish him from the footman. His wife Mary was the cook. These five formed the backbone of the staff. I soon discovered they were all fine honest people who knew their duties and carried them out well. There was a sprinkling of scullery maids, laundry maids, kitchen and stable boys who came and went as they learned their trade and moved on in the world. The only thorn in my flesh was Martha, the upper housemaid.

She was the most unbiddable girl I have ever come across. A great clumsy galumphing thing. She laid the breakfast table as if she was dealing cards. There was always a reason why she couldn't do as she was asked. If I told her to take the coal to the dining room she would do it later — she was on her way to answer the bell in the drawing room. Ask her to dust the hall and she would have to go and change her apron and would not be seen again until tea time. She was lazy and sharp-tongued with a neat way of passing the blame to the other servants. When Martha broke a vase it was Leah who was found sweeping up the shards of porcelain.

By searching out these and other examples of her bad behaviour I quickly found abundant reasons to justify my dislike of Martha. The real reason was deeper and more shameful. When Mr Rochester gave me a bedroom near his I had wondered if he might be minded to inflict some indignities on me. Innocent parson's wife I might be but even I knew such things happened. Sometimes in the mornings as I left my room to go about my duties old Mr Rochester would call to me from his bedroom. At first I hovered in the doorway to listen to his complaints. He had not slept well. The joints of his fingers were swollen and painful. Soon I was entering his room and rubbing his hands. Then it was his shoulders. Matters did not progress much further. To be honest I took no offence at giving him these small attentions. He was an old man who had lost his wife and who missed the touch of a woman's hand.

Martha was never punctual in her duties. For her the clock was just a tiresome picture on the wall. She arrived very early one morning with the hot water and caught me leaving Mr Rochester's room. I wore my nightgown under my dressing gown, and my hair, still golden then, hung loose about my shoulders. I told Martha sharply that the master had called me in as he felt unwell. To give the master his due, he played up to the fiction nicely by staying in bed for the rest of the morning. He drew the line at sending for Carter, the surgeon. That would have cost him money.

I was never sure that Martha believed me.

In spite of this minor worry, for a year or so I was able to enjoy a very pleasant existence, until the course of my life was upset by the cold hand of death. His icy fingers were not laid upon old Mr Rochester as you might expect but upon Mr Rowland, the elder son. Mr Rowland was not my favourite person. He was a whey-faced lanky creature, always indoors doing his calculations or peering through his magnifying glass. He was the kind of boy who pulled the wings off flies, or captured harmless insects as they were going about

9

their lawful business and stuck pins in them. Science he called it. Well, science didn't do him much good. He went gallivanting off to visit a coal mine in the north where they had one of those new-fangled steam engines. In the interest of science, no doubt, he went too close to the machine and got himself crushed by the metal monster. He died of his injuries before they could carry him home.

Old Mr Rochester took it very hard. The lawyers came with long faces and talked to him about the future and advised him to call his younger son, Mr Edward, home. He wouldn't hear of it, just shook his head and poured out more port. The only comfort he could find was at the table. I've lost count of the roast dinners he ate without adding an ounce of fat to his skinny frame. We servants tip-toed round the house and shared our fears in whispers. Our master was a broken man and his lawful heir was in exile. Our futures looked very insecure.

One evening Mr Rochester rose from the table having dined on roast duck with green peas. He had drunk with it a bottle of claret. Afterwards he sluiced down a bowl of Bavarian cream and demolished half a pound of Wensleydale cheese. "Damn fine —" he began. His compliment was interrupted as he clutched at his throat and fell backwards against the sideboard. I will never know whether it was the duck, the pudding or the cheese that had taken his fancy.

The footmen helped him to his bed. Old John sat up with him that night. In the morning old Mr Rochester was dead. Mr Carter, the surgeon, scratched his head as he felt for the pulse that was not to be found. "Don't understand it. He was fit as a flea." Not one to worry overmuch about minor details Mr Carter declared, "I suppose I should call it a Visitation of God but I hate to give Parson Wood any excuse to be more self-important than he already is. I'll call it an apoplexy. We don't want to be bothering the coroner. You were here when he died, Mrs Fairfax, so you can register the death. Tell the parson to arrange the funeral." With that he picked up his hat and his riding crop and took his leave briskly; the hunt was meeting that day.

And so I bid farewell to a second Mr Rochester. I was sad to see him go but it was the threat to my livelihood that caused me the greater anguish. And this time there would be no help from the Fairfaxes. I had crossed the line that divided relations from servants. Relatives could not be left to starve. Servants could — and did.

The lawyers came again but this time with smiling faces. Old Mr Rochester had died without making arrangements for the estate. The lawyers scented dispute and conflict; there would be claims and counter-claims, special pleadings, counsels' opinions and judges' rulings. All such complications were not misfortunes for them, but opportunities for endless work and massive bills. While the lawyers rubbed their hands we servants at Thornfield Hall suffered much uncertainty. At last it was arranged that we should be put on board wages. The amount was generous compared with many other households but our fare would be plain with no leftovers from the dining table to enjoy. There would be no more finishing off a baron of roast beef with the remains of a bottle of good claret.

Mr Merryman left immediately to take up a position with a rich manufacturer of wool in Bradford. His new master was trade rather than the gentry he was used to, but as he said, beggars can't be choosers. He had lost two masters in quick succession and could not afford to be fussy. Some might think it carelessness on his part and be reluctant to employ him.

Our number dwindled as those who could found other employment. Grooms and kitchen maids soon found new masters in the neighbourhood. Without Mr Merryman to insist on my following the conventions I decided to stop having my meals in the housekeeper's room and to eat with the others in the servants' hall. I explained the change as a way of saving Mary and Leah from extra work. It was not a time to maintain the artificial divisions between us and I was glad of the friendship and company of the other servants. We huddled together for comfort and reassurance and asked each other questions we could not answer. Who will employ us? Will the days of hard work and good food ever return? Who will pay our wages?

I spent time persuading Martha, the housemaid, that she should follow the example of Mr Merryman. The deaths in the family could, I suggested to her, be seen as an opportunity for her to improve herself by seeking better employment. I confess Martha's welfare was not uppermost in my mind. She had a way of looking at me that said she had not forgotten seeing me come out of the old master's bedroom with my hair in disarray. It gave her power over me. I did not like it and I wanted to be rid of her.

The deed still sits uneasily on my conscience. I can hear my voice and the exact weasel words I used to persuade her. "An intelligent girl like you, Martha, you should be more ambitious. You've been at Thornfield Hall longer than me. It's not too soon to look for a new position. We've lost two masters. Heaven only knows who the next one will be. You could find work in a house with a mistress, a fine lady to take an interest in you and train you up. You could become a lady's maid. A lady of title perhaps." May I be forgiven. I did not know how things would work out in the end. Sometimes I wake with a start, my body damp with sweat and my head filled with a dreadful roaring sound. Sometimes the palm of my right hand tingles with the memory of the slap I gave to stop her screams.

To help Martha on her way out of Thornfield Hall I drafted letters to possible employers for her to copy and gave her a glowing reference. Some evil spirit must have eavesdropped on our conversation, for the vision of the rosy future that I painted for Martha came true. Lady Ingram, wife of a baron and one of our more exalted neighbours, offered her employment. It was a lowly position, as housemaid, but Lady Ingram hinted that in time Martha might become a personal maid for one of her daughters. She had two young daughters, the Honourable Blanche and the Honourable Mary.

Poor naive Martha believed the vague promises of the baroness! She did not realize that no lady would endure her clumsy ministrations. To have her dress your hair would be a form of torture. Her huge rough hands were more suited to shearing sheep than arranging a lady's coiffure. A lady's maid has to be prompt and cheerful in answering the bell. She has to sit up till late at night while her mistress attends parties. In the small hours of the morning she must smile and listen to her mistress as she unfastens the satin gown and brushes out the dressed hair. The triumphs of her mistress in the ballroom must appear to be a real pleasure to her maid. Martha with her sour face and her love of grumbling had shown no talent in this direction at all. And the damage she could do with a sewing needle had to be seen to be believed.

We had to endure Martha's airs for two weeks until she worked her notice; I let her off working the full month. If I had liked her I might have warned her not to put too much faith in the promises of the landed classes but she annoyed me with her boasting and I held my tongue. At the end of the fortnight I wished her God speed and good riddance and made a note to increase young Leah's wages when the opportunity arose. Leah was a bright, hardworking girl and very quick to learn. What a treasure she proved to be!

Those of us who remained at Thornfield Hall waited with fearful hearts to hear what our future would be. We might dislike our masters at times and think them unjust but there is nothing in the world that a servant fears more devoutly than being without a master. It is a cold and cruel world out there unless you have a place or savings. Over us all hovered the shadow of the workhouse.

Soon the lawyer came from Millcote and summoned us all to the library so he could explain to us what was happening. Old Mr Rochester's younger son, who was living in Jamaica, was to inherit the estate by default. Neither old Mr Rochester nor Mr Rowland had left wills so the laws of inheritance prevailed. There were no other claimants. The lawyer must have been disappointed at the smoothness of the process; the lack of conflict had left him with nothing to do. He could not resist telling us the extent of the property involved. His eyes glowed with avarice as he listed all that Mr Edward would inherit; not just all the land that the Rochesters owned but also a coal mine, two cotton mills on the other side of the Pennines and some property in Liverpool. The Rochesters had some kind of business there that the lawyer was vague and mysterious about. Old John, the coachman, whistled through his teeth when he heard about all these other sources of income. It was news to him and he had been with the family longer than any of us.

The lawyer had reassuring words for us. He announced that our wages and the household bills would be paid. There were some technicalities about grants of probate and funds in escrow — whatever that is — but he promised us that we would not go short of bread or meat or coal over the winter. Word had been sent to Mr Edward in Jamaica of his father's death. Young Mr Edward, the lawyer stressed, was the sole legal heir to the whole estate. This was good news for us; we had been dreading that the Hall would be sold to some stranger. Better the devil you know, as they say.

We were to wait for Mr Edward's instructions. The ships to Jamaica had to sail against the wind so the news might not yet have reached him. Even if young Mr Edward decided to come immediately to claim his inheritance it would be many a long month before he arrived. We should be prepared for a delay.

In the meantime we were to go about our duties and keep Thornfield Hall in good condition and ready for our new master.

We were a joyful band that night as we ate our meal in the servants' hall. We had much to talk about.

"Begging your pardon, Mrs Fairfax, but did you know about those mills in Manchester? I always thought that a gentleman never soiled his hands with business. And the Rochesters are definitely gentry." John, the new young footman, was puzzled by the elaborate layers that society had woven itself into. He had come from a farm where life was more basic and such distinctions did not apply. He was learning what every good servant has to master, the fine gradations of rank. We soon learn to adjust our behaviour accordingly.

"O! They are certainly gentry. They have owned all the land round here time out of mind. I did not know about the mills. Mr Rowland was very interested in the machinery. I knew the Rochesters had business interests. That seems to be very different from trade. The gentry turn their noses up at trade."

"A grocer is trade. Is a lawyer?" wondered young John.

"No. That is a profession."

"How about a mill owner?"

"A rich mill owner can hover on the edges of the gentry. If he has a daughter with a large enough dowry to attract a suitable husband, she has a chance of being accepted. She may marry a younger son, perhaps of a titled family. Someone with a good pedigree but no fortune. If they have children, their children will count as gentry. I think there was talk of finding such an heiress for Mr Edward. But nothing came of it. Old Mr Rochester kept things very close. I am beginning to realize, John, that the Rochesters kept many secrets."

He persisted. "But servants know everything. You know who's not paying their bills and who's carrying on with whose wife."

"Let em carry on with other men's wives, long as they leave our lassies alone." It was Old John, the coachman, who was normally taciturn to the point of rudeness. He stabbed a grubby finger in my direction. "I hope you warned that young Martha, Mrs Fairfax. Told her not to let that old goat Lord Ingram get between her and the door. Poor girl had no mother to make her wise to the world." His words gave my conscience a nasty tweak. I had not thought to warn Martha that in some households the men took advantage of the housemaids. I'd assumed she knew that mistresses took a very hard line with any young girl who found herself in the family way. It was common knowledge that the girl would be put out the door to avoid the master or the son of the house coming under suspicion. I reflected that because a fact was well-known it did not follow that Martha knew it. She was a very ignorant girl who had scarcely mastered setting the forks on the left.

Since I was caught out being in the wrong, I promptly went on to commit a further offence. It is a bad habit of mine. I think I must do it in the hope that a second crime will distract me from thinking about the first. "It is the pretty girls that need the warnings, Old John. You know that." The men sniggered. Martha was not what you might call a pretty girl. They then all turned to look at the sweet face of Leah, who blushed like a rose. The new John couldn't keep his eyes off her.

To change the uncomfortable subject I turned back to Old John. "Tell us about Mr Edward. You've known him for years. I only saw him briefly. He left to go abroad soon after I came to live at Hay." I complimented myself on a successful diversion. The young servants were keen to know what Mr Edward was like and full of hope that when he came to claim his inheritance he would bring some life and society to the hall.

Old John scratched his head as he sifted through his memories. It was some time before he picked one out. "He were always fond of riding," he told us. I might have guessed horses would be Old John's preferred choice of subject! I had hoped for some insight into Mr Edward's character, but Old John had found his voice and there was no stopping him. "Happen he'll buy some decent horses instead of those old nags that can scarcely pull the gig to the gates. He might even take up hunting." His eyes went misty with remembrance of past glory days. "You've never seen the hunt meet at

Thornfield Hall," he told his awestruck audience. "A winter's morning with a weak sun and a flop of dew on the grass. You can't beat it. It's a grand sight."

His audience was dreamy-eyed with visions of Thornfield Hall bustling with life. The clatter of horses' hooves and the crunch of carriage wheels on the gravel path. The women's dresses rustling through the corridors and the high commanding voices of the county aristocrats echoing in the panelled hall. There would be hunt balls, grand dinners and picnics on the lawn.

The servants were not alone in their hopes. The whole neighbourhood was twitching in anticipation, especially those houses where there were unmarried daughters. Letters of condolence with their black borders kept arriving for Mr Rochester and the gentry started calling and leaving cards, secure in the knowledge that the new owner when he arrived would have to return the compliment. Mr Rochester on his tropical island was still in ignorance of his father's death. He was unaware of his sudden transformation from black sheep of the family, whose existence was never mentioned, into a wealthy, young and eligible bachelor.

Mr Edward had been a fine spirited youth, not handsome but strong-featured with wavy black hair. He was shipped off abroad when he came of age. Very sudden it was. The family was tight-lipped about it. A duel or gambling debts, I guessed. Perhaps even some trouble with a married lady. No worse than many a young fellow had got up to, a minor blot on his copybook, a scandal that would soon blow over. It was not to be. At first old Mr Rochester and Mr Rowland would wave his letters about and say he was doing well in Jamaica but they never read them out or let others read them. Questions about their contents were discouraged. When I arrived as housekeeper the letters were infrequent and soon ceased altogether. The silence about Mr Edward thickened and solidified. As I said, the Rochesters are very good at keeping secrets.

My Third Mr Rochester

1822

And so I came to my third Mr Rochester.

The first words from my new master came in the form of a letter. It was written on the thinnest paper I have ever seen. It was so fine you could see through it. What it said was so bizarre and unusual, so far from the normal duties of a housekeeper, that I kept the letter — as evidence I suppose. The task he set me was not one I relished. I folded the letter, fine as a cobweb, and placed it between the pages of the bible I carry in my pocket. By some miracle of good fortune I have both the letter and the bible still.

Spanish Town, Jamaica.

Mrs Fairfax,

Little news of Thornfield Hall has reached me for some years. My father and brother were not good correspondents. I am sorry to hear of the death of your husband. He was a kind and upright clergyman. It is a matter of satisfaction to me that someone with a connection to my family is looking after Thornfield Hall. I am assured by the lawyers that you do so with great competence.

Preparations for my departure are almost complete. I intend to set sail from this benighted island in time to catch the prevailing westerlies. With good weather I will be in Liverpool in about forty days. From there I will come straight to Thornfield Hall. There is much business to be done.

I will have with me a companion who comes to take up residence at Thornfield. She is an unfortunate invalid who suffers from great weakness of mind. Indeed there are times when she loses her wits completely. Alert the local physician that his services will be needed for the new arrival. Remind him that his profession imposes secrecy upon him. Not discretion but absolute secrecy. I will make it worth his while.

Prepare a suite of rooms for her so she can live independent of the rest of the household; she will not be mixing in society. My memory of Thornfield Hall tells me the third floor might provide suitably sized accommodation. Furnish the rooms so that her everyday needs are provided for. All should be clean and comfortable, but not luxurious.

In Liverpool I will hire an attendant who will take charge of her, someone skilled in this kind of work. The patient is not one of my kin. She is merely a connection of my father's from his business in Jamaica. I rely on you to keep gossip to a minimum and ensure the family name remains free from any hint of the taint of madness.

Edward Fairfax Rochester

What a family for secrets! It was shrewd of him to use his middle name and to stress my connection to him; it sealed my lips most effectively. People love a scandal. Once the neighbours got hold of this we would all be tarnished by speculation and slander.

With the help of Leah, I set about preparing the rooms for this lady — invalid — lunatic. I knew not what to call her.

"I have never been in this part of the house before," Leah called out in excitement as she scampered up the last flight of steps. "It's an awful lot of stairs for carrying the coal in the winter and the hot water." We had arrived at the third-floor corridor with its row of black doors.

"You sound like Martha," I told her. "She was always good at grumbling." For a moment Leah thought I was serious. I gave her a knowing look. "I expect John will give you a hand if you ask." I waited until she finished giggling and blushing before I went on. "It was Mr Rochester's suggestion that the lady live up here. We can turn that to our own benefit. We can tell him that with so many stairs we need an extra pair of hands. You've been after a place for your young brother, haven't you?"

I unlocked the door to the first chamber and revealed a good-size room with windows that looked out over the drive. Stray pieces of furniture were scattered haphazardly about. It was large enough to contain an ugly old cabinet and a big old-fashioned bed with dusty hangings.

"O look, here's another door," cried Leah in excitement. She wrenched it open and ran through laughing into the next room. There she exclaimed in delight as she found another door. "It opens into the next room. And the next one! And the next one!" Her voice grew fainter as she ran through the tunnel of rooms until she reached the end. "I've never seen such a thing," she panted after running back. "The rooms are nice though. Bigger than ours at the back."

"The servants always have the smallest rooms, Leah. You know that."

We checked the other side of the corridor but the rooms on that side were smaller. Being on the north side they were dark and cheerless.

"Where do those stairs lead?" Leah pointed to a narrow staircase.

"Up to the attic. Shall we go?"

When we had climbed to the attic we found the ladder that led to the roof. I opened the trap door and beckoned Leah up. She was nervous at first. "I've never been this high before."

We walked carefully on the roof leads for the wind was buffeting in from the east. Leah leant against the battlements and took in the view, the patchwork of fields, the toy cows and the miniature sheep. This, I reflected, would be a splendid place for an invalid who lived secluded from society to come and take exercise and enjoy the fresh air, though a lady who had lived on a tropical island might find the Yorkshire air bracing. Indeed I was finding it chilly myself. I wrapped my shawl round me and summoned Leah to descend the ladder. My mind was made up. The lady would live on the third floor. I would have the walls of the rooms white-washed and I would scour the rest of the house for more suitable furniture. Some wall hangings would make the room seem warm and welcoming.

When all that was in hand I would visit Mr Carter, the surgeon, to seek his services and tactfully put a price on his silence. I had my doubts about his suitability as physician to a weak-witted lady. A splendid man for a dramatic accident on the hunting field, our Mr Carter. There's no one you'd rather see striding towards you if you lay crushed under a wagon wheel or if you'd fallen from your horse and broken your leg. Carter would have you tied to a hurdle and carried away with a splint on your leg in no time. He'd have you back home ready to share your dinner with him and drink a brandy or two as soon as wink at you. Solitary brooding or women's tears were a different matter. I could not envisage that his bluff hearty confidence would be much help to a lady with a fragile mind who sometimes lost her wits completely.

To have the Hall thoroughly cleaned and ready for the new master I had to hire in extra staff from The George at Millcote, as was the custom. When everything was done to my satisfaction I paid them their wages and sent them back to their regular business with a hint that they might be needed again in the future. I pictured the Hall full of life and bustle, with guests coming and going. We stocked up the store cupboards with preserves and pickles. I helped Mary make jellies and desserts. The butcher's boy called more often to be ready for the moment we would give orders for meat for our new master. At last word came that we could expect him to arrive the next day.

We sent a boy to the gates to keep watch for the coach. From there you can see for miles down the road to Millcote. It is the custom for the upper servants to line up to greet family members or important guests. I have Mr Merryman to thank for that piece of servants' lore. Old John came to the entrance hall to be ready to help drive the horses round to the stables and unload the coach. He only came to the front of the house on special occasions. We had warned him to air out in the garden for a couple of hours first; the smell of horse can be very strong. Even after this precaution it was preferable for him to stand close to an open door or window. Mary came up to join the reception party with John, the new footman, and Sam. I asked Leah to make up the numbers though strictly speaking a housemaid is not one of the upper servants. Even with Leah, we looked a paltry number for such a house.

All day we had kept an anxious eye on the weather. True to form, when word came that the coach had been sighted the rain decided to lash down and the wind scythed it across the drive in great waves. I gave the look-out boy two pennies and sent him straight to the kitchen to get warm and dry next to the Kitchener range. As we hovered in the entrance hall, dithering whether to stay in or venture out, Mr Carter appeared from the library; he had been summoned to look after the invalid. He asked for brandy and hot water and went back to warm his backside in front of the fire.

When the hired post chaise bringing Mr Edward arrived at the entrance Carter pushed through to be first to greet the new arrivals and, being Carter, his concern was not for Mr Edward but for the horses. He rushed about ordering that the chaise should be driven round to the stables and demanding to know where in blazes those lazy bloody grooms were. There was much noise and confusion. This was not the welcome I had planned for Mr Edward.

When he stepped from the coach I could see that this was not the gangly youth I remembered. His physique had developed into that of a strong and powerful man. His carriage was erect and his movements athletic. He was swift and light on his feet even after being confined in a chaise for hours bumping along on uneven roads. As he came towards me I saw that his black hair was thick and glossy and his eyes were alert and intelligent. His face still had its craggy attractiveness but it seemed careworn for a man in the prime of life. I felt that the tropics had not agreed with him.

His first words when he arrived in the entrance hall reassured me. "Mrs Fairfax, it is good to be back in England." I bid him welcome and introduced him to my fellow servants. By the time these brief formalities were completed Carter had returned and was busy dripping rainwater on the marble floor.

"All in good order," he announced and gave Mr Rochester a significant nod. "Dry stable and some clean hay. All safely stowed."

"I am glad that is over, Carter." Mr Rochester passed his hand across his face to smooth out the lines etched on his brow and down his cheeks. "The journey was a nightmare. A living hell."

Carter put his hands in his pockets, looked into a distant corner of the entrance hall and whistled through his teeth. It was clear he was sending Mr Rochester some kind of signal, a message warning him to watch his words. "You are not a good traveller then? Do you suffer from seasickness?" he asked cheerily.

"Yes. I suffer dreadfully from *mal de mer*. In future I shall cross no water wider than the Channel — and I shall travel alone."

It was then I realized that I had seen no sign of his travelling companion, the mysterious invalid for whom the suite of rooms had been prepared. Carter must have whisked her up the back stairs. I found I was starting to ask my master about arrangements for his companion but I quickly thought better of it. I swallowed my words, snapped my jaw shut and pulled on my pug face. The master would give his instructions when he was ready.

"More brandy and hot water for your master. Send someone to build up the fire in the library. And get me a towel. My pesky breeches are sodden." Mr Carter was back to his usual rumbustious self. He put his arm round Mr Edward's shoulders and led him towards the library. "Come along, Rochester. You and I will have a bit of a chinwag."

As I set about fulfilling the orders I realized how relieved I was not to have encountered the strange new lady. A new master was enough for one day. Preparing rooms for a madwoman was an easy task; her living breathing presence was quite another thing. I could not help wondering how the disease manifested itself and how the sufferer would behave.

In spite of the poverty and the bereavements I had endured in my life my mind had always returned to its calm orderly self. My crying would stop and I would go back to my usual duties, though I carried my sadness inside me like the hard stone in the heart of a soft plum. Madness had not so much as brushed its fingertips against me. I did not look forward to meeting it face to face.

"Veiled," said Old John as we questioned him over breakfast. He had seen the lady as she descended from the coach in the stable yard. He was the only one of us to have even glimpsed her and he was being singularly unhelpful in satisfying our curiosity. When prodded for more details he added "black" and "heavy". Try as we might we could learn no more than that the lady was hidden behind a heavy black veil.

"I never saw the lady but I came across the nurse," volunteered Leah. "Several times. Once with hot water, then there was supper and the tea this morning and the eggs for breakfast. And soon I have to go back for the trays."

"You only have to say. I'll help." John's soft brown eyes gazed longingly at Leah, who ignored him. Her voice rose with indignation as she continued her complaint.

"And if you please, I have to rap on the door and wait outside until she comes. Then she opens the door a crack and passes whatever it is out or I pass something in." Leah demonstrated with her fingers the narrowness of the door opening. "Not a glimpse or a sign of the lady, have I had."

"And coal!" added Sam. "She's had four buckets already. Blazing fire."

"I suppose the lady feels the cold after living in a hot country."

"It's not affected her appetite. I was told to send up four eggs, lightly boiled." Mary casually threw this nugget of information into the centre of the table where it ricocheted amongst us with the force of a cannon ball. Spoons halted in mid-air as we did the sums in our heads. Four eggs for one lady. Divide by two and it is two eggs for the lady and two for the servant. The servant was getting two eggs while we were eating our customary porridge. I felt all their eyes turned upon me. Eggs for one servant meant eggs for all. Although the hierarchy of servants was very strict we expected a certain equality in our treatment. Here was an injustice. They looked to me to remedy it.

"Did the nurse not think to come down for the lady's breakfast? Surely that is one of her duties?"

"She did not. In fact she wanted to know why there wasn't a bell in the room so she could ring for one of us." Leah's bottom lip stuck out as she looked ahead to being at the beck and call of a minder of the mad. I could feel the sympathy of the other servants around the table for her, and the swelling hostility to the newcomer.

"I will speak to her and explain how we do things at Thornfield Hall and what her duties will be. We must be firm about this. To be plain I think she should have come and made herself known to me by now. Does this nurse attendant have a name?"

"It is Morgan, Mrs Morgan." The voice came from behind me. The wretched woman had arrived unnoticed. I have sometimes wondered if my hearing is all it should be. Being caught at a disadvantage made me angry. The others saw the flash of rage that passed across my features. They exchanged knowing looks and surreptitious grins; they were sure they were about to witness an interesting encounter. I took a moment to compose my face before I turned to greet the woman who had sneaked in behind me.

"And I am Mrs Fairfax, the housekeeper." I spoke in my best icy tones and was pleased to feel the temperature in the room drop by several degrees. "Come to my room," I commanded the frowsty-looking creature before me. "We can talk there." I fixed my eyes on hers and willed her to move out of my way. For a second she stood her ground. Then her mouth twisted, she stepped back and I swept out leaving her to follow behind me.

Once in my room I sat at my desk and kept her standing while I surveyed her. She was a stout little body and none too clean. A few trips up and down the stairs with buckets of hot water would do her no harm. Some very close contact with the aforesaid hot water and the addition of some soap would improve her immeasurably.

"Mr Rochester acquired you in Liverpool I believe." The hostility in my voice crackled like ice. I made her sound like some nasty disease he had caught there in a brothel. "You have no uniform?"

"No. Never have. We didn't have them in the asylum."

"So you have experience of dealing with . . ." Words failed me, but they did not fail Mrs Morgan.

"The mad. Lunatics," she supplied. Mrs Morgan was obviously a woman who liked to call a spade a spade. "All sorts and kinds. There's those as never speak and those as never stop talking. There's some as pull their hair out and —" I held my hand up to stop her.

"You obviously have much experience of asylums but you have very little experience of how things are done in a gentleman's house. Does your charge have a name?"

"Not to my knowledge."

"Have you asked her?"

"Not as such."

"What does the master call her?"

"He just points and says *She. Her. It.*"

I managed to conceal from her that I found this use of pronouns appalling. I never came across a dog but I wanted to know its name.

32

"That is the master's privilege," I continued smoothly. "In service we address our masters and our betters by their proper titles. Until we are told otherwise we shall call her 'the lady' and when you address her you will call her 'milady'. You understand?" She nodded. "Say it. Say M'lady."

She mumbled something close enough to satisfy me so I went on. "I expect to have an interview with the master very soon." This was not strictly true. I had no idea what to expect from my new master but under the circumstances it was very low down in the scale of lies. Scarcely more than a fib.

I took a breath and ploughed on. "The master and I have, of course, exchanged letters about your arrival. In the meantime there are some practical details we can sort out between us. They are too trivial to bother Mr Rochester with. First — arrangements for meals. The lady's meals will be taken up to her. You will carry up the trays and return them to the kitchen. You will eat your meals with the rest of us in the servants' hall."

Mrs Morgan held up her hand to stop me. The expression on my face warned her she should have a very good reason to interrupt me.

"Not always possible, ma'am." (I noted the ma'am. Mrs Morgan was learning fast.) "Sometimes, I am told, she raves something shockin. They reckon it's the moon that does it. Bangin her head against the wall and biting and that."

"In that case I doubt the lady will be very interested in her dinner. I think we should cross that bridge when we come to it." I contrived to sound very composed on

33

the subject. I knew nothing of the behaviour of the mad and my ignorance gnawed at my confidence. Reason, however, told me that Mrs Morgan had been with the lady for no more than three days. A full cycle of the moon requires twenty-eight days.

I returned to my list of requirements. "Now — coal. Sam will bring up two scuttles of coal. You must make that last. And then, hot water. You must take up the hot water for the lady. If the master decides to stay no doubt we will be hiring more servants but until then those tasks are yours." The woman stirred uneasily, no doubt thinking of all the stairs up to the third floor. The movement of her skirts sent the smell of dirt and neglect wafting across my desk. How had Mr Rochester endured sharing a coach all the way from Liverpool with this creature?

Relentlessly I continued. "Then there's the washing. Yours will be charged as usual. It will be deducted from your wages. I know that the master has been very generous with regard to payment." Another little fib. I did not know the exact terms on which Mr Rochester had engaged her but I guessed she had driven a hard bargain. A man of considerable means newly arrived in England with a lunatic on his hands would not stop to count the pennies. I watched her eyes as she calculated how much of her own linen she could pass off as the lady's. Unpleasant though the task would be I vowed I would check all the laundry personally. With a curt, "That will be all," I dismissed her.

This was not my usual way of greeting new servants. Generally I tried to be kind; usually they were no more than children away from home for the first time and struggling to find their way around a house that covered more ground than their whole village. Mrs Morgan and her frightening and mysterious charge were totally beyond my experience. I sat at my desk and remembered how we servants had hoped our new master would bring fresh life to Thornfield Hall. I began to wonder if we should have been more specific about the kind of life and society we desired.

My hope that Mr Rochester would soon send for me proved true. The very next morning I was summoned to the library and told to bring my account books with me. The master sat at his father's great mahogany desk. Glints of red and green from the stained glass in the leaded window flickered behind him. The family bible was in front of him; it sat squat and black in a pool of sunlight. The book was open at the flyleaf where different hands had entered the records of the Rochester births, marriages and deaths. The family goes back a long way; Damer de Rochester was killed at the battle of Marston Moor. My new master's face was mournful as he stared at the list.

I approached him softly. "I am sorry for your loss, Mr Rochester."

"Thank you, Mrs Fairfax. People seem to forget that I have lost . . ." he paused for a moment as he appeared to search for the right words, "both my closest relations within a very short time. They think only of the fortune that I have unexpectedly inherited." His mouth twisted into a smile. People's greed seemed to amuse him.

There was, I noticed, no mention of a dear kind father or a beloved brother.

He ran his finger down the list of names handwritten into the bible and stopped at his mother's name. "I remember very little of her now. She was ill for so long. I was away at school when she died. Was there not a little sister? There is no name or date for her."

"There was. She was christened Elisabeth. She did not survive the three months. Perhaps your parents found it too painful to record her fate. The deaths of babies are particularly hard: their tiny lives so short, their little faces so perfect." I felt the catch in my throat as I thought of my own child. I put my hand in my pocket to feel the soft leather of my little bible. Her name was carefully inscribed in it, the ink smudged with tears and goodnight kisses.

"That is not all that is missing." His finger pointed to the last entry; it was the date of his own birth. There was nothing after that. "I am pleased to see that my name and birth date are still in the book. I heard so little from my father and my brother that I did sometimes wonder if they had crossed my name out. The black sheep of the family sent abroad to mend his ways. I expect you have heard all the stories of my wild misdeeds?" He looked directly at me.

His dark eyes searched my face and for a moment I was overwhelmed by the power of the man. I wanted to blab about the scandal, to offer my theories as to his misdeeds and to denounce his father as an unfeeling wretch; the urge was almost irresistible. By some miracle of self-control I contrived to stay silent. I put on my smooth, expressionless servant's face, lowered my gaze and examined intently the top button of his waistcoat. Sometimes it is best for a servant to act dumb.

My silence seemed to satisfy him. It was not long before he continued. "As the last surviving Rochester it is my sad task to add the date of my father's death. And I see that his death followed so close on the heels of my brother's that he had neither the time nor the heart to complete the record for my brother." He took up his pen and filled in the dates. "I wonder who will write in the date of Edward Fairfax Rochester's departure from this world."

This morbid speculation was too much for me. I stopped being dumb and spoke briskly to him. "Come, Mr Rochester, there are plenty more cheerful things to think of. Why, your marriage will be next. That will be a joyful occasion. And there could be children. There's nothing quite like children to bring life to a house and joy to your heart."

"Enough!" he snapped with one of those sudden changes of mood that I soon learnt to become accustomed to. "There are serious matters to deal with." He pushed the bible to one side and gestured for me to lay the account books in front of him. I prepared myself for a long and tiresome scrutiny of the kind his father enjoyed; the apple doesn't fall far from the tree.

Mr Rochester opened a book at random and turned a couple of pages. His black eyes sparkled as he returned the book to me. "I feel I would be failing in my duty if I did not make at least a pretence of looking at the figures." He smiled and for the first time I saw the frank and cheerful youth that he must have been.

"Now to business. I shall not stay here long. I intend to travel in Europe. No more ocean journeys for me. However, I want to put your mind at rest. Make sure all the servants are told of my plans. Assure them the Hall will not be closed, nor will you be put on board wages. On the contrary, I want Thornfield kept in good working order, ready to receive me whenever I decide to come. I would say ship-shape but the memory of my recent voyage is too vivid." He gave a wry smile and pulled his hand across his forehead.

"I may arrive at short notice. I expect my visits will be brief. Thornfield Hall holds little to attract me apart from business and my duties as a squire and landlord. I will come to attend to my responsibilities and when I come I don't want to walk into clouds of dust and unmade beds. I want the Hall ready to entertain me and my guests at a moment's notice and I will need plenty of guests to divert me. I intend to wrest as much enjoyment from my unexpected change of fortune as possible. I'll try to give you a few days' notice if it is to be a large house party."

I gave him my best blank servant's stare. I remained standing motionless and looked at the patterned window above and behind him as if he did not exist. I said nothing. This time the silence was not a sympathetic one. It was a silence that grew. At first it was an awkwardness. Then it thickened into a dense soup of hostility. I waited for him to break it.

At this point Mr Rowland would have picked up his magnifying glass and a beetle and forgotten all about me. His father would have harangued me about his poverty, the high price of meat and the availability of cheap servants on every street corner. Mr Edward was made of more intelligent metal.

"Is there anything you need to enable you to carry out my wishes?" he asked.

He had asked so I told him. I ticked each item off on my fingers. Did he intend to replace Mr Merryman? If not, another footman would be useful or at least a boy for the kitchen and to help carry coal and hot water. Another housemaid to help Leah. Another pair of hands in the kitchen so cook could start to train her to be ready to help when guests arrived at short notice. Then there was the new lady. I knew not what to call her. And her attendant, Mrs Morgan.

He held up his hand to stop me and fixed me with his glittering eyes. "I rely on you to deal with Mrs Morgan. Her task is not an easy one. I will make it clear to her that she must respect your position. Whatever you need to ensure that the lady is cared for with as much kindness as possible you shall have." His brow darkened and he seemed to struggle within himself. "If there is a problem that you cannot solve by yourself you can write to me. I will send what aid I can." His voice thrilled with emotion, his hand closed into a fist and the veins stood out on his brow. "But before God I swear the less I am reminded of that lady's existence the better." I watched as he struggled to subdue some intense and bitter inner conflict.

Once he was calm he spoke again. "You will be well rewarded — and not just in heaven. You will have a free hand to engage whatever extra servants are needed." He managed to give me his disarming, lop-sided grin. "Now tell me the names of the servants who will have most contact with the lady and with her attendant. I doubt I will know them; there have been many changes among the servants since I last lived here."

"The servants you saw in the entrance hall yesterday will be most closely involved with her care in the house. And probably Old John the coachman, when the lady is well enough to go out. You must remember Old John from when you were a boy. He is still with us."

"I do not think the lady will be going out. She will not mix in society." He looked quite alarmed at the thought of the lady taking the air in a carriage.

"As long as the doctors think she is well enough, I can see no harm in her having a change of scene, taking the fresh air."

Mr Rochester chewed his lip and furrowed his brow and generally acted like a man who wanted to say No. "A closed carriage," I stressed. "With Old John who taught you to ride. She is sick, not a prisoner." I had him there.

He thought for a moment. "So be it. I can trust Old John to keep silent. Collect the servants together and bring them here."

I left the library with my head reeling. My third Mr Rochester was a very different kettle of fish from his father and brother. He might be moody and melancholy, but he radiated power and force of

40

character. I set about carrying out his orders immediately. It was the work of moments to summon the two Johns, Sam, Leah and Mary. There was much smoothing of hair and wiping of hands on aprons as we all trooped in to the library.

We formed an apprehensive semi-circle in front of Mr Rochester as he stood at his desk. He spoke to us in his straightforward manner. "I have to tell you that the lady who arrived yesterday is out of her wits. Many would consign her to the asylum. But she is to be kept here. I would not send a dog to an asylum." We all nodded our approval. The thought of the asylum made us shudder. We had heard of the horrors there. Not just the company of the insane inmates, their wails and fits, but the cold baths, the sleeping on straw, the chains and the manacles.

"I am not such a fool as to think that I can keep her existence a complete secret. There will be gossip and speculation. Let it continue. I can live with speculation. Let the countryside gossip but keep them in ignorance. All you need to know is that my father, through his business, came into contact with her and the Rochester family feels responsible for her. That is a duty I intend to fulfil.

"Do not believe any of the nonsense she may tell you. Keep her safe and close confined. All you need to know is that she is not related by blood to the Rochester family. I cannot emphasize that too much; she is no blood relation of mine. Madness is not part of my family's inheritance. Her care, though, has become my responsibility and I intend to discharge it honestly.

To show you how important this is to me I want you to swear on the bible to keep your lips sealed about the lady as far as outsiders are concerned. Mrs Fairfax, will you set us an example? Who is better qualified than the widow of a good and honourable man of God to go first?" He gestured to the bible in front of him.

"I can do better than that," I told him. It never even crossed my mind to refuse. I took my own little bible out of my pocket. "I will use my own bible. In the front is written the name of my baby daughter. I kiss it every night before I go to sleep." I held the book in my hand and said simply, "I swear." Then I kissed the book and put it away.

The others stepped forward one at a time and put their hand on the bible on the desk and took the oath until it came to Old John's turn.

"There be no use me swearing on that book, Mr Edward. I'm a bit of what you might call a free thinker."

"Is there nothing you hold sacred?" Mr Edward asked him.

"There be plenty things. Horses. Dogs. I tell you what. I'll swear on my dog's life."

A splutter of outrage burst from Mary. Old John slapped his forehead. "O! Mary, Mary, my lovely wife, I clean forgot you was here."

We all laughed and Mr Rochester put his hand on Old John's shoulder. "That'll do for me," he assured the old man. Then Mr Rochester told us all we should have an increase in our wages in return for the extra work and the responsibility. As we left the room we reckoned we were the luckiest and the best-paid servants in Yorkshire.

That evening after our supper we sat around the table and speculated about our future with our new master. Old John from his seat at the end of the table nearest the door waxed philosophical. "Master's got a bee in his bonnet about that there lunatic upstairs. Wanting us to swear! As if we'd go round neighbourhood telling his business to every Tom, Jack and Harry."

"Everyone knows already. Butcher's boy called this morning." Sam peered through his spectacles at the sails of the model ship he was making, a hobby he had learned during his time at sea.

"What you mean by everyone and what master means by everyone is two different things. The Cliffords' cook may know there's a mysterious lady staying here. But she ain't going to tell Lady Clifford. She's going to be saying pork chops on Thursday, milady, and how about duck on Sunday."

"True," says Sam, squinting down a pair of tweezers at a rope as fine as a hair. "Like on a ship. Some things, the captain is the last to know."

Mr Rochester did not stay long. He paid a few courtesy calls on his neighbours, bought a couple of horses and left. I missed him at first, in the way I miss the light when I blow the candle out and am left in the dark. The faces of the ladies of the county grew glum when they heard of Mr Rochester's departure. They made anxious enquiries about the date of his return. We could not help them. He had given us no hint of his plans. For all we knew he had gone to the moon. Only Old John whistled happily as he brushed the two new horses that had arrived in his stable.

Grace

1823

The chill of winter had scarcely arrived before I was struck down with a pleurisy. So severe was it that Mr Carter was called. He gave me some of his useless vile-coloured medicine and ordered me to stay in bed. As if I could have risen from it without the help of two strong men. It was Leah who nursed me through the worst of it. I thanked God that I had not been left in the clumsy hands of Martha.

Slowly the illness left me. My hearing is still impaired but thankfully that is all the injury I suffered. One evening during my convalescence Leah brought my supper on a tray up to my bedroom. Her cheeks were pink and her eyes sparkly. I guessed it wasn't for John with his puppy-dog-in-love eyes.

"Are there visitors in the servants' hall?" I asked.

"Just the blacksmith. Mary's giving him a plate of supper."

I might have guessed it was the blacksmith who had brought a gleam to Leah's eyes. The bronzed biceps, the leather waistcoat, the tangy smell of male sweat mixed with a whiff of horse.

"He does not usually come into the house. Is Old John with him?"

"Old John is still in the stable. A horse needing a drench or something. Blacksmith came to do a job in the house. For that Mrs Morgan." There was a vicious edge to Leah's voice as she named the nurse. What need had a nurse for a blacksmith, I wondered. It was clear that there had been developments while I was ill.

"Ask the blacksmith to come up and see me before he goes."

The young blacksmith arrived. All rippling muscles and a musky aroma that overwhelmed the mild lavender scent of my neat, nun-like room. He was a lad of few words and he was not happy.

"I can guess what Mrs Morgan wanted you to make," I told him. "She had no authority from me."

"In that case." He handed me a key. "I was going to give it to Old John."

"I'll make sure he knows. Have you been paid?"

"For the horses. Yes. I'll take no money for the other thing."

"I'll pay you double when the time comes to take it off. I will make it my business to see you do not wait too long for your money."

When he had gone I took out my little bible and kissed my baby's name and thought about the vow I had taken. I had promised not to talk about the lady to outsiders. Nothing more. I had not promised to stand idly by while she was treated with harshness and kept like a prisoner. When Mr Rochester was absent I was

46

responsible for the Hall and for those who lived there. I berated myself soundly for my lack of supervision of Mrs Morgan. It was true I had been ill but that was no longer an excuse. It was time to gird up my loins as the good book puts it and go to inspect what was happening on the third floor.

I laced my stays extra tight in the morning; it was the closest I could get to girding up my loins — whatever they are. At the top of the stairs I took a moment to get my breath and strengthen my resolve. I thought of Judith going to Holofernes' tent. How she must have fixed her smile as she strove to ingratiate herself with the tyrant! What pleasure she must have felt as she looked down upon her sleeping victim and slowly drew her sharpened knife ready to cut his throat! I fixed an expression of polite concern to my face as I rapped on the door.

"Mrs Morgan. A thousand pardons! I've neglected you." I smiled and gushed at her as she stood in the doorway. Surprise kept her motionless so I glided past her straight into the dragon's lair.

"You have everything you need?" I was all warm solicitude. I made it sound like a question but it was more of a statement. A quick glance round the room showed that Mrs Morgan had not been idle during my illness; she was well-equipped with life's comforts. Many of them were familiar to me; she had looted them from other rooms at Thornfield Hall. There were armchairs, cushions and rugs. There were tables littered with bottles and used plates and cups. A healthy fire blazed in the grate. In the corner was the huge four-poster bed. The new hangings were drawn roughly back, showing the unmade bed piled high with pillows. The deep feather mattress was shrouded in a stained grey sheet. The rug before the fire wore such a crust of crumbs and particles of food that I expected a family of mice with knives and forks to arrive at any minute. The dirty window let in little light and no air. The whole room reeked of neglect and dirt. The already substantial Mrs Morgan had been busy over the winter; she had been working at putting on even more flesh. Of the patient there was no sign.

I occupied myself by wandering round the room apparently without a specific purpose. All the time I had to restrain my hand from opening the window to let in fresh air. I waited for Mrs Morgan to offer to take me to the lady. She did not volunteer an invitation. I decided to compel her into making one.

"And how is the lady? I would like to see her." I saw little point in being subtle with such a coarse-minded creature as Mrs Morgan.

"Asleep."

"So late?"

"She do sleep a lot. When she's not sleeping, she's crying. Better she should sleep."

By now I had manoeuvred so I was by the door to the adjoining room. Before she could stop me I had the handle in my hand and was turning it. To my surprise the door opened. I expected to find it locked. With Mrs Morgan on my heels I went into the next chamber.

I had steeled myself to encounter some unsavoury sights without showing shock or outrage. I did not want to create an enemy unnecessarily. Mrs Morgan had the keeping of this unfortunate woman. She had total power over her. Everything that makes life comfortable or the contrary was in her hands. Food, drink, warmth, sleep, conversation, comfort and occupations were all hers to dispense or withhold. How could I have let this go on unsupervised?

It was difficult to experience the room in front of me without showing horror. I like to think I managed it. Mrs Morgan stood behind me so I had time to get my face under control. The smell had hit me like a blow to the chest: the chamber pot not emptied, the bed clothes not washed, the person not bathed, the window not opened. The naked floorboards were mottled with brown stains that I preferred not to identify. There was no curtain at the window. How could a room so cold and bare smell so bad?

The only furniture in the room was a small iron bed. A great nest of black hair sprawled over one end of it. The rest of the figure was hidden by a thin blanket that no self-respecting horse would have endured wearing. I could not be sure it was a person in the bed until I saw the arm. It was a thin, wasted arm that hung over the side. On its wrist was a heavy manacle; the chain was fastened to the leg of the bed.

"Like I said. She sleeps." Mrs Morgan gazed down at her charge with an expressionless face. I strove to keep mine similarly blank.

"I heard the blacksmith had been."

49

"It was necessary. They do it in the asylum when they have their fits."

Speaking your mind is regarded as a great virtue in Yorkshire. Most of the time, I say what I think. On this occasion a gap as wide as a church door opened up between the thoughts in my brain and the words that came from my lips. What I thought was, "You have chained her like a convict to make your life easier, so you can go and get your breakfast and stuff your face and then feed that poor soul the scraps." What I said was, "So it is a method practised by the medical profession?"

The figure on the bed showed no sign of waking so I retreated to the other room where the air was slightly less poisonous. There I bid Mrs Morgan *au revoir*. I promised her that I would call in again sometime. The message, wrapped in the sweet paper of smiles and compliments, was that I would be inspecting daily and without warning. I thought I had controlled myself admirably but at the end I could not stop myself from firing a parting shot.

"Get that chamber pot emptied." I saw no point in telling her to finish the cleaning of it with a few drops of turpentine. That was a little ambitious. I would settle for empty.

When I returned to my neat, fresh-smelling bedroom I washed my hands and face very thoroughly, enjoying the sensation of clean water against my skin. Then I sat in my chair and looked out of the window at the drive that sweeps up to Thornfield Hall and at the hills that lie beyond the gates. It was a fine and sunny spring day and the light was so clear I could see for miles. The new lambs frolicked in the fields; I could hear the tender bleats of the ewes. Yet my mind was in a turmoil of disgust and doubt and my heart was heavy.

It was a far cry from the storm of wind and rain that had greeted Mr Rochester's arrival as new master of Thornfield Hall. On that day in spite of the foul weather we were full of hope for a new beginning and for a better and fuller life at Thornfield Hall. The weather, it seemed to me, had nothing to do with what was happening in people's lives or how they felt — at least not in Yorkshire. The poets must have got it wrong. After this little grumble my mind cleared and I saw my way forward. I sent word to Mr Carter and suggested it was time he made a visit.

It was my intention to let Mr Carter take Mrs Morgan by surprise. I was confident that he would soon appear now that the hunting season had finished. He was not a man given to forethought so it was unlikely that he would trouble to give advance warning of his visit. When he arrived I let him climb up to the third storey alone while I waited for him in the library with the brandy and hot water handy. He was soon back. He still had the upright carriage of a horseman but I could see the criss-cross pattern of red veins standing out clearly against the pallor of his face. I sat him in front of the fire and gave him a double measure of his usual brandy.

"Any progress?" I asked, well aware that there was none.

He mopped his brow with his handkerchief and swigged back his brandy. As his complexion returned to its normal florid hue the power of speech was restored to him. I discovered it was not the dirt or the smell that had driven the colour from his cheeks. Mr Carter was probably as convinced of the health-giving properties of dirt as Mrs Morgan was. It was a treatment for madness that Mrs Morgan had suggested that had sent the hearty Mr Carter pale. She had put forward the idea of a form of surgery to a part of a woman's body that was never mentioned in polite society; it was reputed to cure the malady of her mind. Mr Carter was outraged.

"That woman had an unspeakable suggestion. I won't sully your ears by repeating it, Mrs Fairfax. The Lord knows I'm not a squeamish man. I've given a hand at gelding a stallion in my time, but to do that to a woman . . ." He shook his head in disbelief and finished his brandy. "I am at a loss as to what to suggest, Mrs Fairfax."

Fortunately, I was not. I outlined my plan to him.

"You do that," he said. He clapped his hat on his head and left. No doubt he went to the stables to stroke the horses and commune with Old John until his usual doughty cheerfulness returned.

I got out my pen and I wrote to Mr Rochester.

I said nothing to the other servants about what I had seen in the suite of rooms on the third floor. They were still spared the sight as the formidable Mrs Morgan kept them outside. Nor did I tell them about my agreement with Mr Carter or my letter to Mr

Rochester. I intended to take Mrs Morgan by surprise; it was an essential part of my plan. The Rochesters are not the only ones who can keep secrets.

The day after I posted my letter I climbed the stairs to the third floor. For the sake of that poor wretch chained to the bed it was vital that I did not antagonize Mrs Morgan. I did not believe her to be capable of reformation but I was sure that, if offended, she would vent her spleen on her defenceless patient. I wore a smile determinedly stuck to my face and carried in my hand a bunch of flowers gathered from the garden.

Mrs Morgan was not pleased to see me but she let me in without protest. We exchanged civilities. In the process I learnt a great deal about her: her rheumatics, the poor quality of Yorkshire coal and the laziness of the servants at Thornfield Hall. After a decent interval I enquired about her patient. She vouchsafed that the lunatic was still asleep. I expressed surprise. It was four o'clock in the afternoon!

Mrs Morgan prated at me with an air of professional confidence. Not at all unusual in such cases. Some lunatics slept the clock round. Lay people, like me, just didn't understand.

I understood all right. A sleeping patient is a quiet patient; she is no trouble, needs no attention. The room was littered with bottles of laudanum and other witches' brews. I waved the flowers in front of my nose. "I brought these for the lady. I think Mr Rochester would approve of such a gift, a reminder of God's bounty and His mercy to us all." Mrs Morgan is not the only one who can turn a platitude to her advantage.

53

I had taken the precaution of bringing a vase with me. A silver one. Glass seemed an unwise choice. Broken glass could provide a dangerous weapon. Mrs Morgan perked up at the sight of the precious metal. More loot for her. I held it out. "If you would be so kind. Some clean water."

As I had guessed, clean water was the one commodity she did not have. The mad lady, she declared, had a terrible fear of water, screamed at the mere sight of it. There was no accounting for mad folk; some were terrified of sparrows and spiders while others made a pet of a rat. With this she lumbered off in search of water for the flowers. It would be perfectly safe for me to wait, she assured me. The lady was not only asleep. She was chained.

Taking my courage in both hands I went into the second room. I held the flowers to my nose as I stood in the doorway and inspected our unusual house guest. She was, I noticed, a tall lady. Her feet hung over the end of the bed. I looked under the bed for her shoes — in vain. But I was gratified to see that the chamber pot had been emptied since my last visit.

She lay face down on the narrow bed. The skin on the manacled arm was so soaked in grease and dirt that it looked more like leather than the covering of a human being. The nails were jaggedly broken and the hand itself was etched with scars and scratches. Her only garment was a grubby linen shift that did little to conceal the sharp outlines of her bones; they stuck out in her meagre flesh.

54

The great mat of dark hair I saved to the last. I was not confident of having the stomach to look at it too closely. There were sure to be plenty of living things that had their dwelling in there. As I crept closer, to my horror, the black mass began to move. It heaved and undulated on the bed. Soon a slice of face appeared and a reddened eye focused on me. My heart gave a great lurch of fear. I was staring straight at the madwoman.

The sound of gasping breaths and heavy footsteps told me that Mrs Morgan was returning. She bustled in complaining about the stairs and brandishing the silver vase. As she heaved into view the woman on the bed struggled to raise herself. The loathsome chain clanked as she struggled to sit up. The rest of the face beneath the hair was revealed. I could not distinguish the features. All I could see was an expression of pure terror.

"No screaming now," commanded Mrs Morgan. She waved the vase in the air. "This is not for you," she told the terrified creature on the bed.

"It is a vase for the flowers," I explained. I snatched the vase from Mrs Morgan's hand and thrust the flowers into it. God knows what foul torture masquerading as medicine had been administered to the helpless body of the poor lady. What frightful purgings and emetics, what blisters and cuppings had she endured? I put the vase on the windowsill where it could be seen from that place of pain that was mockingly called her bed.

"There's nothing quite like flowers to cheer a room. I'll make sure you have fresh flowers every day, every day," I crooned to her, the way a mother does to soothe a fractious child or a groom to calm a skittish horse, as I took my leave. I wanted to convey to the poor woman that she was not entirely alone and that I would return.

I was as good as my word. Every day I climbed the stairs to the third floor. I varied the time; sometimes morning, sometimes evening. On occasions I carried up a meal tray myself to ensure the invalid got her share. It might be lunch or breakfast. Sometimes I appeared with an unscheduled treat. A fresh cake or an ice-cream in the hot weather. Mrs Morgan was never quite sure when I might appear. Every time I took flowers.

In the weeks that followed I like to think there was some improvement in the poor woman's condition. She gained some flesh and had clean linen. I did broach the question of a bath but Mrs Morgan was adamant. Her list of the perils involved in bathing and the dire consequences to the patient was long and vehemently expressed. I do not believe clean lunatics are more unruly than dirty lunatics but I gave way to her; she obviously had a horror of hot water and a profound belief in the beneficial effects of dirt. I was prepared to lose a battle as long as I won the war.

Weeks passed before I received a reply to my letter from Mr Rochester. I expect he took the opportunity to check with Mr Carter; the surgeon would not have stirred himself to write of his own accord. My master was now convinced that Mrs Morgan would have to leave his employment. I was pleased, but not surprised that he agreed to my suggestion about finding a replacement for her. The course of action I had outlined required no great exertion on his part. No doubt if the plan worked he would claim the credit. If it failed, it would be my fault. After the exchange of some letters with the keeper of the Grimsby Asylum a date was fixed for the expulsion of Mrs Morgan.

When he arrived the keeper of the Grimsby Asylum proved to be a monochrome young man. Everything about him was a pale sandy colour. His hair, his eyelashes and his whiskers were all a faded beige. He seemed much too young for his line of work. My opinion was reinforced when he introduced me to his companion, a strong-looking woman with red hair. She turned out to be his mother, a Mrs Poole. Was the boy not fit to travel alone?

I soon changed my mind about him. He wasted no time in getting to work and preparing for the task ahead. Word was sent to Old John to have the gig ready to deliver one departing servant to the staging post on the turnpike road. Young Mr Poole advised me to calculate her wages and have the money counted, ready to put in her hand. Then he questioned me closely about the patient. I was ashamed by how little I could tell him about the lady — not even her name.

"A connection of Mr Rochester's, you say. From Jamaica? Not a relative? The lady has no family who have sent letters or made enquiries about her welfare? Well, they do say an Englishman's home is his castle. It seems to me very wrong that she should be shut up here for so long without anyone in authority knowing. Well, I am here now. And I bring her the best nurse I have." He turned to smile at his mother. Then he turned to me. "Perhaps you will lead the way. Yours is the only face that is familiar to the patient. I do not wish to alarm her unnecessarily."

My heart fluttered as I led the way up to the third floor. I expected much shouting and noisy protests, even some scuffles. Sam and John were standing by in case force was needed. In the event the three of us were through the door and in the room before Mrs Morgan had her eyes open. She was sprawled in an armchair where she'd been sleeping in front of the fire. Robert Poole leaned over her. I thought him very brave to go so close to the evil-smelling wretch. His mother meanwhile went straight to the window and flung it open, letting in a rush of fresh air. A woman after my own heart, I decided in that instant.

The young man fixed Mrs Morgan with his pale washed-out eyes. "I am the keeper of the Grimsby Asylum and I have a letter from your master delivering the lady into my care." With a deft movement he produced the letter from his pocket and wafted it in front of her face. "Where is the patient?"

Mrs Morgan's mouth worked like a carp feeding but no words came out. Just a pop, pop, popping sound. She managed to raise an arm. The flesh on it wobbled from side to side as she pointed to the door that led to the adjoining room. Young Mr Poole gestured to indicate that I should go first.

58

As I went through the door I realized my hands were empty; I had forgotten my customary bunch of flowers. Yesterday's cornflowers in the silver vase brought dabs of blue to the otherwise drab and cheerless room. They were the only sign of freshness and colour in the noisome chamber. The hideous chain still tethered the lady to the bed but today her face was not concealed behind the great mass of hair, for she lay back upon the pillows I'd provided.

"I'm sorry," I told her, "I've forgotten your flowers." She seemed to listen to me. I even fancied her to be disappointed about the flowers but pleased to see me. I drew close to the bed and gestured to young Mr Poole who had followed me into the room. "I have brought you a better gift than flowers. This gentleman is skilled in healing. He is going to help us look after you."

Her bloodshot eyes swivelled in her hollow face and fixed upon her unexpected visitor. He bowed as seriously as if I'd introduced him to a duchess at a ball. "First, ma'am, if you agree, I think we must free you from this chain."

He waited politely. She said nothing. "I shall take your silence as your consent. Mrs Fairfax, would you be so kind as to get the key from Mrs Morgan?"

I ducked back into the first room where a strange tableau met my eyes. Mrs Poole and Mrs Morgan were locked in a silent tussle by the open window. Mrs Poole held Mrs Morgan's wrists in a fierce grip while the fat nurse twisted and struggled to get free. They were eyeball to eyeball and were exchanging killing looks.

Mrs Poole kept her voice low out of consideration for the patient but her words and her temper were high. "This poisonous creature has just thrown the key out of the window," she hissed. "It is an act of sheer spite. It means the poor wretch in there will have to endure the blows of the blacksmith's hammer."

Mrs Morgan smirked at her captor. "You are stealing my place. I'll not make it easy for you. You'll be sorry when that wild woman in there starts her screaming — and fighting. She is as strong as a horse. You'll have your hands full then." She gave Mrs Poole a loathsome leer.

My fingers itched to wipe the self-satisfied smile off her face. It took all my years of hard-won self-control not to slap her with my bare hand. I consoled myself by thinking of the revenge I planned to take on this foul creature. I was going to hit her in a place that would really hurt her. Her pocket.

"You'll pay for the blacksmith. From your wages." I laid heavy emphasis on the word to remind her that her wages were still under my control. She stopped struggling. "Let her go, Mrs Poole. Then she can collect her belongings."

I turned to the now-docile Mrs Morgan. "When you have assembled what belongs to you then you can come down to my office. I will pay you what we owe you." When she turned her back I slipped the spare key the blacksmith had given me to Mrs Poole. She accepted it with a nod and glided quietly into the next room.

I stood over Mrs Morgan as she collected up her belongings. I did not want her to have the chance of stealing the lady's clothes. A flash of clean white linen amid the dingy grey petticoats caught my attention. I took the garment from Mrs Morgan's grimy fingers and held it up; it was a muslin dress of the kind ladies used to wear some years ago. It was a garment more suited to the warm climate of the West Indies. Far too long and narrow for the squat and billowing Mrs Morgan. I held it up against her. Even she could see that claiming the garment as her own was beyond belief. Of her own volition she handed me a couple of similar garments. As the drawers emptied I began to realize how few clothes the lady had. Just a few flimsy nightdresses. No shawl, no pelisse. How had she survived the Yorkshire winter? I was under no illusion about which of them sat in the room with a fire.

Once her bag was packed I marched Mrs Morgan wheezing and huffing under her load down the stairs. In my office I sat at my desk and left her standing on the other side of it like a naughty schoolchild summoned to the head teacher for punishment. I pointed to the pile of golden sovereigns and silver coins on my desk. The sight of the money seemed to cheer her. With a great show I removed a sovereign and a shilling from the pile. "That is to cover the cost of the blacksmith. I was not consulted about the chain. You ordered it to be fitted so you pay for it." Very slowly and with great deliberation I removed two more sovereigns. "That is for your washing. It was agreed when you first arrived."

Her face suffused to an angry red and she clenched her fists. I was glad I had taken the precaution of making sure John and Sam the footmen were in earshot. Her mouth opened and instead of the expected deluge of profanities she made that popping sound again. I fixed her with my best gimlet stare and dared her to say she had been with us the best part of a year without having washing done. I saw her think about saying it. And then she thought again.

"The gig will take you to the toll road. You can pick up the stagecoach there. You will not be getting a reference."

She opened her mouth to complain but nothing came out. Not even the popping sound. She had collapsed into a sack of rags; all the fight had gone out of her. I followed her to the door and watched as she heaved herself into the gig. Old John clicked his tongue and shook the reins. In minutes, she was gone.

I thought of sending Leah to take his payment to the blacksmith. I had promised him his money the day the wearer of the chain was released. I dismissed the idea as the kind of frivolous and interfering matchmaking old women go in for. Instead I sent John, the footman. He was sick with love for Leah, but too young and inexperienced to do anything about it. Handing money over to his rival might give him a moment of power and encourage him to be more active in his wooing instead of just looking at his beloved with puppy eyes. Besides I needed Leah for the cleaning.

"The sovereign is for the blacksmith and the shilling is for you for your trouble," I told John. His smile was all the thanks I needed as he scampered off. For a moment I forgot my burden of responsibilities and shared his carefree delight in a trip outside the confines of Thornfield Hall. As I turned back to the house I picked up my burdens again. The dreadful Mrs Morgan was gone but the poor mad lady remained.

Young Mr Poole came to have a bite of lunch with me. I sent up bread and cheese for his mother and the lady. "It is important for the lady to eat and regain her strength," young Mr Poole told me. "If you have porter in the house that would be splendid. It builds up weakened constitutions. And to tell the truth my mother is very partial to it. It's like feeding children. A mouthful for me and now a mouthful for you. Just to get them back into the way of eating."

"I shall send for some porter straight away. Mr Rochester does not forbid alcohol. Indeed there is some excellent wine in the cellar. Perhaps a glass or two?"

He frowned and pursed his lips, wrinkling up his young sandy face until he looked like a little blond monkey. "That might be a touch strong at the moment. From the bottles I can tell what medicines were given to the lady. What I do not know is how much she was given or how frequently. Could your Mr Carter help me with this?"

"I doubt it. Mr Carter seldom saw the lady. To be honest he is better with horses and dogs than people. Mrs Morgan sent orders direct to the apothecary. I have the receipts. We could work it out roughly."

So we set to with the account books and the invoices from the apothecary. When we had finished Mr Poole whistled through his teeth. "There is enough to kill a horse."

"Perhaps Mrs Morgan took some of this syrup of poppy herself. She was very indolent. I was ill over the winter but when I started to visit she was often asleep. As indeed she was today."

"Let us hope so. Weaning the lady off laudanum is going to be very painful for her. We have to reduce the dose gradually. I must warn you there may be wild behaviour, screaming and crying. Things will be said that you should try to forget. My mother is very experienced at this kind of work. I leave her free to adjust the dosage. There is a certain amount of trial and error."

I accompanied him upstairs to check on the patient and make further arrangements. The lady still lay on the bed but the chain was gone. She was covered with a blanket as the window was open and the cool air blew in from the hills. I could not restrain myself from checking that the chamber pot had been emptied. It had. Mrs Poole caught me wrinkling my nose in distaste at the smell that still pervaded the room in spite of her attention to this basic task.

"One step at a time," she told me. "Perhaps we could have some lavender from the garden tomorrow."

Mother and son put their heads together as they went through the bottles and boxes of medicine. The son held up each bottle in turn, sniffed it and dabbed a finger in the powders and tasted them. When he was sure of the contents he wrote their names very clearly on labels and tied them with different coloured threads round the necks of the bottles. Some of the potions caused them both to frown with dismay. "I would not use this to kill a rat," Mr Poole declared, holding some white powder at arm's length. Once the medicaments were selected they discussed dosages and frequency. There was much talk of grains, drachms and drops.

As they worked I took the opportunity to study the lady. She lay without moving as if the chain still bound her and she watched Mr Poole and his mother go about their business with no more interest than if they were inhabitants of the moon. She looked at them but she did not see. The only evidence of life and movement she displayed was in her hands. Her nails were grubby and broken and the skin of her hands marked with scratches and scars as if she had fought and struggled against her captivity. Now she lay back and played with her hands much as a baby does when he is first discovering them. She knitted them together and then set them fluttering loose like butterflies, enjoying the freedom of movement after the weeks of having her left arm manacled. I looked at the lady's left hand. This time there was no manacle to distract me. Sure enough, dull with grease and dirt, there was a wedding ring. Jewellery, I thought. Genteel ladies always had some jewellery. Had I been so careless as to let Mrs Morgan carry away the lady's other jewels?

Mr Poole bid farewell to his mother and accompanied me to my office. Where Mrs Morgan had stood I invited him to sit. Where I had exerted power over her I listened to him.

"I will write to Mr Rochester. I think it is safe to say the exchange has been successfully completed." He gave me a shy grin and I nodded my agreement. "When I write I shall point out how inadequately clothed the lady is. I shall ask for a sum of money to be advanced to equip her properly. You can deal with that, Mrs Fairfax?"

"It will be my pleasure."

"My mother is a very skilled attendant and she . . ." he paused to search for the best words, "is an enthusiastic reader. Newspapers, novels, even books of sermons, she enjoys them all. But she is not good at making the letters. No one taught her to write. Perhaps you would take on the task of writing a short report on progress to me and Mr Rochester."

"Mr Rochester does not want reports. He prefers not to be reminded about the lady."

"Well, perhaps you will keep me informed when there is something important to say. I trust to your discretion."

"Of course. I will be glad to be involved. I am ashamed of the state of the poor woman — and her rooms. I feel responsible. I thought Mrs Morgan had superior knowledge. My hands were tied until matters became desperate."

"Some people will say it was better than the asylum but to be honest, Mrs Fairfax, things are better in my asylum." He gave a satisfied little grin. "Relatives can make an enormous difference. The lady seems to have none."

"She is married. Or rather she wears a wedding ring."

"No husband has made enquiries about her?"

"No. None that I know of."

"To be honest sometimes a husband can make matters worse. I've been approached by relatives and parents desperate to rescue daughters driven to despair by cruel husbands. They want to bring the woman into our care. If the husband refuses there is nothing they can do. They go to court for writs of Habeas Corpus and the law won't help. The husband can keep her locked away like Bluebeard if that is what he wants." He shook his head at the iniquity of the world.

"Perhaps she is a widow."

"Yes indeed. Let's look on the bright side; she might be a widow. A widow, as I am sure you are well aware, is a free agent." He picked up his hat ready to leave. "If only we had a name for her."

"My master gave no name for her. Mrs Morgan seemed to feel no need for one."

"How can you exist if you haven't a name?"

"According to Mrs Morgan the lady had an extreme fear of water. I am not sure I believe her. I think it was Mrs Morgan who did not value cleanliness."

He thought for a moment. "I suppose all the weeks the lady spent at sea, totally surrounded by water, may have made her morbidly fearful of the element. Such fears can be cured. I can see you like a clean house, Mrs Fairfax. Do not concern yourself. I am confident that my mother will sort out that problem." With that he bid me farewell.

To my relief Mrs Poole proved as unlike her predecessor, Mrs Morgan, as it was possible to be. She did not hide behind locked doors, nor did she demand a special diet for herself, or generally show a total lack of respect for her fellow servants. As soon as she could leave the lady, her patient — we still did not know what to call her — Mrs Poole came to my room, knocked on the door and asked me to arrange for her to meet all the servants involved in caring for the lady. This seemed an appropriate moment to tell her about the oath of secrecy Mr Rochester had demanded of us. She screwed up her face and thought for a minute. Then her face cleared and she announced, "The oath is not necessary for me. I do not gossip about my patients."

That evening we shooed the kitchen maids and the stable boys out after their supper. Only the oath-takers were left in the servants' hall. I said a few words to introduce Grace and then sat down, leaving her free to talk.

"My given name is Grace," she began. "I know that we have to abide by the rules and call each other Mrs this or Mr that when the gentry are around. I just want you all to know that my name is Grace, Grace Poole. My son is the keeper of the asylum in Grimsby. Thanks to the good offices of Mrs Fairfax here we have been appointed by Mr Rochester to look after the unfortunate lady upstairs.

"I want to warn you all that we may have a very difficult few months. The lady has been given large doses of some very strong drugs; they have made her sleep much more than is healthy. My first task is to reduce the amount and number of these medications. She will be very distressed by this. She will be in a kind of pain of the mind as she wakes from her perpetual night.

"I do not know what form her madness took before she was drugged into apathy. As I reduce the drug her malady will probably recur. She may have fits of weeping, she may be violent, hurling herself against walls or she may try to climb out of windows convinced that she can fly. She may hear voices or tell fantastic stories that cannot possibly be true. At the moment, she is filthy, nit-ridden, silent and terrified. She does not move from the bed she was chained to. This is no way for a human being to live. I look for your help in changing this."

We were all silent. I had seen the state of the lady and of her room, but to the others this description was a truly shocking revelation. As servants we were dedicated to keeping everything around us neat and clean and tidy. To find we had such a dung heap within the walls went against the grain of our very existence. To my surprise it was young John, the new footman, who was the first to speak. His voice wobbled; he was as surprised by his temerity as the rest of us.

"Thank you for telling us your name. My real name's Timothy. That's what my mother calls me. Here I have to be called John. It's to save Mr Rochester the trouble of learning a new name every time he gets a new footman." He looked across the table. As usual his gaze fell on Leah. This time it was rewarded with a smile; his courage in speaking must have impressed her. "You don't need to use my christened name," he told us all. "I've got used to John by now." He sat down and looked both sheepish and pleased as a murmur of respect rumbled round the room.

"What can we do?" The question was on everyone's lips.

"You can help her learn again about day and night. Bustle about your tasks in day time. Talk when you are in the room with her. Find reasons to come upstairs to us. The door to the sitting room will not be locked during the day. For the moment I will have to lock it at night. Also for a time meals must be brought up to her. It will be extra work for you but, you understand, I dare not leave her alone more than is absolutely necessary."

The table echoed with a gentle rumble of doesn't matter, no trouble, a good cause sort of noise. Grace's impassive face relaxed into a smile.

"Good to hear it. The battle-axe who guarded the door is gone. Now, when you come, bring the tray into the room. Stay for a chat. Never mind that she does not speak. She has been isolated too long. Does a newspaper come to the house?" She looked to me for an answer. I gave an affirmative nod of my head.

"I'd be glad of a read of it. Better still if someone would come and read it aloud and let the lady listen in. It is good for us all to be up to date and know what is going on in the world. I must warn you though, that being in the same room with the lady is not a pleasant prospect at the moment. I hope to persuade her to have a bath soon and to have her hair cut. In the meantime, ladies, for your own sake keep your hair well fastened back and pin your cap on firmly. You don't want little visitors in your lovely locks."

70

The Lady

1823

It was decided that the first room, where Mrs Morgan had installed herself like a sultan with his loot, was to be cleaned thoroughly. All the bedding and the hangings were removed and washed or taken outside and beaten. Leah and John were in and out moving the furniture, helping with the cleaning and delivering the meals. I had the feeling that a friendship was beginning to blossom between them. Their happy chatter helped dispel the gloom that had attached itself to the third floor.

In spite of our efforts the big four-poster bed in the first room proved impossible to move. Heaven only knows how they first carried it in. There was a big cabinet carved with the twelve apostles and topped with the figure of Christ crucified. I wanted that removed too; it seemed a nasty gruesome thing for a sick mind to live with. Grace granted it a reprieve. The cupboard could be locked so she would use it to store the dangerous medicines.

Soon the lady had a chair in her bedroom, curtains at the window and a table by her bed. There was a cheerful fire in the grate when the weather was cool as it so often is in this part of the world. A kettle provided them with tea whenever they wished it without the labour of descending the stairs to the kitchen.

I believe the kettle was much used during the night at first. The lady, deprived of her sleeping syrup was, to put it mildly, wakeful and restless. Fortunately my deafness protected me from the worst of the shrieks and wails. There was many a morning when Grace appeared haggard and hollow-eyed when the breakfast tray was delivered. "Snappish," she would say when asked how the lady was. "The opium is working out of her system."

My daily visits to the third floor were no longer an ordeal I had to brace myself to undertake. The foul stench, though not completely eliminated, was masked by the scent of lavender and mitigated by the open windows and the increased traffic through the frequently opened door. Grace disliked locked doors. What if there were a fire? she would ask.

The topic that exercised us most was the delicate question of the lady's personal hygiene. She had allowed Grace to wash her hands and face but that was all. Mention of the washing of her hair or a bath sent her into paroxysms of shrieking.

Clean clothing was also a problem. There had been no word from Mr Rochester to authorize the purchase of new clothes. We had done our best from the limited resources we had. Most of the clothes of my first Mr Rochester's wife had been disposed of. The second and third Mr Rochester were bachelors so there was no mistress's wardrobe we could plunder. We managed to ensure the lady was decently covered but you could not say much more than that.

Eventually a letter came from Mr Rochester. It was very brief; the delights of Paris were obviously absorbing most of his attention. He was glad *his* plan to approach the keeper of the Grimsby Asylum had worked so well. There was no need to bother him with details now the unfortunate lady was adequately cared for. We could contact him if there was another dire emergency. He made it quite clear that another emergency would be judged as inefficiency on my part. His letter did not reveal the lady's name but agreed to an allowance of fifteen pounds to be spent on clothes.

I took Leah with me to choose linen for a set of undergarments and samples of fabric for a skirt and bodice for the lady. We also looked at woollen stuff for a warm pelisse; the poor woman must have suffered dreadfully from the cold. In the shop they assumed that the clothes were for Leah and I saw no reason to disillusion them. We had decided that we would do the sewing between us to avoid calling in a seamstress. A dressmaker would want to measure the lady. This was out of the question in her present state. Even if we could get the lady bathed a dressmaker would ask many impertinent questions. She would also be sure to inform all the gentry of the neighbourhood that Thornfield Hall had a dirty new resident of mysterious origins.

When we returned with our purchase Grace shook out the white linen fabric and held it up to show the lady. "This will be for you," she told her as if she was a four-year-old child. The lady reached out her hand to stroke the cloth. Her hand stood out against the pure white of the fabric; her skin was a dark shade of grey. Grace took advantage of the opportunity presented to her.

"We always wash our hands before we handle our sewing," said Grace gently. "Shall we wash yours?"

A bowl of water was brought and the lady's hands were washed with scented soap. It was strange to see such large hands with such long fingers washed and dried like a giant child's. The lady sat placidly through the whole procedure.

Morbid fear of water! Pshaw, Mrs Morgan! I know who was afraid of water.

It does not do to have smug thoughts; they always precede a nasty shock. Grace, grown confident by the lady's composure, reached forward to sweep back the lady's hair so that she could wipe her face. It was a step too far. The lady's hands flew to the base of her throat as if to protect this most vulnerable part of her anatomy. Her face suffused with black rage. She leapt to her feet. The bowl flew across the room and the water splayed out in a great arc. She loomed over Grace and made a lunge at her throat. Murder seemed a short step away.

Grace stood her ground and looked up boldly into the lady's face. "Steady, steady, girl," she said as if she were talking to a restless horse. "I see now. It is your locket. I understand. Your locket. No one here is going

74

to steal it." The lady's hands hung over her like claws ready to maul Grace's face.

A calm, smiling Grace held her ground, the lady's hands dropped and she fluttered her fingers over a locket round her neck to reassure herself it was really there. We had not noticed it earlier. Among the grime and the enveloping mass of black hair, there was no gleam of gold to draw our attention. We had thought all her jewellery gone with Mrs Morgan.

The locket was a very ordinary and well-worn item; the base metal showed through where the gilding had rubbed off. Though its monetary value would be small its sentimental value to the lady was evidently immense. Only when she was satisfied that the trinket was safe did she sink back into her seat. There she sat quietly with an expression of puzzlement on her face, and she gave Grace a very close scrutiny as if she was seeing her for the first time and was agreeably surprised by what she saw.

I was amazed. It was the first evidence I had seen that our grubby and disordered charge was a living sentient being capable of action, thought and emotion. Later Grace and I talked about the incident with the locket.

"It must be very important to her," Grace reflected. "It would be interesting to know who gave it to her. No use asking. She'll tell us when she's ready. She has managed to keep it out of the clutches of Mrs Morgan. That must've taken some doing. No wonder her hands are scratched. I hate to rub your nose in it, Alice, but I think Mrs Morgan got away with some valuables. It is a poor lady indeed who has so little jewellery."

I felt bad about the jewellery. Then I counted up the good things I had done. I had got rid of a nasty vicious nurse and had replaced her with a much more promising one. Grace might look cold and remote but her heart was definitely in the right place. And she appreciated cleanliness. "Do you think she will trust us not to steal from her?"

"Perhaps. For a wonderful moment when she went for me I thought she might say something."

"That would be a great step forward."

"Depends. I warn you her first words may be a disappointment to you. You wouldn't believe the words some of these ladies know. They can cuss and swear like sailors."

We soon had a set of plain white nightgowns ready for the lady. She was quite overcome when we laid the finished garments out to show her. Tears trickled down her grimy face. She looked up at Grace with a question on her face and pointed at her own bosom. "Yes. For you," Grace assured her. "Your very own. To wear."

To our amazement a sound came from her lips. From the mouth that we had only ever seen opened to eat or to scream in anguish came a sound that might have been a word. None of us was sure what exactly the sound was. There was a B and TH and we each made our own interpretation of it. I was torn between Bath and Berthe, the French version of Bertha. I had once met a governess who was so named.

"Just my luck," said Grace. "I get her to say a word and it's in French."

After supper that night there was much excitement. John and Leah ran up the stairs with hot water. Never have I seen servants lug the heavy pails with such enthusiasm. The lady had agreed to take a bath.

Grace came to give me a late-night report. The lady had indeed bathed. The operation had been accomplished smoothly and without distress.

"I look forward to visiting her in the morning."

"Don't expect too much. The hair is still a problem but the rest of her is clean. She is not exactly pink and white. I kept scrubbing. I thought it was dirt until I realized it was the colour of her skin."

"She came from Jamaica. It is hot there. The sun makes people darker."

"Right enough. The sailors who come to Grimsby are all different colours. Anyway that is not the most important thing. Not only is she clean, she said some more words, quite a few more. We were both right. She wanted a bath and her name is that French one you said. She doesn't sound French, but she's not quite English, if you know what I mean. She definitely doesn't come from these parts. I've started to call her Bertha."

By the next morning word had gone round the servants' hall. Bertha she became to all of us.

Although the late Mrs Rochester had contributed little to the lady's wardrobe, she had left a dressing set that we dusted off. A prudent Grace removed the scissors and anything else with a sharp point. She set out the silver-backed brushes and the hand mirror in the bedroom in the hope of persuading Bertha to co-operate in dealing with her hair. "It's a nits' nest," Grace complained. "She'll have to have it cut. You can't get a comb through it and it's going to need weeks of fine-combing to clear out all those pesky little visitors." Grace tried persuading Bertha that her hair would grow back smooth and glossy after it was cut but to no avail. She tried to keep the shaggy black mop restrained in a cap, skewering it on tight with hairpins. A battle then ensued between cap and hair. The hair always won, somehow contriving to throw off all restraint and send hairpins in every direction.

This did not stop us from furnishing the rooms on the third floor with the small comforts of life. Some of the more cheerful-looking books were brought up from the library to occupy the bookshelf in the sitting room and a couple of watercolours of landscapes decorated the walls. With the addition of some colourful cushions the room became a pleasant place in which to spend time.

In the afternoons we ladies took refuge there when the winter wind blew outside. We sat by the fire and drank tea while we sewed garments for the lady. As women will we gossiped and talked and we laughed. At first the lady hovered in her bedroom, watching through the open door. Soon she began to creep into the room and would lurk on the outside of our sewing circle.

Our next project was to make her a respectable dress; she was still wearing the skimpy muslin dresses that must have come with her from Jamaica. Not only were they inadequate for our Yorkshire climate, they were also hopelessly old-fashioned. To be seen in them would cause public comment — something I was keen to avoid.

We had bought samples of grey cloth, thinking that would be the most suitable colour for her status. They were not a success; the fabrics lost their lustre and looked dingy against her coffee-coloured skin. In the end we decided on black; it flattered her, making her complexion glow. It was also a practical choice. You can go anywhere in black and not be noticed; it is the colour of mourning and of domestic service.

The choice of fabric was therefore comparatively easy. The calculations that followed were not. Bertha was tall but still very thin and undernourished. It seemed prudent to allow extra fabric in the seams so that the garment could be let out if she gained flesh. There was much brandishing of the tape measure and counting on fingers as we calculated how much material we would need. In the end we decided that five yards and eight inches would be sufficient.

We sat back and had a cup of tea to revive us after our mental effort. Worse lay ahead. We needed to calculate the cost. Could we afford to pay for a good-quality material? Bertha would need at least one more dress, a pelisse, a cape, bonnets and shoes and boots. Grace and I found scraps of paper and pencils to work out the cost of five and one quarter yards of the dress material at eight shillings and four pence a yard. We hoped that if we worked it out separately we might reach the same answer. It did not happen.

After several attempts Grace threw her pencil and paper aside in disgust. "It's no use," she declared. "It comes out different every time."

I persevered; I was the one responsible for the accounts. I was still muttering "twelve pennies make a shilling and twenty shillings make one pound" while counting on my fingers when Bertha slid Grace's slip of paper in front of me. I had been so busy concentrating on my own efforts I had not noticed that Bertha had taken over Grace's piece of paper. On it was written in neat figures the working out of the sum that had pestered us for the best part of an hour. The answer was two pounds, three shillings and seven pence. I checked through each step of the calculation. It was all correct. Our poor mad lady, who could scarcely speak, could do sums as neat as you please.

We stared at her, dumbstruck. Leah was particularly impressed that Bertha's poor addled brain had succeeded where Grace and I had struggled. "Well, I never," she kept saying and peered at Bertha as if to root out the thread of clarity that ran through the confused fabric of her mind. Bertha seemed not to mind her scrutiny. Calmly she handed Leah the needle she had threaded for her.

Bertha's black dress grew quickly. I always feel an everyday sort of wonder at the way a flat length of cloth can be transformed into a garment in the shape of a woman.

"How shall we make the neckline?" Grace demanded. She held the bodice up for inspection. "You'll want it to look right with your locket," she told Bertha as she approached and held the garment against her to check the fit. Bertha looked slightly overwhelmed but did not run away. "Fetch the mirror, Leah, so she can see."

Leah did as she was bid and held the mirror up. I cannot say that Bertha was rendered speechless by seeing herself for the first time; she and speech were still comparative strangers to each other. She was certainly shocked by what she saw in the mirror. She fled into her bedroom. No appeals from us could persuade her to come out. As she sobbed quietly behind the closed door we whispered gently to each other and at Grace's suggestion carried on sewing.

Half an hour later a red-eyed Bertha appeared from her bedroom. She went to pick up the large shears we used to cut out the pieces of the dress. A quiver went through all of us. Would she run amok amongst us, slashing and cutting at our clothes and flesh? We all knew she was capable of turning violent. No. Bertha held the scissors out to Grace, carefully offering her the handles rather than the sharp blades.

"Cut my hair, please. Cut my hair."

Monsieur Alphonse

1824-5

Our patient made slow but steady progress. A clean Bertha was very different from a dirty Bertha. Now when she circled round us as we sewed in the third-floor sitting room we made room for her to join us. Someone would pat a chair and invite her to sit. Soon we had her threading needles. Then we gave her leftover squares of fabric to practise on and were delighted to discover she could make neat small stitches.

Gradually a few more words came from her lips. To our relief they were not French words, though sometimes the way she said them was a little unexpected. She did not speak of anything complicated or personal, just everyday matters. She was cold, she was hungry. She liked the jelly I had made. When would her dress be ready? What were our names? It took her weeks to learn them. She would master them one day and then forget them overnight.

To our surprise she had been well-trained in politeness. Someone had instilled good manners in her — to say please and thank you and wait to be offered things and to speak only when spoken to. With her short hair and her simple ways she seemed like an obedient child, one who by mistake inhabited the body of a giantess.

And it was definitely a woman's body according to Grace, who confided to me that she was sure that Bertha had had a child. The famous bath had revealed what Grace described as unmistakeable signs. I assume she meant stretch marks. We speculated as to what had happened to it and wondered if or where it — the child — lived. According to Grace, who was witness to Bertha's wildest ravings, she had never talked of a child. We wondered if it had died.

"That's enough to send you mad," I told Grace with feeling. "For a time at least."

Bertha's dress was finished. As she had proved such a skilled needlewoman, better than any of us, we asked her to sew the buttons on and make the buttonholes. Badly worked buttonholes can ruin a garment. When she first put it on she pranced round the sitting room, twirling her skirt like a child on her birthday. I will admit I felt a lump in my throat at witnessing the transformation from manacled madwoman to walking, talking human being.

Once the dress was finished our thoughts turned to further garments we should make. We were keen to continue our afternoons of sewing; they were a pleasant distraction for us. Often I would ask Leah to climb on the big bed and read a chapter or two of a novel to us. This became a popular task. Even Old John would come up sometimes and read the newspaper to us. Grace was very keen on the newspaper; she liked to keep up to date and to know what was happening in the world.

As there was still money to spend on her clothes Leah suggested that we make Bertha some more undergarments. "Not such plain ones this time. She should have some decoration on them. Hers are not good enough for gentry," she insisted.

This raised the interesting question of Bertha's status. Because Mr Rochester had brought her to the house we assumed she was gentry. Her manners were good enough. With her new clothes she might almost pass in the drawing room as long as she sat quiet and no one was unkind enough to ask what she had been reading or what she thought on a matter of current interest. It was not likely that anyone would do such a thing. The ladies only ever talked about their children and their servants — mostly to abuse them. We knew what was said in the drawing rooms of all the county families; we had a network of spies. The footman carried the gossip with the dirty cups down the back stairs to the cook and the kitchen maids. They told the scullery maids who told the delivery boys who spread it faster than the measles. The gossip arrived at our back door more quickly than the newspaper. I was proud that the one topic *not* talked about by the gentry was the mysterious new resident at Thornfield Hall; she was a servants' secret.

"She should have a nice nightgown." Leah was still thinking about underwear. "She doesn't have any stays but then she doesn't need them. She's still so thin."

84

"O but she must have stays." The words came from my lips with unexpected vehemence. I was shocked to hear that I sounded exactly like my own mother. She regarded stays as an essential item in a woman's wardrobe. "Women always wear stays," I found myself informing Leah as if it was an article of faith. "She cannot go out without stays. We do want her to go out, don't we?"

"Indeed we do," said Grace. "Getting her back to the world is the whole idea. At the moment she isn't even curious about the rest of the house. She is not in such pain as she was. I'd be surprised if she wanted to risk exploring beyond this safe haven, but if we are ever to say that she is better, she must go out into the world."

"If she is going out into society, she must have stays." I was adamant on the subject.

Stays were duly procured for Bertha. They were a garment she found very puzzling at first. It was clear that the ladies of the West Indies did not go in much for corsetry. No doubt their climate is too warm for them to feel comfortable when constricted.

Over the next months Bertha's world and her figure gradually expanded. With Grace's care and Mary's food she grew quite buxom. The stays were no longer just a nod to the conventions; they were a necessity. Once she was laced up and dressed with a cap to conceal her shorn locks we thought her suitably attired to venture beyond the rooms on the third floor. How this should be accomplished was the subject of much heart-searching on the part of Grace and me. We rejected the idea of going up to the roof for her first taste of fresh air. Too dangerous, Grace thought. Her dreadful unhappiness was too recent; she might have a sudden fit and try to hurl herself from the roof and fall to her death on the stones below.

I passed on to Grace Mr Rochester's insistence that Bertha would not be going into society. "He was determined that she be kept away from his neighbours. Didn't even want her to go out in the carriage." Bertha might be qualified as gentry by birth but she was obviously never going to be acceptable in the drawing room at Thornfield Hall.

"She might be a high-class lady's maid," Grace suggested. "She sews beautifully."

"She's had a baby. Could be the master of the house had something to do with that."

"You old cynic," Grace taunted me. "As if that ever happens in this world."

"Well it didn't happen in this house. Maybe the master is doing a favour for a friend."

"Maybe," said Grace, who had no high opinion of the gentry. "The men would stick together to conceal their little misdeeds from their wives."

We decided that when Bertha ventured out of the third floor we would teach her to use the back stairs. For all the so-called weakness of her mind she could be trained, much as you would train a child or a puppy. Her first destination was to be my housekeeper's room. It would provide a safe haven that was close to the outside world. Gradually we would introduce her to the idea of going outside whilst keeping her out of the way of society.

"Mr Rochester has warned that he will visit at short notice. He expects to find the house ship-shape. I do not think he wants to meet Bertha on the stairs."

Grace started her campaign by putting crumbs for the birds on the windowsill. As the sparrows and blue tits found them and landed there Bertha sat and watched the birds pecking happily. When the birds flew away she'd stay at the window and direct her attention to the world outside. The window gave onto the main drive up to the house. There were few visitors to the front door and few calls for the carriage to entertain her. Old John liked to keep the horses in practice so he'd drive round with the gig most days. The butcher's boy would come whistling up the main drive and give a cheery wave to the figure on the third floor. His sharp young eyes were the only ones to spot her. He'd come round to the tradesmen's entrance and ask when we were letting our prisoner out. Did we feed her bread and water?

"Only on Fridays," I'd tell him. "Don't you be so cheeky."

The first trip down the back stairs was a tense affair. Bertha, kept confined on one level for so long, had to concentrate on where to put her feet and to keep her balance on the narrow twisting steps. She obviously found them strange and troublesome. So much for Grace's theory that she might have been a lady's maid. A lady's maid would be accustomed to using the back stairs. I was sure that Bertha was more familiar with the wide sweeping staircases of the main house.

After the first flight we had to cross the corridor to take the next flight down. She showed no curiosity about the lofty bedrooms that lined the corridors stretching to the right and left of us. The ground-floor rooms were easier to pass by as the stairs gave no more than a glimpse of the breakfast room. In the safety of my room she took a quick glance through the window and then spent a happy half hour examining the contents of the room. She flicked open the books as if looking for pictures. She did not read them. My knitting seemed to interest her more than anything else.

"I like your house, Mrs Fairfax," she informed me in all seriousness.

"It is not my house. It belongs to my master."

I thought she might enquire about my master but her attention was caught by the embroidery on the fire screen and she said no more on the subject. Soon it was time for her to climb back into her eyrie. Grace said that her charge was as tired that night as if she had tramped five miles.

For some months we made this discreet secretive visit two or three times a week. Bertha still showed no desire to explore further or find out about the owner of the house. One Thursday Leah came flying towards us as we were clambering down the back stairs to bring Bertha to spend an hour in my room.

"Mrs Fairfax, Mrs Fairfax! Go back. Go back. There's a stranger in your room. A foreigner. I didn't get his name. Says he's the master's man."

I told Leah to calm down and to help Grace get Bertha back upstairs. Bertha took some persuading.

Changing plans at short notice was not one of her strong points; she tended to get into one of her states if asked to do something unexpected. Then I hastened down the stairs. Outside my room I smoothed my hair and wiped the panic off my face. After a couple of deep breaths I was able to open the door and confront my visitor.

A man sat in the armchair by the window contemplating the view that we had hoped would lure Bertha into venturing outside the house. The man rose to his feet to greet me. I could see at once that he was dressed with an elegance seldom found in Yorkshire. He gestured at the landscape beyond the window.

"I am pleased to see that my master has extensive grounds. It is not unknown for gentlemen to exaggerate the extent of their estates when trying to attract one to their service. I do not think I will regret my choice of employer."

I cannot describe to you how angry he made me feel. The two words "my master" hit me in the stomach like a blow from a pike. His foreign accent added insult to injury. He is not your master, I wanted to scream. He is my master. He is my third Mr Rochester. I did not choose him as if he were a sweet from a tray. I came with the house; he inherited me. Suffice it to say I simply bid him good morning, introduced myself, and asked the languid creature his business.

He produced a fine linen handkerchief and sniffed it delicately before he spoke. He claimed he was a gentleman's gentleman. To be precise he was Mr Rochester's French gentleman. My face must have shown my incomprehension for he went on to explain his function.

"One sees to the wardrobe. One advises about society. Where to go. Whom to cultivate. My master needed a great deal of help when he first arrived in Paris."

"Would one like tea?" I asked, all innocence. One would. I rang the bell. I do not often ring the bell. The kitchen is so close that if I am not in the mood to go for myself, I will open the door and shout down the corridor. Leah arrived in response to the summons. Her pink face and breathlessness were evidence that she had seen Bertha back up the stairs and had run back down again. "Ask Sam to bring in tea, please. For me and . . ." I looked towards my unexpected guest.

"Monsieur Alphonse."

Leah's mouth opened to protest that she would bring the tea. I raised my eyebrows meaningfully. "Sam can do it," I told her. "There is no need for him to change." Sam was not the most efficient footman but he was the most widely travelled of us all. I wanted his opinion of the new arrival.

Whilst we waited for the tea I quizzed Monsieur Alphonse about Mr Rochester's plans. "My master rests in a town called Manchester. It is a very dirty city. One is come in advance to make preparations for his arrival."

My heart turned over. We had grown slack over the last couple of years. It was so long since Mr Rochester had visited and our attention had been focused on the care of Bertha rather than the dusting. A heavy feeling like lead in my stomach told me I should not offer Bertha's name to Mr Rochester as an excuse for slack housekeeping. He was not interested in her progress or lack of it. I consoled myself with the thought that Mr Rochester, as a man, would not notice the dusting or the lack of it. The consolation was short-lived. The little popinjay in front of me was exactly the kind of person to run his finger along a bookshelf and grimace at the result.

Sam arrived with his shirt sleeves rolled up and his hair disarranged by the wind. I guessed he had been chopping wood. While he clattered about with the tea things I introduced him to Monsieur Alphonse, as we would have to call him. The days of our informality were over — for the moment.

"Mr Rochester always looked after hisself," Sam barked. "And his father and his brother before him. We washed their linen. We polished their boots. They had clean clothes. They didn't need people to fasten their buttons. Not once they were out of nursery."

Pain passed through the gentleman's gentleman. We watched it travel through his slender frame and wince its way across his face. Eventually the power of speech returned to him. "Here it might suffice. The capital cities of the world demand a higher standard. Clean linen is not sufficient for society to open its arms to a newly arrived country gentleman. A gentleman with no title, one must point out. One is there to advise on the nuances of fashion and behaviour. How to tie the cravat. Whom to visit, whom to avoid. When to arrive late. When to leave early."

"Well I visited a lot of capital cities when I were in navy. I managed all right." Sam stared at the well-dressed little man. It was clear there would be no meeting of minds between these two so I intervened.

"We shall need a room for Monsieur Alphonse. Mr Merryman's room is unoccupied. He could have that, could he, Sam?"

"Aye. He could. It's next to mine. I'll show him later." Sam stomped off.

The empty room in the menservants' sleeping quarters puzzled Monsieur Alphonse. When he learnt that Mr Merryman, the previous butler, had not been replaced, he was shocked.

"A gentleman always has a butler. Who decides on the wine? Who serves it?"

"Well, I expect you will. Is Mr Rochester bringing guests? Will there be a house party?"

"One believes not. Hunting and horses seemed to be foremost in my master's mind." Monsieur Alphonse did not need to add the word "unfortunately". The downturn of his mouth told us what he thought of hunting and horses.

"Has he sent instructions for Old John?" Monsieur Alphonse appeared puzzled. "Old John looks after the horses and the stables," I explained.

"No. He said nothing about an Old John."

Now here was a puzzle. If there was one thing Mr Rochester was exact about it was his horses. As I took the little man to meet the other servants I pondered on Mr Rochester's motive in sending him on ahead like John the Baptist. For all his fine talk, he was only

92

what we would call a valet. A valet, that's what he was. I looked forward to hearing what Sam thought of him.

"He's a spy. That's what Monsieur Alphonse is." Sam was adamant. "He's here to report on us. Make sure that we keep the great secret and are not drinking the claret."

We were huddled in the butler's pantry whispering to each other. John's head appeared in the serving hatch, causing us to start guiltily.

"Don't panic. The French gentleman is out of the house and on his way to the stables. He's not very happy about the mud. It will ruin the polish on his shoes."

"Sam thinks he's a spy."

"A French spy!"

"Nah. War's over. A long time since. He's a spy for Mr Rochester."

"Then why did Mr Rochester send him on ahead? Why give us warning? Give us time to hide stuff, plaster over the cracks. Much more likely the master would creep up and take us by surprise. Catch us with our trousers down, so to speak. Begging your pardon for language, Mrs Fairfax."

"That sounds more like master." Sam thought for a bit. A smile illuminated his face. "I know. My guess is that Mr Rochester's fed up with him. He's finding him annoying. He were all right in Paris. Could show him the ropes and speak the lingo. Now he's back in England he seems a bit stupid, foppish like. I bet master wishes he'd left little chap in Paris. He don't want to dismiss him. Bit hard to cut him loose, being a foreigner like. But he just wants him out of his hair — literally."

"So he may not be a spy."

"Mr Rochester may not have sent him with the intention that he spies on us, but that is exactly what he will do. Valets are sneaky little creatures. Take my word for it, he will spy on us. And he will creep round master dropping poison in his ear. He has to be useful to keep his place. Fastening buttons and brushing hairs off jackets is not enough to earn his keep here." Sam pursed his lips and nodded his head up and down as he tested the strength of his theory. Then, apparently satisfied, he turned to John and me.

"We'd best be careful, specially about Bertha. As far as we know he's not taken his bible oath, like rest of us. Until Mr Rochester hisself says so, we'd best keep mum."

John tapped his top lip with his forefinger to show he intended to keep his lips sealed.

"That's right," said Sam, "and batten down the hatches."

We did not feel it necessary to return to the subject. Here in Yorkshire we are naturally suspicious of strangers. We look askance at visitors if they come from a different county in England so there was little hope for the Frenchman. Especially since he was generally thought to be a spy. The sooner Monsieur Alphonse removed himself from Thornfield Hall the better.

My last task that day was to visit the third floor. Bertha was asleep. The interruption of her visit downstairs had disturbed her. It took only a ripple in the smooth surface of her life to upset her thoroughly. She'd had a fit of temper that was quickly followed by a bout of weeping. Grace and I decided against telling her of Mr Rochester's imminent arrival. As Grace said, he was not interested in her, and she was not interested in him. She had never enquired as to the identity of our master or even the name of the house in which she was living. For his part Mr Rochester had made no effort to inform himself about the welfare of his mysterious house guest.

Grace agreed with the general view that Monsieur Alphonse posed a threat of an unspecified nature. We decided it was safer, while the little Frenchman was here, to keep Bertha confined to the third floor and to put a stop on her little expeditions. We did not think she would protest or complain. She was happiest leading a very quiet life with a regular routine.

The valet was to sleep in the old butler's room in the menservants' corridor. Although this was on the third floor it was at the back of the house, well away from Grace and Bertha, whose rooms were at the front. It was possible to prevent his seeing them during the day as long as he did not go exploring in the night.

We worked very hard for the next few days. We cleaned and dusted, polished and waxed. The beds were stripped and the sheets were boiled. The meat was ordered and the vegetables were pickled. The extra hands I had recruited from The George to help with the cleaning ate their meals with us in the servants' hall. We had to go back to our formal ways — and highly uncomfortable it all was. We had to call each other by our official names as we went about our duties.

I entertained Monsieur Alphonse to dinner in my room as etiquette demanded. Mary obliged by sending us the worst food she could create in the hope of encouraging him to leave. We fed him porridge, boiled mutton, cabbage and the coarsest bread we could find. Whilst he struggled to swallow the tasteless slops and chew the hard tack we offered him, Grace slid secretly down the back stairs for her bread and cheese and a pint of porter.

To keep our monsieur busy we set him to sorting out the clothes accumulated by two generations of Rochester men. He tutted and fussed something shocking. He ran the garments through his fingers lamenting the old-fashioned styles and the heavy material. He made the mistake of criticizing the locally woven broadcloth that had clothed the Rochesters for generations. His biggest mistake was to do this in the hearing of Old John. The coachman promptly joined with gusto in the unofficial campaign to make life as unpleasant as possible for poor Monsieur Alphonse.

"Master'll want you to ride with him when he goes to hounds," Old John informed the valet with malice aforethought. "Now he's got his own gentleman he'll want him out in the field with him. All the gentry bring their personal servants. Case they're needed. Help carry them home if they breaks their necks."

The little man blenched so thoroughly he was positively transparent.

"We'd better be thinking of a mount for you." Old John was relentless in his torture. "Nothing too big, but able to handle the hedges. A good jumper. I've got a nice little filly would just suit you. A bit young and frisky but she'll soon learn. Come round stables this afternoon and give her a try."

By the end of the week I was beginning to feel sorry for Monsieur Alphonse, especially when John the young footman told his story to me and Sam. There'd been a knock on his door at night. He'd opened it to find the little Frenchman on the threshold. For some reason Sam chose this moment to slap his forehead as if he'd forgotten to tell us something very important.

"I don't know why he came to me," John continued. "Except I'm the only one as hasn't been actively nasty to him. I've not spat in his food or terrified him with horses. Anyway he wanted to know where he was. Poor chap didn't seem to know. I told him Yorkshire. I had to explain to him it was a whole big county. All he wanted to know was how far he was from London. And how soon could he get there. From London he wants to go to Dover. Apparently there's a boat that'll take him back to his own country."

We looked to Sam for enlightenment. Sam had sailed the world. He would know where London was.

"Must be several hundred miles. Old master used to do it by post chaise in two days, but that were pushing it. He'd be black and blue from the shaking about. And it costs. Specially for a seat inside. It's not so much to ride on top but it's cold and wet up there. I'm beginning to feel sorry for the poor little beggar."

"If only the railway had got to York. They say them steam trains can go at thirty miles an hour."

"If wishes were horses then beggars would ride," I told John. I was brisk with him as I felt bad about the way we had behaved to Monsieur Alphonse. He had come to us as a stranger and we had not welcomed him in. It was time to offer him a friendly hand. "Tell the little chap, if he has the fare, he can get the stagecoach from the turnpike road. We'll find a way to get him there."

"There must be a chaise or a cart going to the turnpike road soon. Stands to reason. Someone from round here must be going."

We sent word round the servants in the big houses. Every delivery man passed the message on with the laundry, the wine or the hay for the horses. The groom told the agent, the butler told his master, the dressmaker told the mistress. By the time Mr Rochester was due to arrive information was filtering back to us. We knew not only who was going to the turnpike road, but also that young Lord Ingram was to be sent on the Grand Tour. A younger son of Lord Clifford's was also ready to undertake the journey. The two were to travel together with a tutor appointed by Lord Clifford. There was, it seemed, a chance for Monsieur to return to the continent.

"We have Martha to thank for telling us about young Lord Ingram," Old John told me. "She sent to say that she misses Thornfield Hall. The Ingrams are hard taskmasters."

"Send her my thanks. Is she a lady's maid yet?"

Old John sucked on his pipe. "Not quite. She still has hopes."

"Mmmm. We'd best work on the Cliffords. The Ingrams are such cheese-parers. Who rules the roost in the Clifford household?"

"By all accounts, she does."

That evening I visited Grace to keep her up to date. Bertha was sleeping and Grace was puffing contentedly on her pipe by the fire. They had not been too lonely. Leah had come in the afternoon and they had done some sewing. Grace showed me the nightdress they had finished. Bertha had embroidered it with strange flowers and exotic birds — the like of which we had never seen before. We decided she must remember them from her own country, Jamaica. The work was exquisite, the stitches neat and the colours and the design well-chosen.

"It is a shame she cannot meet the Frenchman. He is good with colours too. And he dresses very smart. Not really suitable for here in the country, but you can see he has a knack."

Grace and I exchanged meaningful looks. "I am sure Lady Clifford would want her son to be a credit to her in the capitals of Europe," I told her.

Mr Rochester's arrival caused us less consternation than Monsieur Alphonse's had. We had gone into training with the valet and were battle-ready for the master. When he arrived Mr Rochester strode across the gravel to greet us as we waited at the door. It was clear he was in the peak of health and high spirits. There was an indefinable gleam to him that we had not seen before. His black hair was glossy and his eyes sparkling. His clothes fitted him to perfection and his linen was snowy white. I looked at Monsieur Alphonse with increased respect.

I was standing with my back to the house as Mr Rochester greeted me. I saw him glance up at the third storey. "Everything is in good order here," I told him and gave him a significant look straight in the eye. "Absolutely everything. The house is ready if you wish to entertain your neighbours."

"No doubt the whole county is agog to see the returning prodigal."

He gave me his winning smile, which emboldened me to answer, "You could say that, indeed you could say that, sir." As I followed him in I felt the house come alive to welcome its returning master.

The plan fell into place as we hoped it would. A word here, some gentle pressure there, a whispered suggestion, a subtle promise and people will do what you want as long as you work with the grain of their characters. The French valet wanted to go home; Lady Clifford wanted the best for her son. Mr Rochester wanted to enjoy his wealth and position and not be reminded of his responsibility for a deranged woman. The ingredients for our plan to work were there; all we needed was some luck.

Our master spent his days hunting or dealing with business matters. Once Monsieur Alphonse discovered that Old John had been playing a joke on him and that his attendance on the hunting field was not obligatory he languished with nothing to do but clean muddy boots. The unhappy valet must have felt completely marooned on a hostile island. We consoled him by dangling before him the prospect of accompanying a sprig of the grand and noble Clifford family to France. If only Mr Rochester would hold a great dinner party. If only the chosen tutor could be removed.

Help with our plan arrived in the unlikely person of Carter, the surgeon. "A hunt dinner at Thornfield Hall," he roared. "Haven't had one for years. Time we did, Rochester. Landowners' responsibility to host the event." Even if he had wanted to Mr Rochester could not have evaded what the whole county was united in wishing into existence.

"This is your chance to shine," John and Sam told Monsieur Alphonse. "Show us how things are done in Paris. Show us what proper footmen do."

To his credit Monsieur Alphonse rose to the challenge. He came to my office with a long list of requirements. Extra staff were hired in from The George in Millcote. He spent hours in the kitchen with Mary, the cook, discussing dishes and recipes. His experience of eating with me in the housekeeper's room had given him a very low opinion of the food at Thornfield Hall. It was only when Mary produced samples of his recipes that he relaxed a little. "You have been having what you English call a joke with me," he said after tasting her charlotte russe.

The dinner was to be served in a new way. Instead of setting all the food out on the table in the traditional way it was to be served to the guests one course at a time. Monsieur Alphonse explained to me that service à la Russe, as he called it, would require fewer footmen but much more cutlery. Anxiously we counted the knives, forks and spoons; there were enough.

Sam, John and some otherwise unemployed farm labourers were to serve the food at the dinner. Monsieur Alphonse drilled them in their duties with a thoroughness that left them goggle-eyed. He made them scrub their hands until their fingernails shone pink and white and forbade them from putting their clean hands in their dirty pockets. Then he turned his attention to their dress. Their workaday coats did not come up to his exacting standards. He scoured the house, convinced that somewhere there must be livery for footmen. I had great difficulty in keeping him out of Bertha's quarters until I presented him with some dark green coats, from more formal times, stored in the attic. They were shaken out with a good deal of disapproving tutting on Monsieur Alphonse's part. He sponged and he pressed, he let out shoulders and took in waists. When he'd finished with them his little band of footmen looked as smart as soldiers.

One day when there was no hunting, he cornered Mr Rochester about the choice of wine. "Since you have no butler . . ." he began. The master, in his careless open-handed way, passed him the keys to the cellar and full responsibility for the choice. Monsieur Alphonse spent an afternoon down there with a candle and a pen and paper. When he reappeared he brushed the cobwebs from his hair and declared, "If anything could reconcile me to this windswept place it would be the contents of the cellar."

The dinner was an astounding success. The county had not seen anything like it for years. In the absence of a hostess Lady Clifford led the ladies to the drawing room as they retired after the dinner. There they could give free rein to their astonishment. Every detail of dinner had delighted and thrilled them; the sophistication of the table, the delicious food, the immaculate service, the arrangement of the flowers! Yet there was no mistress to run the house! How had it been achieved? The maids and the footmen whispered the answer into the ladies' incredulous ears. It was all down to Monsieur Alphonse. Every lady present made a mental note to entice Monsieur Alphonse from Mr Rochester's service, if it was humanly possible.

In the dining room when the cloth was drawn the men settled down to drink the port. Horses, dogs and the price of corn dominated the bachelor end of the long table where Mr Rochester presided. At the other end sat Lord Clifford with the senior guests. His eldest son moved down the table to join him and Baron Ingram. Talk turned to the Grand Tour the younger son and the baronet were to take and the tutor who was to accompany them. Lord Clifford's loud voice boomed out to express his confidence in his choice. He turned to his eldest son. "He took good care of you, didn't he, when you went a couple of years back? You didn't come back with the pox as many of them do."

"Good God," the Clifford heir exploded. "You're not sending them with that old tart. He tried to bugger me in Rome."

"It was an unexpected stroke of luck," Sam reported to me. "Every enterprise needs one."

The footmen told the housemaids and the housemaids told the ladies' maids. The information reached Lady Clifford's ears as her maid prepared her for bed.

By the next evening it was all arranged. Monsieur Alphonse left with the Cliffords as the chosen companion for the young aristocrats on their way to Italy. He had assured Lady Clifford that as well as speaking French he was fluent in Italian. I suspected it was not true but I was sure he would not be caught out in his falsehood. Once he set foot in his beloved Paris, I did not expect Monsieur Alphonse to stray far from there.

104

The Incident in the Library

1826

Soon after the hunt dinner Mr Rochester set off on his mysterious travels again. We did not know his destination; we guessed it was London. Since Monsieur Alphonse had departed the master had been heard to swear he would not cross the Channel again. Though I missed his lively presence in the house in some ways it was a relief to see him go. The dinner and the overnight guests had made much extra work in the house and there were many tasks ahead of us.

My few conversations with my master had been held in haste when other people were present. He had not summoned me to check on the arrangements for the patient and I for one was glad of it. If the subject of Bertha had come up I think I would have been warm with him. Devoted to him though I was, I did not think he should leave such a responsibility to servants with so little guidance. As it was he rode off in blithe indifference while I stayed and burned with resentment.

Bertha had languished during his visit. She had missed our comfortable afternoons sewing and her trips downstairs. True to her childlike nature she accepted the simple explanation of "visitors" without needing or wishing to know more about them. She was pleased that John now had time to deliver her meal trays and chat with her and that Leah could spend time sewing.

Once the extra servants had been packed off back to The George and the house returned to its normal calm routine Bertha could again be encouraged to explore beyond the third floor. It took weeks to coax her downstairs and months before she would venture beyond the back door. I cannot say for sure how long it took but she had put on so much extra flesh that we had to let out her black dress. "That's what good food does for you," Grace observed. "Not like that stuff you gave poor Monsieur Alphonse." We laughed at the memory of how we had tortured the poor Frenchman and wondered where he was. I guessed he was safely back in Paris while his two charges were loose on the continent.

By summer Bertha was walking in the garden regularly. I fretted a little that the gardeners and their boys would see her and tell others of her existence. I comforted myself with a technicality. My oath had specifically referred to telling people about Bertha. I wasn't telling the gardeners anything; they just happened to see her. Grace and I were sure they would not gossip to the gentry. As Grace said, it is difficult to get more than a grunt out of a gardener at the best of times. In the chilly autumn sunshine Bertha kicked her way through the fallen leaves, wearing the woollen pelisse we had made her. When she came in her cheeks glowed like red apples.

The next step was for her to go out in the brougham. At the start of this curious enterprise I had, in my ignorance, asked Mr Rochester about taking the unnamed lady out in a closed carriage. What an inspired stab in the dark that turned out to be. At the time that I asked him he had reluctantly agreed. Now I was sure that Mr Rochester, if asked, would shout No loud enough to frighten the crows. On his recent visit it was clear he wanted to avoid any sight, sound or mention of the poor woman. So I didn't check that he had not changed his mind. In my experience as one of the so-called lower orders it is sometimes better not to ask for permission. Just assume you have it.

Old John enjoyed polishing up the neglected carriage and giving the horses an outing. We took it in turns to accompany Bertha as we bowled down the lanes and through the villages. Safely hidden behind the broad brim of her bonnet she waved to the children who played in the road. There was no family crest on the carriage to identify us. We were just another group of ladies travelling to visit relations.

Sundays are always difficult days for a housekeeper. You need enough staff in the house to safeguard the premises and to look after the master or attend to any visitors. On the other hand it is the right of every servant to attend church on Sunday, if they so wish. I am strongly in support of this opinion; you will remember my husband was a clergyman. Most servants did want to go. I found it was the younger servants who were most enthusiastic about churchgoing. I was not under any illusion that they wanted to hear the word of God or listen to the parson preach. They wanted a few hours off work and the chance to flirt with the servants of the other great houses.

Grace claimed she was indifferent to religion and that she was paid extra for not having time off on Sundays. She was happy to stay in the Hall with Bertha. She didn't need to tell me she was extremely well paid. I did the books. That is not the point, I told her. What about Bertha? Might she not benefit from hearing God's word? Grace was not convinced. I confess I became quite rabid on the subject. In the end we agreed to try taking Bertha to the church in Hay on the following Sunday. It was my late husband's church, a fact that gave the expedition a special piquancy.

Our plan was quite simple. We would dress Bertha in full mourning; in effect she would wear widow's weeds. I still had mine. No one would know who she was or what she looked like under the yards of black crepe. Her face would be completely veiled. We gave her gloves to cover her hands as we feared her dusky skin would stand out among the rest of us; we are all winter-white descendants of the Vikings. No one would speak to her or ask awkward questions. I knew that from experience. There is nothing like bereavement and misery to make people shun you.

It went like clockwork. We sat up in the gallery and enjoyed the rare sensation of looking down on the gentry in their pews. They would not turn their heads to inspect us; they were too busy inspecting each other.

The other servants nudged each other and muttered and wondered at this black crow in our midst but we knew they would not give the game away. After the service we filed past Mr Wood, the parson, who stood in the doorway exchanging compliments with some of the congregation. I had a sudden fear he might speak to us; it had been my husband's church after all. I need not have concerned myself. He had eyes only for the gentry and stood on tiptoes to call out over our heads to Lady Clifford in the hope of an invitation to lunch. We slipped past him unnoticed.

When we arrived back at the Hall we climbed up to the third floor and Bertha threw herself on the sofa where she writhed and squirmed. I thought she was having one of her hysterical fits. Grace had the smelling salts in her hand before we realized she was laughing, laughing fit to burst.

"I did enjoy that. I felt so free. No one could see me. I just a big bundle of black. No one could see my dark skin." She squealed and giggled and clutched at her side; it is not easy to laugh when wearing stays. "It is nice being widow, isn't it, Mrs Fairfax?"

"Sometimes," I admitted. "It has its compensations."

"And you, Mrs Poole. Are you a widow too?"

"Sort of," said Grace. Her answer satisfied the uncritical Bertha but it made me wonder. Grace had always avoided telling us any details of her former life.

We all three felt we'd got away with something rather clever. We'd played society at its own game and by its own rules and we had won. It was only later that I realized what a useful lesson we had learned.

That November Mr Rochester returned for the start of the hunting season. When he wasn't dealing with business he was out on the hunting field. He bought extra horses and hired more grooms to look after them so that he could hunt three days a week. So intent was he on the sport I wondered if he was hoping to break his neck.

This time there was no Monsieur Alphonse to unnerve us and no great dinner to cater for. The few visitors were all men of business, happy to eat a roast dinner by the fire in the library. As often as not Mr Rochester would dine out after a day's hunting. He was not short of invitations, especially from families with daughters. We managed very nicely with just an extra scullery maid and Leah's younger brother, who was kept busy cleaning boots and fire grates and carrying coal. Even Bertha earned her keep repairing the linen.

It was at this time I decided to make use of Bertha's unexpected talent. She was not good with letters; we might as well have given her a bucket with a hole in it as give her a book to read. But with figures Bertha was as keen as mustard; she could work out yards and inches and the pounds, shillings and pence to the last farthing — in her head!

In the long dark evenings she and Grace would come down to my room after supper and Bertha would check over my figures in the account books. Her eyes were much younger than mine and her addition was much more reliable. She had no understanding of the figures; she did not know if a side of beef cost three pounds, thirty pounds or three hundred pounds, but she could add and subtract fast and accurately. While she flew through her sums Grace and I would sit and knit and drink tea and generally spend a pleasant peaceful hour or two before it was time to take our candles upstairs.

One evening Bertha could not read one of my figures. Had I written seven or nine pounds for the butcher's bill? From memory I could not be sure. While the master was home we were buying much more meat. I went to get the invoice to check. When I found the bill I handed it to her. She held it so the light from the candle shone on it. She studied it for such a long time without speaking that I put my knitting down to look at her.

Her finger was tracing the letters of Mr Rochester's name where the butcher had written it in flowing script. "Is that an R?" she asked. "And an O. What does it say?"

"My master's name. Mr Rochester. He owns this house. Did you not know?" I did not realize what a storm I had unleashed.

"He is here? In this house?" There was no time to answer her. She rose to her feet and pushed back her chair with such force she sent the table flying. Through the door and down the corridor she went. Some instinct sent her up the main staircase, through the empty dining room and into the library, where Mr Rochester sat alone with a glass of port and a book. Her hands must have been round his throat before we had disentangled ourselves from the upturned furniture.

By the time Grace and I arrived Mr Rochester had grappled her to the floor and was holding her wrists behind her back.

"A garter." He waved an imperious hand at me. "Give me a garter. God dammit, woman, don't pretend you don't wear them. I want to tie her hands."

I have done many things for the Rochesters. I have rubbed old Mr Rochester's knobbly hands; I have watched without comment as Mr Rowland pinned butterflies on boards and I have cared for some poor mad friendless creature without any guidance or thanks from the man who made me responsible for her. All these things I have done. But here I draw the line. I will not take my garters off for him. I set my face and stood firm and still.

Grace saw which way the wind blew and decided to oblige him. She passed him a garter and one of her stockings. Somehow or other between them they got Bertha upright and in a chair. There was foam round her mouth as a torrent of angry words spewed out. I have never heard her say so much. And such words! I blush to remember them.

"Get her out of here. I told you I never want to see her or be reminded of her. Lock her up. Throw away the key." His dark eyes flashed fire at us.

Grace took her charge by the shoulder, "Come, Bertha." Mr Rochester jumped at hearing the name.

"Don't believe what she tells you," he snarled at Grace. He pointed an accusing finger at Bertha. "The truth and she are long parted."

112

Grace ignored him and continued to talk soothingly to Bertha, promising her sleeping draughts, a warm bed and feeling better in the morning. Then she held her by the arm and led her like an obedient burly child from the room.

I was left alone with Mr Rochester. He had pulled off his cravat and loosened his collar, his hand clawing at the red marks on his neck. He leant against the mantelpiece, his chest heaving as he struggled to calm his breathing. I felt I should speak to my master, that there should be some comment made on the scene that had just been enacted. The savage expression on his face warned me to stay silent. Whatever I said would simply add fuel to the fire and by talking I might reveal more about my part in the incident than was good for me. Finding out Bertha had been in my room checking the accounts would not please him. I pressed my lips together, made him a bit of a curtsy and left.

I spent a tense and restless night. I had crept up to the third-floor rooms and tested the door. It was locked. The silence behind it was ominous rather than consoling. When I rose from my troubled slumber I was in an agony of expectation. The master was sure to summon me and ask me to account for the events of the previous evening. I was mentally packing my bags and wondering where I could go.

None of it happened. I was not summoned; I was not dismissed. There was no angry scene.

I discovered that Mr Rochester had left first thing in the morning. He'd roused Old John from his bed and got him to saddle his favourite horse, Mesrour. He had ridden off while the frost was still on the fields. Old John was devastated. "Summat must have happened. For him to go off like that."

"Summat did," I told Old John and gave him a highly censored version of events.

"Must be bad blood between them two. Fighting in library. Well I never." As soon as I was able I went to visit Grace and enquired about Bertha. "Snappish, is she this morning?" It was Grace's favourite understatement for the demented behaviour of her charge.

"Not anymore. Last night she talked and raved and cried and talked some more. Then she wept and wept until she fell asleep with exhaustion. Now she doesn't want to wake up."

"When she does you can tell her Mr Rochester has gone. Left without a word this morning."

"So we are off the hook."

"Looks like it."

Grace whistled through her teeth. "Interesting. If you had been sitting by your library fire when a crazed creature closely followed by two of your servants came to attack you, wouldn't you at least ask a few questions? How did she get here? Why wasn't she watched? That sort of thing."

"Why did Bertha suddenly attack him? It happened as soon as I said his name. She's not the world's best reader but she obviously recognized it on the bill. She must have heard the family name before."

"We don't use the name much. You call him the master, most of the time. Or worse. My master. I have

114

nothing to do with him." Grace tossed her head and looked very smug when she said this. It is easy for people who have a generous salary and a son to help them in their old age to act so independent and haughty.

"Old John thinks there must be bad blood between her and Mr Rochester. Something shocking in the past. Has Bertha said anything?"

"She has said plenty. I couldn't stop her raving about him. It poured out of her, with plenty more choice words that a lady like you wouldn't understand."

"What sort of thing is she saying?"

"Mr Rochester kidnapped her. He locked her up on his ship. He drove her mother to her death. He stole her father's money. According to our Bertha he's done enough to get his neck stretched at the next assizes." Grace ticked each crime off on her fingers as she spoke.

"But there must be a germ of truth in there. Something that stays Mr Rochester's hand. He does not suffer fools gladly. You would expect him to have a major rage, a huge attack of temper. Something stopped him. There's something more he wants to keep hidden than her presence in his house. That's why he went away in a hurry. He made us swear to keep her identity secret. We call her Bertha. Bertha who? There's one of the Rochester secrets at the heart of this. The Rochesters love secrets."

"O yes, they've got a secret, one great big secret." Grace paused to add drama to her announcement. "Bertha claims that she is Bertha Rochester. Says she's married to him. That she is his wife."

115

I did a most unladylike thing. I gulped. A huge mouthful of air made its way into my mouth and down my gullet. I felt it travel like a rolling ball down inside my stays. Grace gave her harsh laugh. "I thought that would give you a turn." She appeared to enjoy my embarrassment more than was strictly necessary.

It was some time before I found my voice. "Do you believe her?"

"If I believed everything my patients told me . . ."

"It's true that the master went to Jamaica as a young man. There was never a word about his marrying." My voice trailed away as I recalled that news about Mr Edward had never been forthcoming from his father and brother. Enquiries about his health or his whereabouts had been abruptly discouraged. There was one slender piece of evidence to support Bertha's claims. "She wears a wedding ring."

"True. So do I." Grace waved her left hand in my face. But you'd be hard put to it to find a Mr Poole. The Mrs is a courtesy title. I wear the ring to avoid impertinent questions. I put it on myself when I moved to Yorkshire."

"You are not from these parts?"

"No. I am from further north. I came here when my son was born. That's how I know the word 'husband' has many different meanings."

I waited in case she would tell me more about herself; she did not take the opportunity so I returned to the subject of Bertha and her claim. "Just imagine for a moment that what she says is true and she is indeed Mrs Rochester. Then she is the mistress of this

116

house. She should be in the drawing room, receiving visitors, ordering the dinners, sleeping in the big bedroom. I should be taking orders from her!"

For a moment we were silent as we considered the alarming prospect of Bertha being in charge of us, rather than of our looking after Bertha.

"In a good spell she might be able to manage." Grace was judicious. "She would need a lot of help. There'd still be work for you and me."

"It can't be true," I told Grace with confidence. "Mr Rochester has made it clear that she is nothing to him. His father and brother never announced his marriage. That's not the kind of thing you keep secret. The master does not admit to having a wife and he certainly does not acknowledge that Bertha is his wife. How can he keep her in the same house as if she is a stranger?"

"Lots of married folk do exactly that. It's how they manage when they dislike each other. He treats her the same way many men treat the wives they no longer want."

"Never. He has not spoken her name or acknowledged her existence. What kind of a husband does that?"

"A husband who hates his wife and yet cannot be free of her. He keeps her locked away and pretends she does not exist. A man can do that with a wife. Ask my son. He knows. The law can stop a man who mistreats his maidservant or his mother but it cannot and will not stop him ill-treating his wife."

I did not have enough knowledge of the law to dispute with Grace but I assured her with some warmth that my brief experience of marriage had not been of obedient slavery to a capricious master. Marriage had opened the door of a cage for me. I had been glad to escape from the many rules for good behaviour imposed upon me by my mother, who was obsessed by the notion of gentility.

"We do not have any proof. Just the word of a woman who is generally regarded as mad," Grace admitted. A broad smile broke out on her naturally stern-looking face. "I've just remembered. I saved the best till the last. Bertha claims that she had a baby."

"That does tend to happen if people get married." I contrived to look demure and innocent as I spoke. Although I count Grace as my closest friend I wanted to pay her back for the unladylike gulp she had shocked out of me.

"Pshaw!" She waved a dismissive hand. "Not just an ordinary baby. A black baby!"

"Now that I do not believe. She really is making it up. And just where is this unlikely baby?"

"It seems it died."

That silenced me.

The Honourable Blanche Ingram

1827

In the absence of our master tranquillity soon returned to Thornfield Hall. Our routine was strenuous — we worked long hours — but we worked with good hearts and were free from anxiety. We were all skilled in our trades and worked to a high standard. Criticisms and quarrels were few. Old John grumbled that he had too many hunters in the stables and no one to ride out on them. In truth he loved to see the heads of the bright-eyed creatures gazing out of every stall. The new grooms managed to exercise them without breaking their legs — the horses' legs, that is. Old John had no care for the grooms' legs. On occasions Mary cooked for us some of the delicious recipes that Monsieur Alphonse had shared with her. Just to keep her hand in, she said, in case there should be another big dinner. Leah and John were beginning to look at each other with big moony eyes and Sam was busy building a model of Nelson's *Victory* no more than six inches high. All was harmony in the servants' hall.

Matters were as satisfactory on the third floor. Bertha had returned to her usual state of placid indifference to her surroundings. She ate her meals and went to her bed as Grace directed her. In between she gazed at the sky, smiled at Leah or me when we came to sew in the afternoons and said very little. In all she was the most undemanding presence it was possible to imagine.

We spent companionable evenings by the fire in my room. Grace had her pint of porter and her pipe. I had my knitting. Bertha would be busy checking the sums in my accounts. This was an activity that absorbed her completely. She would crouch silently over her task, the tip of her tongue protruding through her teeth, and she would work with great concentration. She worked quickly and carefully and never made any mistakes.

We heard no more from her about being married to our master. The name of Rochester never passed her lips and in view of the kerfuffle it had caused previously we avoided using the master's name in her hearing. An ordinary person needs a reason to throttle a man when he is sitting quietly by his fireside. But, as Grace says, the mad do not work like that. I thrust the thought that Bertha might be Mrs Rochester to the bottom of my mind and bid it stay there.

In this way the months ticked by happily until the autumn. The trees were bare when the letter arrived from Mr Rochester. To my surprise he gave warning of a visit. Perhaps Bertha's attack on him in the library had persuaded him that arriving unannounced was a little unwise. Not only did his letter surprise me, it also caused me considerable dismay, as I foresaw much labour and many responsibilities ahead of me. He planned to hold a great ball at Thornfield Hall at Christmas and to invite the hunt to meet at Thornfield on Boxing Day. I was pretty confident that the hunt master would oblige him by accepting his invitation.

The previous hunt dinner had set a standard that would be difficult to repeat and this time we had no Monsieur Alphonse to help us. I had set a brisk pace of work all year and so we were all on top of our routine tasks. The store cupboard was full and the house was clean and the bedding mended. Well done me, I thought, and braced myself for a busy few weeks.

Once again I raided The George at Millcote for extra menservants. They willingly agreed to leave their meagre festivities at home to come and wait table at Thornfield Hall; they knew they would feast royally on our leftovers. With much laughter they mimed scrubbing their fingernails and standing with their hands folded in front of them, their faces a careful blank; Monsieur Alphonse's training had not been forgotten. With Mary's help I wrote lists for the grocer, ordering everything from arrowroot to vinegar. The butcher, after much thought, put rings with my name on four great geese and a fine young black bullock. I felt sad as I watched him trot away unaware that his days were numbered, but I was confident about my arrangements for the food and its service.

The table decorations caused me much heart-searching. I really missed Monsieur Alphonse. He would have found a stunning way of decorating the buffet table with the dull evergreens, the ivy, holly and branches of fir that were all that was available to us in winter. The gardener shook his head sadly when I asked for flowers. "Too late now," he told me, "even if we heat the glasshouse from now till Christmas."

My other problem was Bertha. Grace and I talked it over. Should we warn her Mr Rochester was coming? Should we say nothing? Could we turn the key in the lock and keep her on the third floor? I am ashamed to say the thought of the chain went through my mind but I quickly dismissed it. Better that Mr Rochester be savaged on his hearthrug than we should resort to restraining the poor creature with manacles. The more we struggled to find ways to keep her away from Mr Rochester the more insoluble the problem seemed.

In the end it was Bertha who decided matters; we had underestimated both the sharpness of her ears and of her understanding. She had picked up the gist of our whispered consultations and had come to her own conclusion. When she heard me lamenting my lack of inspiration for decorating the table she announced that she would undertake the task.

"I make flowers. My mother taught me." She mimed curling petals in her fingers and twisting them together to make a stem. With a flourish she presented me with an imaginary flower. "In Jamaica we wear them in our hats when we go to church. Red. Pink. Yellow. Not black like here."

I demurred. It felt rash to entrust such an important feature of the entertainment to a woman whose wits wandered. It was Grace who came up with the solution.

"Let Bertha make one. If you like it she can make more."

122

Within the day Bertha produced a red rose bud fashioned from scraps of silk but so lifelike you wanted to put it in water to give it a chance to open. I complimented her on her handiwork and asked what materials she would need to make enough to decorate the dining tables.

"Coloured silk, gold thread." She started to count off on her fingers the things she would need. "Starch, glue." When she came to the end of her list, she stopped and started as if there was something she wanted to say, something she found difficult. Her big hands flapped in the air as she struggled for the words. "These flowers. For Mr Rochester's tables?"

Grace and I froze at the name. Bertha's mouth twisted and for a moment I thought she was going to spit out the words "my husband". It was a relief when she went calmly on.

"I hear you whisper. Sometimes I not well but my ears work." She cupped her hands on the sides of her head. "Mr Rochester come. I stay up here. He take no notice of me. I take no notice of him."

As Grace said afterwards, you can't say fairer than that. On the surface it appeared our problems were over. In my heart I was not convinced. It was all too glib and easy.

The short days of December rushed past with unaccustomed haste. All was busyness and bustle at Thornfield Hall. From the number of letters and notes that arrived from my master I realized that the Christmas ball had a special importance for him. My heart went out to the stagecoach drivers who had ploughed through the rain and snow to bring us the post from London.

A great packet arrived with the invitations. I recognized Mr Rochester's handwriting; he had written the names himself. I was curious to know why he had chosen to exert himself on this particular task and rifled through the envelopes in search of clues. I could see no unexpected name among them. They were all to the usual county families.

I handed the letters out to Sam and John to be delivered. John, a farm boy, was pleased to have the chance to ride a horse, but Sam was less keen. Old John was even less eager to trust him with one of his precious horses. "Go gentle on his mouth," he told Sam. "Sailors' hands," he muttered to me in explanation. "All they's good for is heaving on ropes."

"The Ingrams are coming and the Eshtons," Sam announced on his return. He made a pantomime of rubbing the nether parts of his anatomy and walking stiff-legged for a bit. "Ingram Hall is as unfriendly as ever. You'd think they'd invite me in for a bit of a warm by the kitchen fire. Not leave me to wait in the chilly entrance hall while they write their reply."

I sympathized with Sam and enjoyed a moment of smugness; Thornfield Hall would always provide a better welcome to servants going about their masters' business. They would be offered a warm by the range and food and drink.

"I reckon it's that Miss Blanche is the reason for all this Christmas party. She came and gave me a haughty stare as I waited. Word is she is just back from a London season. She is very striking on the eye."

"You don't think . . ." The thought died in my mouth. I did not finish the sentence. Sam did it for me.

"That Mr Rochester has a fancy for her as a wife. Could be. It's not unusual for a man to want a wife and he can certainly afford one. The Ingrams' estate adjoins the Rochesters' land. It's entailed but you never know. Baronets don't always make old bones. The Rochesters must've got most of their land by marrying their neighbours."

It did not take long for Sam's speculation to travel round all the servants. It added extra spice to the preparations for the Christmas party. Grace said nothing but I knew that she was thinking the same as I did. It niggled away in my mind. What if by some amazing circumstance Bertha's claim to be Mrs Rochester were true?

There were nearly fifty guests at the Christmas ball. They arrived with their horses and their coachmen and their valets and their maids. They were sleeping three in a bed in the servants' quarters. You have never seen such a quantity of food eaten. It arrived in cartloads in the morning and by evening it was all gone.

Martha, my old *bête noire*, arrived under the guise of lady's maid to the Honourable Blanche Ingram. True to form she bragged and boasted to the rest of us about her high status in the Ingram household and how wonderful it was to work for the aristocracy, people with titles. I congratulated her on her success and annoyed her by taking all the credit for myself. "Aren't you pleased you took my advice and looked for better employment?" I asked her. We were in the kitchen where the table was piled high with provisions and the air was full of busy bustle and the happy chatter of our staff. Martha gave me a scowl. I knew that matters were not so comfortable below stairs at Ingram Hall. Then the bell rang and the flag on the board went up to show someone had pulled the bell cord in the East bedroom. "That's your lady," I told her and watched to be sure she answered the summons.

As is the custom I entertained the senior upper servants to meals in my room. Baroness Ingram's lady's maid, a French lady with a very high opinion of herself, was quick to take me aside with what she described as a friendly word of warning. Martha, she informed me, was not really a lady's maid. She was one of the parlour maids and therefore should not be admitted to my room but should eat in the servants' hall with the rest of the lower orders. If the French maid thought this was the action of a friend I should not like to have her as my enemy.

The baroness, she explained, had temporarily promoted Martha to oblige her elder daughter. The Honourable Blanche did not wish to be seen to arrive without her own maid. Martha was to pretend to be Blanche's maid; she was to go up the stairs to Blanche's room when the dressing bell rang. Once there she was to occupy herself by tidying the room until the French lady arrived. It was "*absolument interdit*" for Martha to touch Blanche's hair or her dress. "On pain of punishment," the French lady added and gave me a knowing smirk. "She has a rare temper on her, has the young lady Blanche. Even her mother is frightened of her. And the rage of the old baroness is something formidable."

For once in my life I tried to be kind to Martha. The memory of this small act comforts me when I am reminded of all the terrible things that happened to her later. I asked Leah to convince Martha that all her old friends at Thornfield Hall were eager to see her and keen to hear her news. They wanted her to dine with them in the servants' hall, and not "with that hoity toity lot in the housekeeper's room". Martha was persuaded and so she spent a few happy evenings in praising the frosty grandeur of Ingram Park while enjoying the warmth, comfort and good food of Thornfield Hall. I envied her as I sat in my tiny room, surrounded by the so-called cream of the servant class. I soon grew weary of their talk of Sir This, Earl That and Viscount What's-his-name. It made me grateful that my master was plain Mr Rochester.

Plain Mr Rochester he might be, but the arrangements for the Christmas party at Thornfield Hall were a triumph. The house shone with the rich lustre normally reserved for homes that are loved and cherished by their families. I cannot say that I loved Thornfield Hall; it could be a dark and gloomy place when the weather was wild and the skies lowered. My pleasure in the place was more of a professional nature. Thornfield Hall was run to high standards; the beds were aired, the linen clean and the fires generous.

Downstairs in the kitchen red-faced scullery maids and harassed cooks put the finishing touches to a lavish dinner. All that was needed to make a sparkling and memorable occasion were some pleasant guests and some lively conversation.

I went to check on the dining room while the guests were upstairs dressing for dinner. My heart swelled with pride when I saw it. John was just finishing lighting the candles. "It's a picture, isn't it, Mrs Fairfax?" It was indeed. The purple drapes were drawn and the walnut panelling gleamed in the candlelight, making a perfect background for the great dining table. It was covered with a white linen cloth, ironed to perfection and laid with fine china decorated in crimson and gold. The crystal glasses and silver cutlery shone so clean and polished that they dazzled the eye.

Along the centre of the table flowed a stream of sweet-scented greenery cut from the boughs of conifer trees. These branches in defiance of nature bore flowers in red, yellow and amber, the colour of flames. Each flower was cunningly fashioned out of silk with gold stamens at its centre. They were so convincing I wanted to pick one up and smell it. All the flowers were the handiwork of Bertha, who had laboured happily in her third-storey room, her big hands twisting and shaping the scraps of silk. How strange that a mind that had been so disordered and was so feeble in its understanding could make such enchanting tiny masterpieces!

128

"It's a shame Miss Bertha can't see it now while it is all so perfect." John blew out the taper, his task finished.

I let him spend a moment in silent admiration before I asked him to tell Leah to come to look at the finished table, for it was she who had laid the tables and set out the greenery. She soon arrived, gliding silently along the corridor. Behind her came a tall figure in a maid's uniform of black dress, white pinafore and cap. At first I thought it was Martha and wondered what she was doing coming to the dining room at this hour, for the dressing bell had rung. She was supposed to be upstairs pretending to dress Miss Blanche. As the figure came closer I realized it was not Martha. It was Bertha. I felt my face turn as white as my hair and my heart leap against my stays. My mind did some swift calculations and told me not to shriek out loud in protest. Silence, as so often is the case, seemed the best course of action — or inaction.

"I wear a disguise," Bertha whispered as she slid past me. Her eyes were alight with childish glee.

"Grace said it was all right." Leah pointed to the end of the corridor where a dark figure, which I assumed was Grace, lurked. "She will take her back upstairs."

"It's so risky," I hissed. "Mr Rochester might come to make sure all is in order."

"There are so many strange servants here. He would think her one of them."

That was true. The house was full of familiar uniforms topped by unfamiliar faces. Bertha gazed at the dining room like a child at a sweetshop window and

129

then allowed herself to be led away. I watched as Grace shepherded her to the stairs. I knew that I would have to pretend to be angry with one of them. But which one? And when? I had far too many other demands on my time to think about it at that moment.

A door banged and I heard feet patter briskly down the corridor. The sound of the footsteps ceased as the owner arrived on the thick Turkey carpet of the dining room. I heard a tongue clicking *tsks* of annoyance and impatience and the sound of a woman's dress rustling. I turned to see the Honourable Blanche, in her white evening dress, with her hair loose about her shoulders, attacking the table decorations. She was pulling and tugging at one of the flowers attached to the green branches.

The events of the evening seemed to be in a conspiracy to test my self-control to the utmost. I wanted to strike the Honourable Blanche straight between her black eyes and tell her firmly to stop, tell her she was behaving like a selfish, naughty, undisciplined child and was spoiling handiwork that had taken many laborious hours to create. I did not, of course. Years of training took command and I enquired as civilly as I could manage, "Can I help you, madam?"

"I need a flower. To finish my ensemble. This colour. It will match my shawl. I can't get it off the branch." She was twisting and pulling at the bloom with her fingers. As she wrenched at the flower the greenery twisted about on the table like a demented snake, knocking over the carefully laid glasses and scattering the cutlery.

130

"Allow me, madam." I took the scissors that hang on my belt and cut the poor flower free. When I handed it to her she held it to her nose to smell it.

"Huh! I thought it was real." She looked a little less thrilled with her find until she held it against a loose tress of her hair to test the effect. The result obviously pleased her. Away she went without one word of thanks passing her lips.

I set the table straight again and remedied the damage she had done. Fortunately nothing was broken. I don't suppose the alteration would be seen by a blind man on a horse as my mother used to say, but for me in some obscure way the effect was spoilt. I was pleased that Bertha had seen her handiwork before the Honourable Blanche had manhandled it. After some thought I decided I would not put myself to the trouble of being angry with either Grace or Leah about Bertha's brief visit to the dining room.

As I turned into the corridor I stopped and melted back against the wall the way servants learn to do. Before me, very close, stood Mr Rochester and with him was the Honourable Blanche. They were both tall and their two dark heads were bent together examining the flower. Their talk was low and intimate until suddenly Blanche broke away with a laugh. She tossed her hair and brandished the flower as if she was a gypsy dancer, rather than the daughter of a peer of the realm. My master watched her as she sped away down the corridor. The expression on his face was soft and lingering but I could see the hunger in his eyes. He's smitten, I thought, definitely smitten.

131

Later that evening after the dinner had been served the master sent word to thank the servants for the magnificent meal and invited us to sit in the hall and listen to the singing. He requested that I join the guests in the dining room as befitted my rank. I slid into a quiet corner and watched as Mr Rochester and Miss Blanche sang a duet. They both had fine voices. She was very striking, tall and straight with raven black hair and an olive complexion. Her white dress was draped with an amber shawl tied over one shoulder. It matched the amber flower in her hair, the flower that she had prised from the dining room decorations; it contrasted well with the jetty mass of her curls.

As they sang I could feel the guests around me make a match of them. The unspoken feeling that here was a pair who should be married circulated the room. For many the thought was tinged with envy. There were mothers who had hoped for Mr Rochester for their own daughters and there were men who would have liked the lovely Blanche as a prize, if they had the fortune or the mettle for such a match.

Outside the room, in the hall, was the throng of servants; some were my old friends who worked permanently at Thornfield Hall and some were casuals, hired in for the occasion. Some had arrived only yesterday from their own houses with their masters and mistresses. I wondered if hidden among the genuine ladies' maids, disguised in a black dress with a white apron, was a large ungainly woman whose status was still a mystery to me, a woman who was neither a child nor a mature adult; a woman who was neither a servant nor yet the mistress of the house she lived in.

The next day the hunt came to meet at Thornfield Hall. The weather was still and clear and a light frost sparkled on the grass. The courtyard at the front rang with the clatter of horses' hooves. Every gentleman was mounted and his groom led his spare horse. Old John was in a heaven of delight to see the pink jackets and to hear the crack of the whips and the expectant barking of the hounds. Into this melee of men and horses arrived Miss Blanche in a black habit, riding side-saddle on a black horse. She made a magnificent sight — as I am sure she intended.

All the gentlemen turned to look at her but it was Mr Rochester who steadied his horse and raised his riding-crop to salute her with a pretty speech about the goddess Diana. He could not have made his preference for her clearer if he had gone down on one knee and proposed in front of the assembled gentry. For a moment I contemplated my future with Miss Blanche as the mistress of Thornfield Hall. She had already displayed a nature that was selfish and impulsive. Rumour, in the reliable form of her mother's maid, gave her credit for a formidable temper. My future looked bleak.

At that moment Mr Rochester's horse started. As he struggled to restrain it the horse reared and turned back towards the house. Mr Rochester's eye was drawn upwards; something caused him to stare briefly at the third storey. When he had composed his horse he moved away abruptly from Miss Blanche and went to talk to Carter, the surgeon.

Afterwards I learned from Grace that Bertha had been leaning out of the window to watch the hunt set off. It was Bertha who had caught Mr Rochester's attention. Grace pulled a face as she told me; she expected to feel the brunt of Mr Rochester's wrath in due course. He wanted Bertha kept out of sight and out of mind. Bertha seldom took much interest in the goings on at Thornfield Hall but that day she had opened the window to get a good look at Miss Blanche, who exercised a fascination for her.

"It's her complexion," Grace explained. "Somehow Bertha has the idea that her skin is dark and unattractive so she is pleased to see that Blanche, who has a similar complexion, is much admired."

"That is true. Mr Rochester gives every impression of admiring her. Does that console our Bertha?"

"I hope so. She went on to ask a most interesting question. She asked if this was one of those countries where men could have two wives."

I raised my eyebrows and looked significantly at Grace. Was this further evidence to support Bertha's claim that she was Mrs Rochester?

"Don't get too excited," said Grace. "The next thing she asked was the name of this country. And before you say anything, as well as going to the dining room, we did slip into the hall with the other servants to hear the singing."

I waved a careless hand to dismiss the matter. They had not been caught. I laid it to rest with all those other

134

undiscovered misdeeds of servants. What concerned me now was Bertha leaning from the window. If Mr Rochester was angry about it he would no doubt summon me and I would have the uncomfortable task of passing on his displeasure to Grace. I would not be happy to do that. I had come to regard her as a true friend.

The next evening Mr Rochester did summon me to the library. He was not his usual vibrant self; his face was pale and drawn as if with fatigue. He lay back in his chair, his feet to the blazing fire and brandy in a glass by his hand. He kept me standing while he studied the flames in the fire. Fond of him though I was, I could feel resentment bubbling up inside me. It had been two in the morning before we finished the washing up from dinner. I had found a kitchen boy, Leah's brother to be precise, asleep on the stairs. The poor lad was too tired to make it to his bed. I coughed to remind Mr Rochester that I was still standing. I hoped he would realize that my legs were aching and that if he had any complaints they would be best kept till morning. I was in no mood to be meek and respectful. I had a mind to bite first.

Fortunately my master had called me to express his thanks to us all. He bid me sit as he handed the tips to me. There were shillings and sixpences for the youngsters who had run errands and washed dishes. There were half crowns for the extras from The George and sovereigns for the rest of us. He made no mention of Bertha hanging out of the window.

When we had dealt with these matters of business he poured me a glass of port and turned the conversation to other matters. His reputation in the county? How was he judged as a landowner? As a gentleman? He wanted to know his standing among the gentry. He had me flummoxed there. What was I supposed to say? I assured him he was rated highly, particularly at this moment, having entertained his neighbours so royally.

Then he wanted to know what was thought of the Cliftons, the Eshtons. I could see where he was going. He did not pull the wool over my eyes. As I expected he worked his way round to the Ingrams last. Once there he started with the father, moved onto the mother and finally arrived at his target, Blanche. She was just eighteen. Was that too young to be married? He had met her in London where she had just had her first — very successful — season. She was much admired as a beauty and word was she had already turned down several suitors.

That'll be her mother's word, I thought. In spite of all these reported offers Blanche had returned home to Yorkshire empty-handed. Perhaps her dazzling beauty had not entirely concealed the meanness of her nature nor the emptiness of her father's bank account.

I told him what I understood about society and marriage. It was a subject in which I could claim some expertise; my mother had drilled me in its lore. "I know it is very bad for a girl if a man pays her attention and then does not propose. It can damage her reputation and her chance of marriage with another gentleman. Marriage is the only goal of girls in society. For them it is a serious business. They are trained to be wives and mothers, to run households and to manage servants. It is so important for them to marry well because there is nothing else for them to do. They cannot be parsons or lawyers or join the army. Their futures depend on their reputations — and their portions. Ill-natured gossip can blight their whole lives."

Mr Rochester's craggy face revealed little but he paid careful attention to my words. It was clear to me that there had been something lacking in my master's education; it was short of a feminine influence. His mother was an invalid, dominated by her husband. His father was an arrogant, close-fisted and insensitive man with little interest in society or the opinions of others. His brother was a virtual recluse with his magnifying glass and his insects and his steam machines. There was no sister to give him a glimpse into how girls were raised. I thought it only fair to enlighten him about the unkind ways society treated women. "People . . ." (I meant women but I did not wish to slander my own sex) "are quick to speak ill of a girl and they are just as quick to speak ill of the gentleman concerned. If he pays attention to a girl and it comes to nothing, people will say that he has proposed and been rejected. They will nudge each other and whisper that there must be a reason. His credit is not good, his fortune is too small, insanity runs in the family. There is no smoke without fire. That sort of thing. It seems to me best if a couple behave so discreetly that when their marriage is announced there is an element of surprise."

I left it at that. He bid me goodnight and I was pleased to escape from the room with the coins jingling in my pocket. I looked forward to distributing them to my fellow servants with Mr Rochester's compliments. The rest of my conversation with him I would keep discreetly to myself. I was confident that he had reached the point with the Honourable Blanche where he had to propose or risk being regarded as a blackguard by society in the county. It would be best if the announcement of his engagement came as a surprise to my fellow servants.

How wrong I was! In the morning he announced he was leaving for the continent. To my knowledge he had no business that called him to France. Many men grow skittish at the prospect of matrimony and many an English gentleman goes abroad to take his pleasures. I did not then know the exact nature of the furies that drove him to brave crossing the Channel in the middle of winter. It was some years before I discovered the real and secret reason for his abrupt departure.

Adele

1831

For a few years after the Christmas ball, life at Thornfield Hall was remarkable only for a lack of incident. The seasons followed each other in their usual course and brought with them their allotted tasks. We washed and polished in the spring and in the autumn we pickled and preserved the harvest. In truth it was very dull. We even missed Monsieur Alphonse; he had brought some novelty into our lives. Now there was nothing to break up the monotony of the days, weeks and seasons. Even though I am old enough to know better I longed for change. I should have restrained myself; change is not always for the better.

Mr Rochester came perhaps once a year. His brief visits were easily managed. He sent word in advance that he was coming so we could prepare for him without panic and he stopped entertaining. The gentry called when he was here, but there were no more lavish parties, hunt dinners or house parties for the other landowners. When he was at Thornfield he dealt with business matters and arranged for money to run the household. He pleased Old John by buying and selling

139

a few horses and then set off again on his mysterious travels.

As Mr Rochester was away so much we grew ambitious on behalf of Bertha and gave her more freedom than ever before. As long as she was accompanied by Grace, Leah or myself, she was free to visit the garden. She showed no propensity to wander beyond the gates and displayed no curiosity as to what lay behind the garden walls. Like a well-trained child she knew her limits and that to push beyond them would lead to trouble; either we would be angry with her or she would come up against something she could not cope with.

Inside the house she never strayed beyond her familiar places, the third-floor rooms, and the back stairs that led to my housekeeper's room. On the whole she remained placid and docile. Sometimes in the winter she became tearful and would stay in bed and cry a lot. Grace reckoned it was a sort of homesickness, a longing for the sunshine of her native land but this time it was in the spring that Bertha became "snappish".

Bertha raged. She threw her meals to the floor, refused to wash, and took to hiding knives and scissors. Grace's son came and prescribed a new medicine which seemed to help. What really cured her, according to Grace, was the news that John and Leah intended to marry. They were adamant that the wedding would not take place until they could afford a cottage of their own. In the meantime Leah was working on her bottom drawer so that she would have the necessary bedding

140

and linen. "Bottom drawer" was a new phrase to Bertha but once she understood its meaning she was eager to help. She set to work hemming sheets and embroidering nightdresses.

Bertha's episode of insanity had already ruffled the waters of the calm millpond of life at Thornfield Hall. The next event caused shockwaves that brought profound changes to all our lives. Mr Rochester wrote to say he would be arriving at the end of the summer and that he would have a companion with him.

I stopped reading his letter at that point and made a short sharp prayer. "Dear Lord, please do not let it be another madwoman," was the gist of my request. "I have coped with one but two such individuals in the same house . . . That is too much to ask!" I protested to an indifferent heaven. I read the rest of his letter with trepidation. It was such a relief when I learned in the next paragraph that our visitor was to be a child. A little girl of about seven years old. She was to come and live with us. I was in ecstasy. It would be so lovely to have a child around stuffy old Thornfield Hall. To hear her chatter in the corridors, to bake treats for her and to have the care of her pretty dresses. She would bring such joy to the house. I've never met a child yet that did not smile and laugh more than it complained. If only I could say the same for adults.

The news made me think of my own baby girl. She was still a baby to me. As I thought about her I realized she would be fifteen now. If she'd lived she'd be an adult. I did not like to think of her as growing up and leaving me and marrying and having children. I decided to keep her in my heart as the angelic-faced baby she was. In this way she would avoid all the pain of childbirth and the great toil and the many heartaches that are the lot of women.

The little girl was called Adele, a ward of Mr Rochester's. Everyone said she must be Mr Rochester's bastard child, begotten on some French dancer. I did not care. The way I look at it, when there are no parents, a child should be loved and cared for by the nearest body who is handy, willing and able to carry out the task. I was handy and I was willing and able.

I searched the attic for something to furnish a room for her and found nothing that would delight a little girl. The Rochesters had produced nothing but sons for generations. The only toys stored up there were hobby horses, swords and drums. There was not a doll to be seen. Bertha and Grace came to my aid; they made a bedspread and curtains of pretty patchwork with a design of bluebirds so that her room would look welcoming for her.

I need not have worried about supplying Adele with pretty things. When she arrived with Mr Rochester she brought with her trunks full of beautiful dresses and a maid to look after them. The unpacking revealed frilled dresses, velvet capes and a whole colony of dolls. Her wardrobe surpassed many a grown woman's trousseau. I hoped that such exquisite garments concealed tucks and extra fabric so they could be let out and lengthened as the child grew. There was no way we could replace them from the limited resources available to us. Yorkshire has many things to be proud of but French

142

chic is not one of them. We would be hard put to satisfy someone as fussy as Adele proved to be. In the morning she could not come down for her breakfast until her hair had been curled to her satisfaction.

The child and the maid, Sophie, both spoke French but not English. We had to do much pointing and miming but we managed. Adele was a bright little thing and within a few weeks she knew how to ask for what she wanted and to misunderstand completely when anything unpleasant was on the agenda. I admit that she completely stole my heart.

Before he left Mr Rochester charged me with finding Adele a governess who would teach the child English and give her enough education to enable her to go to school one day. It went without saying that Adele was to be kept in ignorance of the lady on the third floor. Madness would be frightening for the child. Once I got to know Adele I realized that the deception would not be too difficult a task. She was a child who noticed only what was of interest to her. If she could not wear it, eat it or play with it she ignored it.

Mr Rochester was very emphatic that the existence of his inconvenient lodger be kept concealed from the governess. According to my master, "No self-respecting governess would stay in an establishment that housed a madwoman." Mr Rochester was adamant in this opinion. I wanted to remind him that I had to share the house with such a woman and ask if he thought I was short of self-respect. It seemed wiser to restrain myself from making such a sharp remark. He could be a very tetchy man at times.

I tried to convince him how much Bertha had improved. I wanted to tell him about her sewing, her attendance at church and the docile way she behaved most of the time. He would not listen. He waved his hands in the air to waft my words away from his ears. He would not visit. He never even admitted that her name was Bertha. "That woman," he called her and accused her of wickedness beyond compare. "When the fit is on her," he said, "there is no limit to the evil acts she is capable of."

So he packed his bags. Before he left me to cope with what he regarded as a dangerous lunatic and an inconvenient foreign orphan child I asked for a substantial increase in the allowance for expenses. Adele and her maid would not be cheap to maintain and there was a potential governess to be paid and catered for. Mr Rochester did not argue or protest. I have noticed how easy it is for rich men to be generous. He wrote a note for his agent to give me what I asked for, pulled on his gloves and picked up his riding crop. When he was mounted on Mesrour and ready to leave he called out to me, "Get a governess. The brat is going to school as soon as she speaks English." He touched Mesrour with his heels and set off. "Don't forget. A governess."

As is my custom when I have problems to sort out I went up to the third floor and sought advice from Grace. She sat by the fire and smoked her pipe while Bertha put the finishing touches to some embroidery.

"A governess! To be kept in the dark. That'll spoil things for us. There'll be no more cosy evening chats for us round the fire here. You'll have to sit in your room with her and make conversation. You will have to be on your best behaviour. No more drinking porter." Grace cackled with laughter at the thought. It was true that I had developed a taste for her favourite drink.

"Get a really inexperienced one," she advised me. "Some girl straight out of school who doesn't know how things are done in the gentry's houses. Then we can sort of mould her into our ways. Keep her away from the back stairs. That shouldn't be difficult. Governesses are so touchy about their position they want to use the main staircase all the time, like family. Confine her to the school room of a morning. Get her to walk in the garden in the afternoon so we can have our sewing sessions. I know! Pretend there's a ghost on the top floor. Every old house has a ghost. Listen to this." She gave a strange hollow laugh that had much menace and no humour in it.

The ghoulish laughter echoed round the walls. It sounded so strange that Bertha leapt up and fled to her room. "That's right, Bertha," said Grace. "That was just a practice. We are going to use it as a warning sound. When you hear that noise, you go to your room, shut the door and wait for me."

I did not rush to find a governess; I was enjoying the company of little Adele. She shared her meals with me in my room. In truth I spoiled the child while I had the opportunity to do so. Grace's advice about finding an inexperienced tutor seemed a good idea to me. I looked in the advertisements in the *Yorkshire Herald*. There were two possible governesses who had advertised. I wrote to them asking for their references and testimonials. They both replied. One lady of twenty-five had been a governess in four different households. She listed the names of the people she had worked for; too many for my purposes. The other governess had never even left her first school. She had been both pupil and teacher in the same establishment, Lowood School. For appearance's sake I wrote for her references though in truth I was determined to employ her. Naivety was her greatest qualification as far as I was concerned. And that is how Jane Eyre came to Thornfield Hall.

She arrived very quietly in October, sort of slid in one night. Unlike Adele she brought very little with her and what she brought was black or grey or white. A real Quaker's wardrobe compared with the froth and pink frills that had spilled out of the child's trunks. I gave Miss Eyre the room next to mine; it seemed both sensible and kind to keep her close to me. It was agreed that she and Adele should eat with me in my room. This arrangement meant I could continue to have the pleasure of Adele's company and could keep an eye on how she was getting on with her new governess. I was not going to repeat the mistake I had made with Mrs Morgan. I was going to supervise this new member of staff very closely at first. The governess appeared to be both pleasant and respectable. I wanted to be sure she was also kind and understanding with the child.

Miss Eyre, as I always think of her, was a sweet creature: very small with a slight figure. I do not believe she had ever been properly fed or kept warm; I intended to remedy that. I felt very motherly towards her and at times I wondered how from being a woman who had lost her daughter I now had two motherless girls in my care. In her first three months at Thornfield Hall Jane gained flesh and her face filled out. You could never call her pretty but she became attractive as any young person in good health always is.

Adele was thrilled to have someone who spoke her own language, who could sort out the occasional difficulty over food so that we knew when Adele said "*pain*" she meant bread and we should stop offering her porridge or kippers. Miss Eyre never over-worked Adele but she had no real sympathy for the more theatrical side of the child's nature. She disapproved of Adele's concern with her appearance, thinking it frivolous and flighty. Her ambition was that Adele should become as sober, hardworking and serious as she herself was. I guessed her own childhood had been harsh and joyless, but that was no reason why Adele's should be so. When I was given the opportunity I joined the child in playing with dolls and conspired with cook to give her treats to eat. When the child had a cold I begged a morning off for her. It was granted with reluctance. Miss Eyre intended that Adele should have as much practice in English as possible so that she could go to school. I, on the other hand, wanted to delay the child's departure as long as possible.

The little Miss Innocent Governess that I thought I had engaged was not as malleable as I'd hoped; she concealed a central core of tempered steel. Her little mouth would set in an inflexible line and her requests were so polite and reasonable that it was impossible to refuse her for long without seeming ill-natured and difficult. One of her first requests was to be shown the entire house. I was reluctant to oblige her. I fobbed her off with excuses but she soon found a way to persuade me. She needed to know the layout of the house, she explained, "in case Adele wanders off or plays hide and seek. I need to know where to look." There was no putting her off. I managed to give Grace plenty of warning so she could keep Bertha close and have no fire in the sitting room that day.

I took Miss Eyre round the dining room, the library, the hall and through the bedrooms on the next floor. She still wasn't satisfied and asked to see the third floor if you please. I took her into the first of Grace and Bertha's rooms. We had put tapestries round the walls and they were draped so as to conceal the connecting door into Bertha's room. We did not stay there long. Once I had Miss Eyre back in the corridor I waved vaguely along its length and told her the rooms beyond were always locked; they were storerooms. I told her that this part of the house was thought to be haunted. She gave me a sharp look as if to say she didn't believe me. Next thing I knew she had found the stairs to the attic and had climbed the ladder out on to the roof. Once there she took deep breaths and gazed out at the moors beyond the lawns and the great meadow with its thorny trees and bushes. It was my first inkling that she was a fiend for fresh air.

Adele preferred to take her afternoon walk in the company of her maid. That left Miss Eyre free to

148

wander the lanes and fields on her own. When the weather was bad and Adele took refuge near the fire with her dolls Miss Eyre chose from sheer awkwardness to take her exercise indoors and to prowl up and down the third-floor corridor like a caged animal. She would pace backwards and forwards for an hour at a time, keeping Grace and Bertha confined in silence to their room. I could not understand her restlessness.

"Men," Grace diagnosed with her characteristic sniff. I gave her a look of disbelief.

"What men? You mean Old John. Or young John even. Perhaps the young blacksmith!" We giggled at the thought.

"No. Not one man in particular, but men in general. Think about it. An all girls' school, all female teachers. I bet the only man she's ever met was a weedy curate or an elderly man of the cloth. No disrespect to your late lamented, Alice. She's just discovered that the world contains men. It's got her juices going."

I think Grace was right about the cause of Jane's restlessness, for it disappeared when Mr Rochester arrived. Until then it caused us considerable inconvenience. I kept telling Jane that the corridor was haunted, that strange sounds were heard at night but she was not to be deterred. When she was walking the corridor our happy chatty afternoons of sewing had to stop. We prayed for fine weather so that she might take her exercise outdoors.

Not only did I lose my afternoons of cheerful conversation but my evenings also were blighted. After Adele had gone to bed Jane would spend an hour or

149

two with me in my room, as is the custom for upper servants; her status prevented her from spending her evenings in the servants' hall. This was a great trial for me as Miss Eyre was not only keen on fresh air and exercise but also incurably inquisitive about Thornfield Hall, its inhabitants and its history. I am by nature honest and straightforward in my dealings with people but I was charged specifically by my master to keep the presence of Bertha hidden from her.

At first the silly girl had thought I was the owner of Thornfield Hall. That shows how innocent she was of the ways of the world. Then she wanted to know all about the real owner, Mr Rochester. No one likes to draw a portrait of their employer; one either flatters or complains. There were too many barriers for us to hold a proper conversation: the presence of Bertha, my suspicion that Mr Rochester was married to her and the fact that I was desperately longing for my evening glass of porter.

Miss Eyre was a formidable inquisitor. When she interrogated me about the character of Mr Rochester I felt like one of Mr Rowland's moths or butterflies, impaled on a pin so that I could be studied through a magnifying glass, and poked with tweezers. To avoid answering her questions without lying or breaking my promise I took to reading my bible and to knitting. I reasoned that Miss Eyre's upbringing would not allow her to interrupt someone who was reading the bible. As I clicked away with the needles I had to endure the discomfort of seeing Miss Eyre mentally dismiss me as a stupid old woman.

150

After some evenings of bible-reading and Miss Eyre my need for real conversation became desperate. I longed to discard my mask and engage in a free and open exchange of ideas, news and gossip with no dark places of concealment. Grace, as usual, came up with a solution. She suggested we meet in my housekeeper's room after Miss Eyre had retired to bed. She would bring Bertha with her; they would come in their nightgowns, ready for bed.

As my excuse for staying behind after Jane I told her I was responsible for the locking of the doors and the checking of the windows. It was, I insisted, much too important a job to leave to anyone else. I would light the governess's candle and watch as she climbed the main staircase while Grace and Bertha crept down the back stairs with their candles. We would congregate in my room for a chat and a glass of porter.

In this way we managed the last three months of the year. We grew quite comfortable in our routine in spite of the strain of keeping secret Bertha's presence on the third floor. Then in January Mr Rochester arrived; he heralded a year of tumultuous events.

A Year of Tumultuous Events

1832

I am not normally superstitious but this new Year had an unfortunate start. Mr Rochester's arrival was blighted by some kind of fall from his horse. His ankle was badly sprained and he was forced to rest the injured joint. He took to the chaise longue by the fire in the library. Jane had been using the room to give Adele her lessons. Governess and pupil had to move out. I had a fire lit in an apartment upstairs which they could use as a school room. I doubted Adele would give much attention to her books; there was a man within reach. She would be in an agony of impatience to be in his presence so she could practise her winning ways on him.

All day the house was busy with callers for Mr Rochester. When it grew dark and started to snow, the visitors ceased. Mr Rochester sent to ask me about Adele. There was no point in my telling him what a charming child she was; gushing about children would be anathema to him. Instead I reminded him about the new governess and was told to bring Miss Eyre and Adele to take tea with him in the dining room at six o'clock.

I was keen that Jane should make a good impression on our employer as I wanted to keep her. In spite of her occasional pacing of the third-floor corridor, she was exactly the naive and inexperienced governess I had hoped for. Naivety and inexperience, however, do have their drawbacks. On this occasion I had to explain everything to Jane as if she were a child. She had to be told to change her dress; the dull black stuff one she wore was completely unsuitable for an upper servant who was summoned to appear in a gentleman's dining room.

I offered to fasten Jane's dress so that I could go with her to her room and make sure she put on something more appropriate than her glum everyday wear. When I looked in her wardrobe I saw she was not exactly spoilt for choice. I tried to persuade her to wear the grey dress but she was adamant it was only for a very special occasion such as a wedding. For a young girl she could be very determined at times. We were left with the black silk dress. I am very fond of black silk. I wear it myself — all the time. Black is a very serviceable colour and silk gives it a lustre and a texture that makes it more flattering than the matt black of mourning. But I am a white-haired widow, a housekeeper past forty, while Jane is scarcely eighteen and as far as I know not in mourning for anyone. I could not understand why she chose clothes that were so gloomy. Eventually I persuaded her to wear a brooch to lighten the effect and with that I had to be satisfied. Once dressed, she followed behind me to the dining room like a tiny fluttering shadow. There we found Mr Rochester

153

resting his injured foot while his dog, Pilot, basked in front of a handsome fire.

As I expected convalescence and discomfort made Mr Rochester even more imperious and unpredictable than usual. He did his best to ignore us when I introduced Jane to him so I found myself making fatuous remarks to fill in the silence. Jane, on the other hand, showed surprising coolness and composure. What a relief it was when he ordered tea to be brought! Once tea was served Adele took charge of the proceedings, asking about her present and leading Miss Eyre round the room by the hand to show her all the delightful ornaments.

I retreated to a sofa with my knitting and watched from the corner of my eye. As I expected, Mr Rochester decided to interrogate his new governess. He sent Adele to play with Pilot and bent his formidable attention on Miss Eyre. She withstood it very well, responding without embarrassment to his orders. Some of the things they said, in all apparent seriousness, about little men in green were beyond me but I spoke up to support Jane when he asked who had recommended her. I told him that she had advertised and that I had answered. Her references were from people of standing in a town over a hundred miles away. He seemed content and did not take it amiss that she had no connections in the immediate neighbourhood.

My master decided to put Jane through her paces. He sent her to the piano but her playing did not impress him. He demanded to see her paintings and seemed to find them interesting. Suddenly it was nine o'clock and he was rebuking her for letting Adele stay up so late. When we left I was not sure that Jane had passed whatever test it was that he had set for her.

Later that evening Jane came to my room to quiz me about Mr Rochester; she thought him very changeable and abrupt. I fudged my answers, though I did let it drop that Mr Rochester was the younger son and that he had broken with his family and gone abroad. In the end she accepted my vague talk of family troubles and the gloominess of Thornfield Hall as reasons for his infrequent visits and abrupt departures. I refused to be pressed further on the subject. It went against the grain to be so niggardly with the truth to Jane but my bible oath stood between me and telling her what she really wanted to know.

To my relief Mr Rochester did not send word that he found Miss Eyre unsatisfactory and that I should immediately look for a replacement. Indeed there were signs that he approved of her. One evening when he was entertaining he sent for her drawings to show the dinner guests. After his visitors had left, he summoned Adele and Miss Eyre; Adele's long-delayed present had arrived from Paris. Soon afterwards he rang for me to join them. Whether my presence was required to entertain Adele or to act as chaperone I cannot be sure. Mr Rochester had not previously shown much regard for the proprieties.

I enjoyed watching Adele explore the contents of her parcel. In silent concentration she peeled away the silvery tissue paper and inspected each item with the seriousness of a connoisseur. Short bursts of talk from

Mr Rochester travelled across the rich Turkey carpet to the alcove where I sat. Mr Rochester was so voluble I thought he must have taken too much wine but my attention was focused on Adele. At the bottom of her box was a pink silk frock of such exquisiteness it could have come only from Paris. Her little face lit up in ecstasy. Her expression told me it was imperative that the dress be tried on and I nodded my approval. She scampered off, her feet pattering her out of the room, taking her to Sophie and some serious time at her toilette.

Without other occupation my attention was drawn to the conversation taking place between Mr Rochester and Miss Eyre. His desire to dominate showed in his posture; he stood with his arm leaning against the mantelpiece while Jane was seated directly in front of him. The subject of their conversation was not clear to me but it was evidently of a weighty nature. Whatever it was they discussed, it was apparent she would not let him bully her. He commanded her to speak and she stayed dumb. I would not have dared to defy him so openly. When he had persuaded her to speak I distinctly heard her inform him in no uncertain manner that he was both "human" and "fallible". True though the words are of all of us I would not dare to say them to my master's face. He would engulf me in an avalanche of thunderous rage. Miss Eyre, however, escaped censure. Perhaps as a result of the few respectful "sirs" she sprinkled among her answers.

Adele, in her pink dress, arrived like spring after a cold winter. She twirled and curtsied and gave her thanks with style and polish, an unconscious contrast to Jane's monochrome solemnity.

Mr Rochester spent the whole of the short month of February with us; he had never spent so long at Thornfield Hall before. He blamed the slow healing of his sprained ankle: I thought he had another motive. I've confessed that I found Adele enchanting and so I easily convinced myself that my master too had fallen under her spell. Why else would a short-tempered and irascible old bachelor summon a seven-year-old girl to his fireside every evening?

Mr Rochester was nearly forty. He was at the time of life that men leave off sowing their wild oats and begin to wonder what memorials they will leave behind them. Most men of my master's age and means were married and had families. They were looking to the future, thinking of their sons' inheritance and their daughters' dowries. My master had proved skittish about marriage. He had paid court to the Honourable Blanche, and then at the moment when all expected an engagement to be announced he had fled to the continent. Marriage might not be to his taste but he had a duty to provide an heir for the Rochester estate. Society expected it of him.

The only child with any connection to Mr Rochester was Adele. I did not know the exact nature of that connection. Mr Rochester had told Jane about Adele's background while walking round the garden. (His ankle must have recovered enough to permit such exercise.) He felt it right that Miss Eyre should know the child's parentage in case she found it unacceptable to act as governess to the illegitimate child of a French singer. Jane was such a strict little thing he must have thought she might up sticks and gallop off in a huff of sanctimonious disapproval at Adele's mother. Mr Rochester had insisted that he was not the father. Miss Eyre was quite emphatic about this. I veiled my eyes to hide my amusement as she told me. Sweet innocent that she was, she believed him. I don't suppose she knew what people did that made them into mothers and fathers. To be fair to the girl, afterwards she took Adele on her knee and let her chatter away in a manner she did not normally permit.

By contrast with Miss Eyre, all the county families and all the servants were convinced that Adele was Mr Rochester's daughter. Not a legitimate daughter, to be sure, but the closest living thing he had to a blood relation. They had decided that her mother was some flibbertigibbet of a creature who had abandoned her and gone off to Italy. I began to dream of a future for the child. It did not take me long to transform her in my dreams from unacknowledged bastard to heiress to the Rochester thousands.

In the evening when Adele and Jane were summoned to entertain Mr Rochester, and I accompanied them to act as chaperone, I studied my master's behaviour carefully, looking for signs of softness and affection for the little girl. I looked in vain. True, he was less abrupt and imperious than he had been but I saw no special favour in his treatment of Adele. In spite of all her wiles

158

he never sat her on his knee, or stroked her hair or told her stories.

I began to wonder if my master might have a different reason for his prolonged stay at Thornfield Hall. Might the attraction be Miss Eyre? Was Adele summoned to his presence so that Miss Eyre might accompany her? It was not so much her person — though she was much improved from the half-starved waif who'd arrived in the autumn — it was more her ability to listen intelligently and to contribute sparingly to his conversation that appealed to him. He could spend an evening talking to Jane without breaching any of the strict conventions that govern the behaviour of men in the company of an unmarried woman. Jane teased, provoked and soothed him by turns but she never flirted with him. I watched with envy the easiness of their conversation and thought wryly of how I was currently deprived of my talks with Grace, my trusted companion. Jane and Mr Rochester spent their evenings in comfort by the fire in the library. I had to wait till the early hours of the morning when Grace and Bertha scampered down the freezing cold back stairs in their nightgowns.

When Adele was busy with her dolls I started to eavesdrop on my master's conversations with Jane. The proverb is right. Eavesdroppers hear no good about themselves. Between the two of them they decided that I was not merely unintelligent but I was definitively stupid; my thoughts were dominated by small children and knitting. My master did not hesitate to whisper it loud enough for me to hear. Apart from this slight to my *amour propre* their behaviour was impeccable. They were straightforward and friendly with each other. There were no compliments or coquetry, no lingering looks and languishing sighs. The parson could have joined them without causing a ripple in the subject matter of their conversation. Indeed they were much concerned with questions of what is right and what is wrong, and God's law and man's law. I studied Jane, her face glowing and her eyes alight, and I could feel some strong emotion like a captive bird beating its wings within the walls of the dining room in Thornfield Hall. I could see that Jane regarded her employer with more warmth than is usual from a paid servant.

And why not? He was intelligent and widely travelled. Peremptory and changeable he might be, but he had vigour of the mind as well as the body and a rare way of speaking frankly to all. Infuriating he might be with his moods and his demands but when his lopsided smile flashed across his face and lit up his black eyes you could forgive him almost anything. Indeed I was half in love with him myself. Sternly I reminded myself about my age, my white hair and my knitting which in Mr Rochester's mind condemned me to wear the dunce's cap.

The short month drew to a close and still Mr Rochester stayed on. I added a special warning to my list of duties. As well as keeping Bertha's existence a secret from Miss Eyre I also had to warn her about the inadvisability of growing too attached to her employer. I was sure my words would be as welcome as a late frost.

160

With the first tentative signs of spring our spirits lifted as the temperature climbed a few degrees. One evening we arranged that Grace and Bertha should come to my room after the rest of the household had gone to bed. We would share a bottle of porter and have a chat by the remains of the fire. Bertha settled herself down and set about stroking the cat; Grace puffed on her pipe. The conversation turned to Jane, who was proving more complex and troublesome than the innocent girl I had expected, especially in relation to Mr Rochester.

"Poor cow!" Grace can be very coarse at times. "All you can do is warn her. Gentry do not marry governesses. It does not happen."

"She knows the rules. Her education was very strict. I would not like to see the master break her heart." I glanced at Bertha. "He has broken enough of those." I thought also of the magnificent Blanche but I was not sure she had a heart.

Grace showed little sympathy for broken hearts but she did have a suggestion. "He might make Jane his mistress. From governess to mistress is not an unusual step. There's many a household chugs along happily with two mistresses and a schoolroom full of children."

"He shows none of the usual signs of a man in lust." I remembered the hunger in his eyes as he watched Blanche Ingram and her stolen flower whirl away from him in the corridor outside the dining room before the Christmas party. His behaviour to Jane might have been rude and peremptory but it had also been impeccable. He had done nothing to expose her to malicious

161

speculation. Adele and I had been present at all their conversations.

"Anyway Jane's too virtuous to be a mistress," I told Grace. "She's so innocent she wouldn't know what to do."

"She could learn. He'd enjoy showing her." Grace sent her tongue round her lips with a lascivious smacking sound. This so amused her she slapped her own rump and gave her harsh laugh. Bertha jumped when she heard it and hastily put the cat down. The laugh was her signal to return to her room. Nothing could persuade her otherwise. Our conversation came to an abrupt end.

As we made our way along the gallery towards the staircase to the third floor we saw smoke coming from under the door to Mr Rochester's room. I panicked. What to do without giving away the fact of our secret meetings? Bertha's presence on this floor would sound the death knell for us all. She must at all costs be kept from both Mr Rochester and Miss Eyre.

Quick as a flash, Grace pushed Bertha towards the stairs, took my candle from me and gestured for me to go into my bedroom. I found I could not move my feet so she gave me a hefty push through the door. As I stumbled into my room I saw her set the candle on the floor outside Miss Eyre's room and scratch at the door. Her fingers made the sound of an animal's claws against the wood. I shut my door and listened as she ran in the direction of the third-floor stairs while giving her ghostly laugh. In this way she suggested a supernatural presence and warned Bertha to retreat to her room. I leant against the wall to Miss Eyre's room, my ear pressed close. As I waited to hear the sound of her stirring from her bed my heart thumped in such a panic I thought it would leap straight out of my chest.

It was a small reassurance to hear her door open. The candle flickering on the threshold must have enticed her out into the corridor to investigate. Once there she would see the smoke billowing under his door and go to rescue Mr Rochester. I heard her cries of "Wake! Wake!" There followed a crashing sound and, at last, the reassuring sound of the baritone voice of my master swearing like a soldier on finding himself drowned in his bed. The muffled murmur of a conversation taking place in his bedroom travelled across the corridor to my anxious ear. I let out a great sigh of relief. The fire was out. They both lived and breathed. Then I heard a door open and bare feet slap along the corridor.

I did not dare look out, but I was sure it was Mr Rochester on his way to the third storey to confront Grace and Bertha. The eerie silence that followed let me enjoy the illusion that Grace had everything under control. I heard Mr Rochester return and some time later Jane returned to her room. At last I felt able to undress and take myself to my bed.

The blame fell, as we knew it would, on Bertha. It was Grace's laugh that had revealed her presence near the scene. Mr Rochester had gone straight up to the third storey, sure that the culprit would be found up there. My confidence in Grace's quick thinking was not misplaced. Grace, already in her nightdress, pretended she had been asleep. Bertha, in her white gown with her great mane of black hair loose, looked and acted every bit the lunatic. She turned snappish the minute she saw Mr Rochester. She growled and raged at him so he got no sense out of her.

"She surprised even me," claimed Grace. "She acted every bit the mad wife. The best thing is, that's exactly what it was — an act. As soon as he was out of earshot, she stopped. It warms my heart to think how much better she is. Most of the time, at least."

I questioned Jane at breakfast and she told me briefly her side of the story. She had thrown the water in the ewer and the basin over the flames on the bed hangings and cast the empty jug into the air so the crash of it shattering would rouse our master. For good measure she had fetched the water jug from her own room. She'd proved that she, like Grace, had a cool head in an emergency.

After that she was very silent at breakfast, sitting with downcast eyes and pink cheeks. I thought her discomfort might be caused by the raucous laughter coming from the servants' hall. Various coarse comments about how much of the master's manhood Miss Eyre had seen when she had roused him from his bed travelled down the passageway. We all knew he never wore a nightshirt and slept naked as nature intended. Why not? He had us servants to wash the sheets.

I consoled myself by reasoning that speculation on such a topic would be unthinkable to the innocent Miss Eyre. I doubted she would know the meaning of the words used. With her customary composure Jane set about her duties with Adele as usual, though later I learned that she had questioned Grace severely about the incident. She had found Grace helping to repair the damage caused by the fire but Grace blocked her at every turn.

Mr Rochester gave it out that he had left his candle burning and knocked it against the hangings in his sleep. Grace and I stuck to the authorized version of events; it was the truth after all, if not the whole truth. He ordered a door to be made at the foot of the stairs to the third storey and for it to be kept locked, making it clear to those of us in the secret that he blamed Bertha for the fire. Then he simply packed his bags and left.

At dinner time I noticed that Jane could scarcely eat her food and blushed and started at every ring of the bell. In the evening I'd had to send Leah to remind her to come to my room for tea. When I went to draw the blinds I casually remarked that the weather was fine for Mr Rochester's journey. Jane started as if I had taken a hot poker to her. To put her out of her agony I explained that Mr Rochester had left immediately after breakfast for the house party at the Leas, Mr Eshton's place. I am sure she was dismayed and disappointed but she concealed it well, beneath her usual demure demeanour.

Disciplined though she was, she could not resist asking me if there were ladies at the house party. I confess I laid it on pretty thick. The beautiful Honourable Blanche Ingram would be there. I gushed on about how accomplished she was and how much Mr

Rochester admired her. It gave me no pleasure to take the light of happiness from Jane's eyes and douse the flames of her burgeoning love. This was the lesson I'd failed to give Martha before I unloaded her onto the Ingrams. I did not intend to repeat my mistake with this naive governess, especially as I had handpicked her for her very innocence of the world. My uneasy conscience made me spell it out to her in the strongest possible terms that a gentleman does not marry a governess. He may make her his mistress but he will not marry her.

One good thing came out of the fire — the locked door to the third storey. Mr Rochester intended it to keep Bertha in. We used it to keep Miss Eyre out. She was not given a key, since we had strict orders to keep the governess out of the secret. I gave a key to all my trusted fellow servants. They needed to have access to the stairs to deliver meals, coal and hot water and to bring down the slops and the dirty dishes. Miss Eyre, without a key, would not be able to pace up and down the corridor of a wet afternoon. Grace and Bertha need no longer spend hours in silence and would have occasional opportunities to leave the confines of their narrow prison.

We had ten days of peace after Mr Rochester went to the Eshtons. Miss Eyre was very quiet, busy with a painting that seemed to occupy all her spare time. Adele was happy spending her afternoons with Sophie in the garden when it was fine or inside with her dolls when it was not. She ate her supper with me and Miss Eyre in my room so I had some opportunities to spoil her, ordering Mary to cook food I thought she would like. After her meal Adele would give me a formal curtsy and a kiss on each cheek before departing for bed. I was left to spend an hour of stilted conversation with Miss Eyre in my room. We both had secrets to conceal but I was confident I had guessed hers. She was sick with love for Mr Rochester. I profoundly hoped she had discovered neither the secret I kept from her nor the suspicion I harboured that Bertha was married to Mr Rochester.

Cut off from the talk in the servants' hall, I relied on Leah to keep me up to date with the ebb and flow of feeling among the other servants. The only real development concerned Sophie, Adele's maid. In spite of the language difficulties Sophie was welcome in the servants' hall. Leah informed me with a sly smile that Sam, the footman, was spending a lot of time with Sophie. "Teaching her English, he says." Sophie was a pretty girl with a gift for making the best of herself.

Mr Rochester had supplied Adele with a handsome new doll from Paris with a luminous wax complexion and blonde ringlets. Miss Eyre did not seem to understand about dolls. I suspect she had not been allowed one as a child. Her reaction had been to warn Adele not to take it too close to the fire for fear it would melt. Adele, duly warned, kept away from the hearth but was distressed by the scantiness of the doll's clothes. She was sure it felt the cold. I secretly conveyed this urgent need for clothing to the third floor. Bertha took it up with enthusiasm. Behind the locked door to the stairway our sewing afternoons began again to take place. Soon we were busy making tiny garments. We raided the storage rooms for scraps of brocade and velvet from old curtains and cushions. Bertha proved as gifted at making dolls' clothes as she had been at making the flowers for the Christmas decorations.

The first outfit for Adele's newest doll consisted of a matching dress, cape and bonnet in purple velvet. The doll was also supplied with a complete set of underwear including four lace-trimmed petticoats. When these items found their way into Adele's hands she was in ecstasy.

With her sharp eye for material advantage Adele soon discovered that she had other dolls with gaps in their wardrobes. A doll would be smuggled up to the third floor to be measured. Later a little pile of clothes would be left outside her door one night and by some miracle they would fit perfectly. We told Adele there was a special group of fairies that did the work and she obliged us by pretending to believe. I do not think she was fooled by the fiction, but, being a pragmatic girl she indulged us to make sure the clothes kept coming.

One by one the dolls were smuggled up to have their measurements taken and their features noted. Grace nudged me to watch Bertha as she tenderly undressed and measured a baby doll and then gently dressed it again. This done she hugged it to her breast and gave a distant smile. It was strange to see her big hands around such a tiny body, but more notable was the expression of ineffable serenity on her face.

"I was sure she'd had a baby. Perhaps we should have got her a doll when she was really bad," said

Grace. "Hugging something can console people. It seems to take away a bit of the pain."

A happy few days we had. Miss Eyre was too busy to notice that Adele's dolls had almost as many changes of clothing as their owner did. She was deep in her own project; she was painting something and a very secret something it was. She would slide it away the minute I came into the room. I thought it might be a portrait of the master. Leah, who had managed to sneak a look, put me straight on that. "It's a lady. With a lot of black hair and a very cross face." It sounded like the description I had given of Blanche Ingram, though I had not mentioned her bad temper.

A letter from Mr Rochester disturbed our peaceful interlude. He wrote to say he was returning in three days' time and that he would be bringing a large house party with him. This news immediately cured Miss Eyre of her dejection and gave me the shock of the century; he had never invited people to a house party at Thornfield Hall. As a bachelor he was constantly invited to other people's houses; he seldom felt the need to return their hospitality. I quailed at the thought of the organization involved and set off at once to put matters in hand. Three days was not very long.

We servants sprang into action like a well-oiled machine. The hunt dinner and the Christmas ball had given us valuable practice. We all knew what to do or where to find someone who could do it. I blessed Monsieur Alphonse for his strict training of our local boys. The only novice was Miss Eyre and I kept her busy in the pantry making sweets and jellies. She was a dab hand at delicacies. Adele, bless her, did not have time for lessons; she had to check her dresses and practise her party pieces. She was sure she would be needed in the "salon" to entertain the guests.

The list of guests contained mainly those who had attended the Christmas party some years back, the one where Mr Rochester paid Miss Blanche some extravagant compliments. This repetition in the guest list is inevitable in the country, where there is such a small supply of suitable people to invite. The only real change was that old Lord Ingram had died and his son, Theodore, was now Baron Ingram of Ingram Park. The futures of the Honourable Blanche and Mary looked gloomy. The new young peer was reputed to have run up many debts on the strength of his future inheritance; the estate was entailed to him. Now that he had come into his fortune his creditors were circling their prey. If they decided to pounce there would be little actual cash left to provide his sisters with marriage settlements.

I hoped my master would be more discreet in his behaviour this time. Miss Blanche was twenty-five now and still unwed. Her triumphant London season was a long way behind her. Her opportunities dwindled as her years accumulated. I guessed that, given half a chance, she would snap her jaws tight round my master. Once again I was concerned for my own future. If the Honourable Blanche became mistress of Thornfield my livelihood depended on her whims and temper. I was saving to buy a pair of cottages, one to live in and one to rent out. In this way I hoped to have

170

an income to support me in my old age. With luck I could avoid cold and hunger; my life, however, would be very meagre compared with my present circumstances. Like most honest working people I dreaded the thought of being forced into the workhouse. The world can be very unkind to old women.

The House Party

1832

It was one of those mild serene days toward the end of March or the beginning of April when the guests arrived for the house party. My first glimpse dashed any hope that my master would be more discreet with the Honourable Miss Ingram. While the other ladies were content to travel in the two open carriages Miss Blanche rode her horse. Her purple riding habit swept the ground and her veil streamed behind her. By her side rode Mr Rochester on his black horse, Mesrour, while his dog, Pilot, bounded ahead. They made a splendid sight; it was hard to imagine a more flagrant way of announcing their interest in each other.

Even among the flurry of arriving guests with their many maids and footmen I noticed Martha. Again she travelled under the guise of the Honourable Blanche's maid, but it was a very different Martha this time. She had lost all her bounce and swagger. There were black rings under her eyes and her cheeks had caved in as if she had lost teeth. The grim set of her lips suggested she was holding back tears all the time. Since my conscience bothered me about the girl I set Leah to find out at servants' meal times what was wrong and report back to me. Custom condemned me to entertaining the upper servants in my room.

I had many other calls upon my time in the evenings so I asked Mr Rochester if Miss Eyre could accompany Adele to the drawing room after dinner; the child was desperate to meet the ladies. Since Mr Rochester had no wife or female relative to act as hostess, it was the custom for there to be a female servant of some status present when there were lady guests, so they could call on her if need be. Mr Rochester gave my suggestion a warm reception; he thought it such a good idea that he warned me he would drag Miss Eyre to the drawing room if she resisted. I showed Jane where she could slip quietly in and advised her to dress in her best costume. Adele did not need such advice. She arrived in style, her hair curled, her petticoats rustling and her immaculate pink dress decorated with a rose.

The footmen and the maids brought us regular reports of what was happening in the drawing room. Mr Rochester was flirting outrageously with Miss Blanche and she was lapping up his attentions. With her brother, the new baronet, she had spent a happy half hour abusing governesses in general while poor Miss Eyre sat within earshot. Now she was singing a duet with the master and very fine singers they both were. Now they were planning charades and we had to ransack the third floor for costumes and props. I scampered as fast as my legs would carry me to keep the visiting servants away from Grace and Bertha's end of the third floor.

Word came down that the answer to the charade was Brideswell. Mr Rochester played the groom and Miss Blanche acted as the bride. They were married in dumb show. Was he determined to ruin her? Or was he making such a spectacle of his courtship that the alliance would be inevitable? The prospect of matrimony had made him flee abroad before. This time even he would not have the brass neck to turn tail. The expectations of his neighbours would force him to lead his dusky bride up the aisle.

As the days went by I still had no real inkling of why my master behaved as indiscreetly as he did. I did not believe he loved Miss Ingram or cherished her for herself. She was a puppet in some kind of show. I might have felt sorry for her if she had not been such a nasty, vain and shallow person. After the duets and the flirting and the charades Mr Rochester had still one last trick to play on his guests. He pretended to be out on business but returned secretly. He had disguised himself as an old gypsy woman who had come to tell the ladies' fortunes. Or rather the fortunes of the young and single ladies. He did not waste his time on that awful old battle-axe the Dowager Baroness Ingram.

The bold Miss Blanche volunteered to be first to brave an interview with the gypsy. "What a drama she made of it! You'd have thought she was going to wrestle a bear," said Sam, who had been in charge of the negotiations between the ladies and the gypsy. "And when she came out! You should have seen the gob on her!" he guffawed. We all cackled with laughter. The haughty Miss Honourable driven into a bad case of the sulks by a gypsy.

Sam revealed that the gypsy — or rather Mr Rochester — had at the end specifically asked him to go for Miss Eyre to have her fortune told. Sam was full of approval for Jane's behaviour. "She didn't make a performance of it. I offered to stay out in corridor in case she was scared. Not her. She sent me back to the kitchen to get on with my work." What words were exchanged during that interview we never learnt.

While Mr Rochester was dressed up as a gypsy even the staff thought he was away on business in Millcote. In his absence — as we thought — a Mr Mason arrived and claimed to be an old friend of the master's from Kingston, Jamaica. As is the custom we admitted the visitor, who joined the others in the drawing room. Once the pantomime of fortune-telling was over, our master welcomed the new arrival and showed him to a bedroom near his own. The arrival of this visitor from Jamaica changed everything, but we did not know it at the time. The revelations he set in motion reduced the posturing of the gentry in the drawing room to a mere shadow play. It was on the floors above and below them the real drama was played out.

In the morning the unexpected guest had gone. Gratitude was my first thought; one less mouth to feed. I am a little deaf so I had slept through the disturbance in the night. Sam whispered that he had been involved. He gave me a nod and a wink and a "tell you later". To be honest I was too busy catering for the house party to

175

have time to think about anything else. We were working from five thirty in the morning to eleven or twelve at night. We had little time for gossip and tended to sleep well. The house party was over before I discovered there had been strange comings and goings in the night, horses saddled, a post chaise summoned to wait outside the gate as dawn broke.

It must have been the season for sudden departures. In the afternoon a manservant we did not know came with news for Miss Eyre. The two of them set off in the early hours of the next morning before I was about. Her disappearance made me quite angry, as she had not had the courtesy to seek me out and ask my permission. She had gone straight to Mr Rochester; governesses like to think they are family, not servants. The master had given her leave to go and paid her ten pounds from his own pocket. I was annoyed because it made a muddle in the accounts. To be fair to Jane she wrote to me later, explaining she had been summoned to a dying relative.

When the Easter recess of Parliament came to an end Sir George Lynn, who was member for Millcote, left Thornfield Hall. After that the house party quickly dwindled; the Eshtons and the Dents soon found reasons to leave. We were left with the dregs, the Ingrams. I might have known they would hang on, eating our food and burning our coal in preference to their own. My worst ordeal was a final meal alone with the Ingrams' upper servants. They were shallow imitations of their employers: full of stories of exalted visitors and complaints about how hard it was to get "proper staff". They spent their time abusing their fellow servants as either lazy and slovenly or ignorant of the necessary skills to do their jobs properly. I smiled and nodded and managed to keep my pug mask intact while inside I wanted to curse them and sentence them to the cruellest torments of cold, hunger and poverty. I was proud of my staff at Thornfield. They were honest, punctual and reliable and they knew their trades.

At last the Ingrams left. As befitted their rank Mr Rochester waved them off and we servants stood outside in a respectful line. We had done well in the customary tips from the previous departing guests but we were not optimistic about these. The Ingrams ran true to their usual tight-fisted form. Miss Blanche sat in the coach with a face that would sour milk. I could not blame her; she must've expected a proposal while she was at Thornfield Hall. Poor Martha followed behind them in the dog cart. She was balanced on the top of the trunks and crying fit to burst.

"Can I have a word?" It was Leah by my side, all pink and embarrassed. Her news did not surprise me. She and John were in love. Nature had taken its course.

"What does John say?"

"He wants to speak to parson straight away. I wanted to tell you first."

"Thank you, Leah. I appreciate that. First Adele arrives and now a baby will be coming to Thornfield Hall. The old place will be full of life. Let us hope your baby arrives when Mr Rochester is away. The gentry don't really like babies being born in their houses —

except their own. Let's hope you have your own cottage by then."

"My baby's not the only one. Martha's in the family way. That's why she's crying all the time. I only just persuaded her to get in the dog cart to go back with them. She wanted to stay here. She's further on than me. She thinks she's due about harvest time." Leah shrugged her shoulders and held out her hands in a gesture of helplessness.

"I don't suppose the daft girl has any idea of her dates. The clock was just a picture on the wall to her. As for looking at a calendar!" I raised my eyes to heaven. "I saw she looked unhappy but I didn't notice her thickening out."

"You were busy and you can hide a lot under an apron. At least I hope so."

"Any mention of the father?"

"She had plenty to say about him. It's the new Baron Ingram, of course. Young Lord Theodore as was."

"He'll not be speaking to the parson."

"No. Gave her five guineas not to tell."

"Who else knows?"

"The dreaded Blanche. Says she'll give her a reference if she goes quietly. They don't want the baroness to know. Apparently it's not the first time young Theodore has put a maid in the family way. Following in his father's footsteps. Martha showed me her arms. They're black with bruises where Blanche has pinched and twisted them."

I felt the heart drop out of me. Poor Martha was with child by a man who was scared of his mother and who got his sister to do his dirty work. All this because I'd been squeamish about being seen leaving old Mr Rochester's bedroom. As if my reputation counted for anything against the fate of the unwanted baby of a silly girl who let a coward seduce her. In seconds I'd made my mind up.

"I'll send word to her tomorrow. Tell her to give her notice in and get her reference. She must come here. I'll not see her go to the workhouse. You know how hard they are on girls who are not wed. We will look after her. I'll put her on the books as a laundry maid to cover her food. She'll have to work until her time comes but no one here will torment her. I don't know about after the baby comes. She'll have a reference from a titled lady. That must be worth something."

I knew there would be times I would regret making the offer of a safe refuge. Martha could annoy me faster than a buzzing fly in the dairy. I would have to grit my teeth and bear her irritating ways; I must reap what I had sown. As I always did when I had a problem I climbed the stairs to the third storey. To my surprise the upper door was locked and I had to knock. Grace unlocked it but kept the door half closed to warn me not to venture further. She put her finger to her lips to signal I should be quiet.

"Snappish?" I whispered.

Grace drew her hand across her throat in imitation of a murderer's knife and rolled her eyes. She was wan and haggard from watching her unpredictable charge. "A doll would help."

At first I didn't understand her request. Then I remembered Bertha nursing the tiny doll, her eyes and her mind faraway and peaceful. "I'll ask Adele."

"I have important news."

"So have I."

"It'll have to wait. Can't talk now."

With that I had to be satisfied.

Adele was taking advantage of Miss Eyre's absence. She had taken to her bed, exhausted by her efforts at entertaining the house guests. Her dark curls billowed round her face as she lay back against her frilled pillows like a small empress holding court. It was a matter of regret to her that she could not join me for the evening meal but she was suffering from *la grippe*. Could Sophie bring her supper up to her? Of course I agreed; I wanted a favour from this tiny tyrant.

In my experience children do not like to part with their possessions. They tend to scream and shout and clutch their treasures to their chests but my request for the loan of a doll was met by Adele with her usual perfect equanimity. She had an army of dolls; she could afford to be generous. She lined up all the candidates. This one she could not part with at the moment as she too was suffering from the *grippe*. That one had been very naughty and so she could not be allowed out.

"It is for cuddling," I told her to speed up the process.

"Cuddling? What is cuddling?"

I mimed the action. "It is to cheer someone up, Adele. Does that help you choose?" It did. A *bébé* doll,

180

then, not a *jeune fille*. Definitely a *bébé*. She was desolate that the doll's clothes were not up to her usual standard. I assured her that would not be a problem. I expected that when Bertha recovered she would start sewing again.

There was much laughter and joshing in the servants' hall that evening. We were glad to be reunited and free to talk without having to watch our tongues. John came in for lots of jibes and back-slapping once Leah's news was out.

"You'll be making an honest woman of her no doubt." Old John's choice of phrase was not the happiest; he was not one to mince his words. Mary scowled her disapproval at him. John was a farm boy, and had been courting Leah for some time. They were simply following the country custom of waiting for the baby to start before they got wed.

"I'll be talking to parson soon as I can get time off," John announced. Leah looked at him with admiring eyes. As he spoke, he flushed with pride and embarrassment and I saw that the boy had become a man. Marriage was a brave step for them to take. Married servants are not tolerated in many households. Mistresses expect their servants to be available at all hours, not tucked up in their own cottages at night. Fortunately Mr Rochester did not concern himself with such details. In effect I was mistress of the house — until I was replaced. I told John to take time off the very next day and used the moment to tell them about

Martha. "Leah's not the only one to be having a baby. I hear Martha's —"

A cry of anguish stopped me. Old John had his head in his hands and was wailing through his fingers. "Don't tell me Martha is up the duff. We should never have let her go to those Ingrams." He raised his head and glared at me with his clouded blue eyes. "I warned you about that old goat." I saw tears tremble on his weather-beaten face.

I felt my cheeks flame with guilt and a pain like a dagger cut through me. Old John was right; I had done wrong. It was a most uncomfortable moment so I took some small relief to my feelings by correcting him. "It wasn't the old goat. It was the young goat."

They sat with solemn faces while I told them all the rest: the threatened bad character, the five guineas and the bruised arms.

"I'll make that young whipper-snapper pay," Old John vowed. He saw from our expressions the question in our minds. How? How could an obscure elderly groom affect a man who was now a peer of the realm?

"You don't believe me," he snapped. "Then you don't know horse people. We stick together. Every coachman, every groom and every hunt servant will turn their hand against him. That little sprig of Satan. He likes the races. He likes to mix with the viscounts, and the colonels, and the honourable this and the dishonourable that. And he likes to show off. He's been betting large sums on old nags. He's no judge of horse flesh." I knew that in Old John's book, this defect was the equivalent of a mortal sin.

182

Old John muttered on, "They let him bet on credit. They know the estate's entailed to him. They'll wait. There'll be interest. They won't be so patient when we put the word out against him. They'll be fighting to be first to get their share."

I was amazed; I'd never heard Old John put more than four words together in his life.

"If he thinks he'll have trouble with that old trout of a mother if she finds out about Martha, he wants to see what'll happen when his creditors panic and come stampeding for their money. His ma'll have something to say when they auction Ingram Park over her head and turn her out in the cold. That estate'll go for a knockdown price. It'll not cover what he owes." A grim smile came over his face.

"Time for the servants' revenge," Sam announced.

"What's that?" Leah asked.

Sam leaned across the table to explain. "Well, you know the whole point of our existence is to make their lives comfortable. The servants' revenge is when instead of doing just that, the servants start to make their lives uncomfortable."

"How?" John was a newcomer to these tricks of a servant's trade.

"We'll tell them at Ingram Park. They'll think of something. An important letter mysteriously delayed, the bedroom fire gone out, the tea cold — with spit in it."

We all felt a bit better after that. When I told them that I was going to ask Martha to come back a rumble of agreement went round the room. Old John seemed to speak for them all when he said I was doing the right thing. "I am sorry about earlier, Mrs Fairfax. I had a bit of an outburst like, but Martha's father was my oldest friend. I should have kept a better watch on her. There's no one else."

"You tried," Mary consoled him. "Martha didn't take kindly to being told what to do. And she surely didn't like being told what not to do. She has a rare sharp tongue on her, that girl." Mary shook her head.

Old John was not to be pacified. "In my day if a lass swore a man was the father, he was. He had to do the right thing. That was it. No questions asked. I seen the parish constable take the girl in one hand and the warrant in the other. Church or prison. That was the choice."

"That how you got him, Mary?" It was Sam, who could never resist a joke.

"So we are all agreed?" I spoke after the laughter died away. "We find a way to look after Martha here until the baby comes. After that who knows? We must do our best. John, after you've seen the parson, ride over to the Ingrams' place and tell Martha what we've agreed. I'm sure in the circumstances Old John will let you have one of his better horses. It's twenty miles to Ingram Park. Nothing to a farm lad like you."

"Master could get there in a morning. He's a fine horseman. He could be there every day wooing his lady love, the lovely Miss Blanche. But he isn't."

"Master doesn't like to show his hand. He plays his cards close to his chest. This Mr Rochester has more than one secret." I pricked up my ears at Sam's words.

184

He gave the satisfied smirk of someone with superior knowledge. It could not be the fact of the existence of Bertha; all of us present had sworn the Bible oath. It must be a further secret. Had Sam discovered that Bertha claimed to be our master's lawful wedded wife?

Sam leant forward confidentially to enlighten us. "There was a rum do the other night. You remember that Mason fellow who said he came from Jamaica? Mr Rochester woke me up in the middle of the night. Sent me off in the dark to get a post chaise. Told me to make the driver stay outside the gates so the noise of the wheels didn't wake the guests. Master sent me straight back to bed when I got back with it. I didn't go, of course. Hung about in the dark."

"Anything interesting?"

"I saw Miss Eyre come out to make sure the road was clear." Rude whistles greeted this piece of news. "By the way, where is she?"

"Summoned to a dying relative."

"That's her story."

"Go on. Tell us the end of the tale."

"Well, you know that Mr Mason?" We all nodded. "Master and Mr Carter came out into yard and they were sort of holding him up between them to help him walk. When they got him to the chaise, they bundled him into the coach. Mr Carter climbed in after him and they drove off."

"Sounds as if he was drunk."

"Funny," said John. "He was all right when he rang his bell late that night. Asked me if I had a key to the third storey. Told me to unlock the door."

"Did you?"

"Aye. A guest tells you to do something, you do it. He said the master knew all about it and he couldn't wait any longer to see his sister, Bertha. He knew her name and where she was kept. So I thought it all right."

His sister! We were astounded. Bertha had a brother. We had myriad questions and many speculations. Most of our comments were not complimentary. A brother who let you rot for ten years without a visit or a letter was not much of a brother to our minds. More secrets, more Rochester secrets. One gem of information came out of it. We realized that we now knew Bertha's second name. Bertha Mason. She was Bertha Mason. We could hardly wait to get the full story of the night's events from Grace.

Bertha's Story

1832

My master left for London, claiming he was going to buy a new carriage in readiness for his marriage. He still did not give the name of his bride but it was assumed that he would marry Miss Ingram. If he had gone to Ingram Park occasionally we might have been more inclined to find the alliance credible. To be honest we all breathed a sigh of relief that he was gone and that with Miss Eyre away we could fall back into our more relaxed ways and could talk more freely without looking over our shoulders to see who was listening.

It was a day after the master's departure before Grace and Bertha could cope with a visit. The evening was still light and the sunset across the moors blazed a magnificent scarlet. Bertha was in the room, but not in the room, if you get my meaning. She was looking out of the window but what she saw I did not know. I was sure it was not the green fields and the great open spaces of Yorkshire. She was dressed but her hair was loose, lying around her shoulders like a big black cloud. Her eyes were rimmed with red and the scratches on her hands showed that she had been tearing at herself with her fingernails, something she only did when she was very disturbed. The baby doll Adele had loaned was nestled against her bosom and every now and then she would look down tenderly at it and adjust its position. There was no other outward sign that Bertha had suffered one of her episodes of wild and uncontrolled behaviour. Both women looked exhausted, their faces grey from lack of sleep, fresh air and exercise. This enforced secrecy was very hard on them; it's no way for people to live.

Since Grace seemed disinclined — or too tired — to talk I started the conversation. You know how it is when you have not seen your friend for a long time. Once you have started talking you cannot stop. There was so much to tell. First the good news: Leah's baby on the way and John doing the right thing with love in his heart. Then the bad news about Martha.

Grace laughed when I recounted Old John's description of the parish constable offering a man the choice between marriage and prison. "Not much of a choice is it? I think I would choose prison. An unhappy marriage is worse than jail. Course now it's not enough to point your finger at a man and say he was the one who did the deed. You have to have evidence. Still, Alice, if there's anything I can do to keep Martha from the workhouse, consider it done. I know what it's like in there. I would not wish it on my worst enemy. Here's my hand on it."

Her hand when she gave it to me was dry and papery, a sure sign of the strain of the last few days; she had been living off her formidable willpower. "So you have not been wasting your time with fripperies while I've been locked up here?"

I could not ignore the jibe. "I have not been idle. I have been running a house party." I lowered my voice. "I hear you had a late night visitor." Grace nodded and looked towards Bertha to make sure she was still occupied at the window. "Did he claim he was her brother?" Grace nodded again. "Did he give you his name?" This time Grace shook her head.

"Your Mr Rochester called him Richard or Dick." She gave me a sour look. "I can think of some better names for him."

"He's a Mister Mason. So Bertha must be Bertha Mason." I sat back with a pleasant feeling of triumph.

"No she's not. She's Bertha Rochester." Grace had trumped my ace. I felt my jaw drop in a most unladylike way. I snapped it back shut.

Bertha chose this moment to move away from the window. I thought she had heard her name. She came to lie on the big four-poster bed, her doll still clasped firmly to her breast.

"Leah to have a baby," she murmured. It always surprised me, what she took from a conversation and what she ignored. "Will she let me hold it?"

"I expect so."

"It is so nice to suckle a child," Bertha said wistfully and gazed down at the doll.

On hearing that remark Grace rose and went to sit next to her. I joined them to make a cosy circle with Bertha and her pretend baby on the bed. "Now Mrs Fairfax is here you might like to tell her your story,

Bertha," Grace began, speaking earnestly and seriously to her charge. Bertha nodded and I put on my listening face.

"Start with Mr Edward coming to Spanish Town," Grace prompted her.

"We have house in Spanish Town. I live there with my father, my mother and my big brother."

"Is that all your family?" Grace asked.

"No. I have little brother but he stay at plantation. He . . ." Words fail her. She twirls a finger at her head.

"So you were living in Spanish Town when Mr Edward came."

"Yes. He come to see my father on business. I was young then. I go to dances, parties. I have many admirers. Nice dresses. Mr Edward not handsome but he very strong and he does business with my father. Pa call me in and say he think it good thing for me to marry Mr Edward. I have a nice dowry. Thirty thousand pounds. Papa talks to Mr Edward. It is all agreed. Everybody is happy.

"First year very nice. He love me a lot." She stopped talking and gave me a hard look. "You know," she said and bounced up and down on the bed. "We do the jiggly thing."

"I know," I told her. "I know what you mean."

"Then it not so nice. My mama keep asking why there no baby yet. She keep on at Mr Edward. She give me things to drink. She put magic in Mr Edward's whisky. Every time she ask he get very angry with my mama. Mr Edward stop working in business. Papa very angry with Mr Edward. Now he drinking whisky all

190

time. Papa sends us to live on plantation." She shudders.

"Plantation not nice. Nice flowers and bright birds but many slaves. Sometimes my brother come and he take Mr Edward to slave cabins at night. For the women. That very bad thing."

She starts to count on her fingers. "Three, no four years go past. Baby comes." A great smile lights up her face as she remembers. "I so happy. He lovely baby. Big brown eyes, curly hair, strong hands. He grip my finger tight." She put a hand to her bosom and pulled up the locket she had fought so hard to save and had since worn continuously.

To my amazement she opened the locket; she had never done that before. Inside was a tiny lock of curly black hair. It was different in texture from any hair I had seen before. It looked as if the inexpert hands of Martha had been working on it with an overheated curling iron. Like a dutiful child offering cake at a tea party, Bertha held out her locket for Grace to inspect and then showed it to me. We gazed in turn at the sad memento and silently handed it back to her. She closed the locket and slipped it round her neck and back into her nightgown.

I sat frozen in my chair, dreading what might come next in her tale.

"I feed him myself." She slapped her bosom. "With these. Mr Edward not happy."

I smiled to myself. The gentry were notorious for not letting their wives feed their own babies. The poor children were sent off to take their chances with wet nurses. This peculiar system caused much hardship — babies dead in the first three months and women pregnant and giving birth again within the year. I assumed Mr Edward's anger was caused by his sharing this strange English prejudice against a baby temporarily taking over a woman's breasts. I was a long way from the mark. Bertha had a surprise for me.

"Baby very dark. Black really. It happens sometimes in my country. Pale lady has black baby. Black lady has pale baby. We know that it happen in Spanish Town. But Mr Edward he go mad. He point at baby. Baby cannot be his son. He tell me now he rich man in England. His father and brother dead. He say we must go to England. He need son and heir. He say he cannot take black baby to England."

I try to imagine Mr Rochester presenting the local gentry with a very dark baby he had brought with him on a ship from Jamaica. I hear him explaining that the dusky child is his firstborn son and therefore the true heir to the Rochester fortune. I can see the nudging, the head-shaking. There would be whispering behind hands that would soon break out into outright scorn and contempt. People in Yorkshire do not take seriously any births that occur outside the county boundary. If you are not born in Yorkshire you do not really exist.

"He say I been going with slaves. He say that to me! He is the one who is down the slave cabins with my brother up to no good." Bertha's voice grew shrill with indignation. Grace patted her hand and mopped her brow. She gave her a sniff of smelling salts to soothe her. Bertha's voice when she took up her tale again was quiet and subdued.

"One night I sleep very deep. Baby not wake me to feed. In morning cradle empty. Mr Edward tell me baby dead. Died in night. Has taken body away. I go mad. He give me potion to drink. I sleep. When I wake I find I am on big ship. In little room. In dark. Door locked. He bring food but I sick all time. These hurt." She tapped her breasts. "All big with milk. It leak out. My frock all wet. No little mouth to suck them. I cry and cry."

Tears dripped down her face as she remembered the voyage to England. I pictured her locked in a tiny cabin in the bowels of the ship, dependent on Mr Rochester for all her needs. We had all heard about the dreadful journey the people from Africa had been forced to endure before the navy put a stop to the trade. The suffering was beyond my imagining.

"When the boat stop I in smoky cold town. Mr Edward put me in coach with nasty smelly woman and bring me here." She gestured to the window. "No bright flowers, no colourful birds, most time no leaves on trees."

My heart went out to the poor soul. I knew the agony of losing a child. At least I had been able to lay my baby girl to rest and had a gravestone to mark her existence — not just an empty cradle and a tuft of hair.

"I very tired. Can I go to bed now?" Bertha turned her childlike gaze to Grace, who led her away to prepare her for bed. Bertha sat quietly while Grace brushed her hair and dressed her in a clean nightgown.

Through the open door I watched as Grace tucked her into bed like a giant child and dropped a kiss on her forehead. Within seconds Bertha was asleep. She was reaping the blessing of her limited intellect; she could not keep an idea in her head for very long. Grace returned to the sitting room, closed the door to Bertha's bedroom and pulled the tapestry across it.

Grace gave me a mocking grin. "Would you like a cup of tea?" she asked, smooth as a society hostess. "Or something stronger. You've gone a little pale. Your beloved master does not come out of that story very well, does he?" She sniggered as she put the kettle on the fire.

That put me on my mettle. "We don't know her story is true. We've no proof, no evidence, no . . . What do the lawyers call it?"

"Corroboration." Grace, as always, was well-informed on legal matters. "You should read the newspaper more," she told me. "Not just recipes."

I let her win that one.

"I have ears to hear." Grace waggled them with her fingers. "I have now heard Bertha's story and I have heard both the brother and your sainted master himself acknowledge the truth of it. She is the legal wedded wife of our Mr Rochester. I do not doubt any longer."

That really knocked the wind out of my sails. When I recovered the power of speech I begged Grace for more details. I wanted evidence. I did not want to believe that my master had been so cold-blooded and determined in his deception of us all. Grace took a swig from her

194

glass of porter, wiped the foam off her top lip and began.

"Two nights ago, the dim-wit that I now know as Richard Mason, arrived up here late at night. He claimed that he was Bertha's brother and that he was here with Mr Rochester's permission and agreement. Stupidly, I believed him; the door to the stairs had been unlocked for him.

"It was John who unlocked it for him."

"Tell him not to do that again. I did try to keep him out but his knocking on the door woke Bertha. I could hardly turn her brother away. Anyway this cobweb of a colonial thought it was a good idea to visit his poor mad sister in the middle of the night. When he hasn't so much as sent a message all the time I've been here.

"Once he was here he had much to say about his own troubles and tribulations. You should have heard him complain. The sugar crop failing, the plantation mortgaged, the slaves in rebellion. Never a word for his sister and her sufferings. The way I see it he was hoping to get her to persuade Rochester to give him a loan, a little slice off her dowry. That shows you how out of touch he is. As if she has any influence on Rochester! Apparently their father gave thirty thousand pounds when Rochester married her. Our colonial boy would like some of it back, if you please.

"It seems the bottom's dropping out of the sugar trade. The navy has put a stop to bringing slaves from Africa. The poor plantation owners cannot buy new slaves!" Grace's face made clear her opinion on the slave trade. "It seems that the only way they get new ones is by breeding them. Understandably the slaves are not too keen on doing that. Life is not as comfortable as it was for the plantation owners. Mr Mason would like a little help with paying his bills. The smell of money has brought him here. Rochester is a very wealthy man now."

She glared at me. "Guess where Bertha's baby went when one morning he disappeared, leaving his cradle empty. It seems he miraculously made his way to the slave quarters. Remarkable, isn't it? Walking away from freedom at a month old!"

"You mean the baby did not die. They just took him away and then lied to her."

"They took him to the slave quarters. The child was brought up as a slave. Ten years ago."

I sat frozen with horror.

Grace continued. "There was a rebellion this Christmas. It was serious; I read the reports in the newspapers here. Anyway in the upheaval the boy escaped. He must have made for the hills with the other runaway slaves. I hope he's safe there. I hope he lives long enough and grows strong enough to take his revenge on Mr Richard Mason and Mr Edward Rochester."

I was silent. I found it hard to believe that my master could be a part of such wickedness. The cruelty of the crime was for me beyond words. Grace found the words; she enunciated them savagely.

"This Richard Mason, this apology for a human being, was so obsessed by his own misfortunes that he let slip that the baby Bertha thought was dead, was in

196

fact alive. Just let it slip. Didn't confess to the crime or break the news to her properly. Just popped it into his list of complaints. He was so mightily miffed that he had borne the cost of feeding the boy for ten years for no return. Just as he was old enough to be of some real use as a worker the perishing lad took it into his head to run away. And so poor Mr Mason lost all his profit. I think we are supposed to weep for him."

"Bertha heard this?"

"Yes."

"What did she do?"

"She went for her embroidery scissors. She stabbed him in the shoulder. I think she was aiming for his heart. They didn't go deep enough to satisfy her; they're only small scissors. So she gnawed at the wound with her teeth. When I got to her she was telling him she would suck the blood out of him. There was terrible screaming and scuffling and rolling about on the floor. Mason shouted for help. Then he called for Mr Rochester. He probably thought I would stand by and let Bertha finish him off. I was certainly tempted to. The shouting must have woken Mr Rochester. He arrived very quickly and helped me pin down Bertha. He did a very neat trick with a cord and bound her hands. I sat her on the bed and stayed with her while Mr Rochester dragged the wounded wastrel next door. Mr Rochester spent some time trying to bandage up his friend and stop the bleeding. They were talking about what had happened."

"So you went to the door and put your ear to the keyhole."

"No I did not. There was no need. They left the door open. Mason was on that big four-poster bed, whimpering and fussing and crying like a baby. He was only too happy to give his side of the story. It all matches with what Bertha has told us about being bundled onto a ship. She must have spent more than a month mourning her dead baby with nothing but the sea for company. If she was not mad when she started the voyage she would be at the end of it."

"You've still not proved Mr Rochester is married to her." I did not want to believe what I had heard and so grasped at straws. "It might be a fantasy of Bertha's. She might have had an inconvenient baby and Mr Rochester obliged the brother by smuggling her away to England to avoid scandal."

"True. But I heard Mason refer to Bertha as 'your wife' and Rochester did not deny it."

I made one last feeble attempt to avoid the awful truth. "The family never said he was married." Even as I spoke, it sounded hollow.

"You can see why. They must have known she was slow in her mind. Perhaps Rochester didn't. In the right circumstances Bertha manages, but when things go wrong . . ." Grace shook her head slowly from side to side. "And things have gone very wrong for her, the poor soul."

"And I left her to the unscrupulous Mrs Morgan and the negligent Carter." I hung my head in shame. "A baby dying is very hard to bear. I know that. To be plucked away from your family and taken to a strange place at the same time doesn't bear thinking about." I

198

got up and went to the window to feel the fresh air. I looked out over the Rochester lands and thought about my master. "My master" — how long had I taken those two words for granted? Not anymore. What was it the lawyers had said when Mr Edward came into the inheritance? Business interests in Liverpool. Factories near Manchester. Then there was the connection with Jamaica. Why send your younger son there for a bride? There were plenty of wealthy heiresses in Yorkshire. The West Indies, slaves, sugar, cotton. It all added up. The Rochester wealth did not all come from good honest farmland.

To tell a woman her baby had died when it lived, to drag her across the ocean and then shut her away from the world: these were the acts of a monster. My — I mean Mr Edward had always been a fair and generous employer to me. He must have had some reason to carry out such cruel deeds. I rallied to his defence.

"Don't forget the baby, living evidence that Bertha had been unfaithful to him. Bertha says she wasn't. She would say that, wouldn't she? We only have her word for it."

"To be fair, Mr Rochester himself is dark and swarthy. Some couples wait twenty years before a baby arrives. It doesn't mean the wife found a handy young footman to do the business."

I fell silent. "No one will ever know the truth of that for sure."

"Some things we do know." Grace spoke earnestly to me. "We suspected she might be his wife. Now we know for sure. I heard Mason and Rochester both speak of her as Rochester's wife."

I accepted defeat at her hands. No one else in the world could have told me such a thing and be believed.

Grace was still putting forward her case. "They had no reason to lie. I am a servant. To the gentry that makes me blind and deaf; they speak freely in my presence. It was only when he came back with the governess that Mr Rochester realized he'd been indiscreet. He forbade both Miss Eyre and Mason from speaking to each other. Then he locked the door to Bertha's bedroom so I heard no more."

"That tallies with Sam's version. He saw Miss Eyre act as lookout when they put Mason in the coach. Miss Eyre is away at the moment. She's been summoned to a sick relative. She never said a word to me but went straight to the master. Master! That word again. I must think about this. It's not fair to say I only read recipes, Grace. I do read the newspaper. I do know what's going on in the world and I do try to sort out right from wrong."

I was glad that Mr Rochester was absent from the house. There were many things I wanted to think about calmly and clearly. For a start I had to stop referring to him as "my master". He was my employer. I vowed to call him "Mr Rochester" in future though I found it very hard to break the habit of so many years.

I wrote back to Miss Eyre, whose relative was taking a long time dying, and assured her we would look after Adele. I also told her that Mr Rochester had gone to

London to buy a coach for his intended bride. It seemed kind to give her a warning so that she could prepare her face for when the official announcement was made.

Then there was Miss Ingram to consider. Mr Rochester's courtship of her was of a strange nature. He lavished attention on her in public and then proceeded to ignore her when there was no audience; he made no effort to visit her at Ingram Park, no fond notes travelled backwards and forwards. It was not a promising start to a lifelong union.

My own conscience troubled me. Could I stand calmly by and watch Mr Rochester commit bigamy? A wicked piece of me wanted to see the Honourable Blanche's face when she discovered that there already was a Mrs Rochester. Baroness Ingram's servants would have their hands full on that day if it ever came. They would need more than smelling salts. The hysterics would be spectacular; the ornaments and the hairbrushes would fly. I reminded myself I was bound by a bible oath to keep Bertha a secret. Now I understood why that oath had been so important to my employer.

Grace and I mulled the problem over together and could make no progress. In the end we decided to share our news with the other servants who had taken the oath. There could be no harm in that. "Just the fact of the marriage," Grace warned me. "I don't think we should tell them about the baby. It's too sad and too complicated."

"Agreed. We don't know the rights and wrongs of that. She wouldn't be the first woman to look elsewhere after a few years of a sterile marriage. It is more sensible though to pick someone with a passing resemblance to your husband."

Grace pulled a knowing face at me. "How long were you married, Alice, before your daughter came along?"

I ignored her. "Let's stick to our business."

Grace ticked the points off on her fingers as she went through them. "All we know for sure is that they were legally married. Just because it happened in Jamaica doesn't make it any less binding. We have a witness, Mr Mason. Rochester was there when he called her his wife. He did not deny it. So it's not just Bertha's word."

"It is enough. I will tell the others."

That evening I shooed the stable lads back to their dormitory after supper with a flagon of weak ale and a long string of instructions and warnings from Old John. The rest of us gathered round the big table with our favourite comforts. Tea for me, ale for Old John and Sam. John and Leah had each other's hand to hold and the knowledge of a tiny growing child to keep them happy. Mary, the cook, needed nothing more than the opportunity to rest her hands and her feet. Bertha was still too troublesome in the evening to be left so Grace could not join us. I had armed myself in preparation for a shocking piece of news; I had my bible in my pocket and my stays laced tightly.

John, the young husband to be, was horrified by the news that Mr Rochester was married to Bertha. The

202

first banns for his own wedding to Leah had been called and he was full of idealism about enduring love and the sacred nature of marriage. "Isn't there something about marriage being until death us do part? That's what it says and that's what it means." He gazed soppily at Leah who beamed back at him. "If master tries to marry someone else, we should stop him before it's too late. It's . . . what's it called?"

"Bigamy. You can get sent to prison for it. But not for long. Magistrates think having more than one wife is punishment enough. Chap in Harrogate just got caught. Mind you he did have three wives and was busy acquiring his fourth." Sam grinned at the idea of four wives. "Makes me glad I was a sailor. One in every port."

"That reminds me. Where is Sophie this evening?" Old John gave Sam a knowing leer.

I wasn't having that sort of talk so I quickly spoke up. "She is with Adele. In theory she knows nothing about our mysterious lady. She was not here when we took the oath. Unless someone has been blabbing." I gave Sam a significant look. I was pretty sure Sam and Sophie shared more than the initial letter of their first names. I turned to Old John. "What do you think about this?"

"You know I'm a bit of a free thinker. Not a churchgoer at all. Well, for what it's worth, here are my thoughts. A man in master's position needs a wife. No disrespect to Miss Bertha but she's not a fitting wife for a gentleman of standing. The way I see it he should marry Miss Blanche, if that's what he wants. There's no way he could get his hands on her without a wedding. She's a fine horsewoman but she has a mighty wilful way with her. He'll need a tight rein on her. That's his lookout. I don't see why a few words from a clergyman years ago in Jamaica should stop him. It's a lot of mumbo jumbo."

"And Mary. What about you?"

"It may be mumbo jumbo but it's how the world works. You're married. You stay together. Through thick and thin." She gave Old John a savage look. "You don't think I'd be here now if I'd not taken that vow. I'd be over the hills and far away while you were still mixing bran mash for your beloved horses. I haven't lived with the smell of horse shit for years from choice. I did it cause I have to. It's my duty."

Old John's jaw sagged and his eyes opened wide. Mary was usually the silent partner, loyally nodding her agreement to her husband's views. She patted his lean arm and smiled at him. "It's good to give you a shock every now and then."

"And, Leah, what do you think?"

"To be honest I think that Miss Blanche is a nasty piece of work. I wouldn't choose to have her as mistress here. I saw the bruises on Martha's arms. I don't know what the master sees in her but I do know that Miss Bertha has been very unhappy. And I can't help noticing that now she really only goes wild when Mr Rochester is here. Seems to me, married or not, they'd be better off living hundreds of miles apart."

I saw the glimmering of a solution on the horizon. The youngest and most inexperienced of us had provided an answer. I patted the bible in my pocket and tried to remember where I would find the phrase "Out of the mouths of babes and sucklings".

Sam had the last word. "Don't forget, Mrs Fairfax, that a husband must support his wife. Remember that, young John." He wagged his finger at him across the table. "Once you are married you must put clothes on her back and food in her mouth — and do the same for all the children." When the laughter died away Sam continued, "To be fair to Mr Rochester he has provided for her. He's kept Thornfield Hall going and paid our wages all these years. Generous wages at that."

There were murmurs of agreement round the table. I was not as whole-hearted as the others in my acquiescence. He'll still have change from the thirty thousand pounds, was my uncharitable thought. I had kept that snippet of information to myself. Thirty thousand pounds is a lot of money and people can be very silly when they get greedy.

"Think on," Sam continued, wagging his finger in the air, "if this secret gets out, we are dead ducks. Master has nothing to lose. He can send Bertha to an asylum, close up Thornfield Hall and go and live it up on the continent with one of his French tarts. What'll happen to us then? We'll be out on the street. We'll not find it easy to get places round here. Scandal sticks."

Now there was something we could all agree on. We decided that we should continue to call our upstairs lady Miss Bertha, and not Mrs Rochester. We should keep a tight hold on our lips and be especially careful when Martha arrived. It would be easy to forget that

205

she knew nothing of Miss Bertha and she had not taken the oath of silence as we had done.

I reminded them that Mr Rochester had said only that he was buying a coach for his bride. No formal announcement of an engagement had been made. I warned them that he had talked of hiring some new servants. No doubt the Honourable Blanche expected to be mistress of a considerable establishment. So far it was all talk. Our jobs were safe as long as we kept the oath. The secret we nursed gave us security for the moment. There was no need yet for us to think of breaking our silence.

Later I sat in my room alone and thumbed through my little bible looking for the saying about babes and sucklings. I could not find it. I think it must be in the prayer book. When I look in my bible, especially the Book of Proverbs, I usually find a saying that encourages me to do exactly what I was thinking of doing. They are such useful phrases to trot out in your defence or to ease your conscience. "Pride goeth before destruction and an haughty spirit before a fall" suited my purpose very nicely; Mr Rochester was a very haughty man. I also liked "He that maketh haste to be rich shall not be innocent." There was some very guilty money in Thornfield Hall. I wasn't quite so happy with the warning that he who digs a pit will fall into it. That was exactly what I intended to do: dig a pit and watch Mr Rochester fall into it.

Summer

1832

Grace helped me refine my plan. She eased my conscience by pointing out that we were mere bystanders to the unfolding events. It was only sensible to prepare for what seemed likely to happen. The decision to set the wheel of fate turning was not ours. It was Mr Rochester's. On her instructions I wrote to her son at the Grimsby Asylum. We had questions only a lawyer could answer and Grimsby seemed sufficiently distant to keep our enquiries in the strictest confidence. We avoided the local solicitors. They were too much in debt to the Rochester domain to be trusted with our secret.

Young Mr Poole arrived under the pretence that he was visiting Miss Bertha and changing her medicine. Bertha's gnawing of Mr Mason was common knowledge among the servants. Fresh medicine reassured them that she would not be allowed to develop a taste for human flesh. I was confident that no one suspected the real purpose of his visit.

The three of us sat in my room out of earshot of Bertha, who had returned to her regular harmless occupation of making doll's clothes. Leah was keeping her company on the third floor.

"You asked about divorce," young Mr Poole began. "A very rare occurrence. Almost unheard of. As I understand it a wife must prove that the husband has committed adultery and — I stress the word 'and' — various other unspeakable crimes."

"Such as?"

He blushed, reluctant to use such words in the presence of his mother. "Violence, beatings, er bestiality, er sodomy?" He looked enquiringly at us. We shook our heads.

"It is easier for a husband to divorce his wife. Adultery alone is enough." Again he looked at us.

"Go on," I said. Mr Rochester might really believe his wife had been unfaithful to him. He could cite the dark-skinned baby, though he would not be able to produce the boy as proof.

"It's a possibility then?"

We nodded and young Mr Poole went on to explain that first the husband must bring a case against the offending man for what is called "criminal conversation". When that has been proved he can get a private bill through Parliament. The costs would be more than four hundred pounds. Would the sum be an insuperable obstacle to Mr Rochester?

Grace and I shook our heads. The cost was not the problem. The offending man was. A proud man like Mr Rochester would never publicly admit that his place in the marriage bed had been taken by anyone. To admit that his place had been taken by a black slave was unthinkable.

"So we are left with judicial separation. Both parties are free of their marital duties. They can live apart." Our eyes lit up. "They are not free to marry another, though." Gloom descended on us again. Baroness Ingram's daughter would not accept the despised position of mistress.

"Then of course there is Chancery but it is notorious for delay."

"What is Chancery?"

"It is an arm of the law to enforce trusts. Wealthy families draw up legal agreements at the time of the marriage to protect their daughter and their daughter's property. They specify arrangements for money in the case of disagreement between husband and wife. Especially when a dowry is paid. Sometimes that money is kept to provide an income for the widow. A jointure, I believe it is called. I take it no such trust was drawn up in this case."

"Not as far as we know. If it had it would be done in Jamaica."

Grace frowned. "Her scoundrel of a brother would have used it, if it existed."

"Then we are left with the last tool in the box. Persuasion. Let the parties come to an agreement. It is the best solution." Grace's son smiled at us benevolently as if we were the naughty children and he was the all-seeing parent.

Grace and I looked at each other. I raised my eyebrows in query to Grace.

She gave an enigmatic smile. "We can be very persuasive." The temperature in the room dropped a few degrees; she spoke so chillingly. I did not give much for Mr Rochester's chances.

"Tell us more about trusts, Mr Poole. I think I can see a way forward."

We sent young Mr Poole back to his lawyer with very precise instructions. He was not optimistic about a speedy result. Lawyers were notoriously slow, he warned us. "Put salt on his tail," Grace said.

"That's for killing slugs," I protested.

"Exactly," said Grace. "If lawyers cannot find a better way to rescue men and women from unhappy marriages, as far as I am concerned, that's exactly what they are. Slugs."

The long days of summer were full of arrivals. Letters came from our lawyer in Grimsby; Grace and I pored over their contents in stolen minutes. We had to dig into our savings to pay the lawyer's fee for what at times felt like a desperate gamble. Mr Rochester arrived with the new carriage, a splendid affair with purple cushions. He made jokes about it suiting Queen Boadicea. I was not sure Miss Blanche would appreciate his comparing her with the warlike queen of a primitive tribe but I could see Mr Rochester's point; there was something regal and ferocious about the woman.

He was full of strange fancies and enthusiasms at this time. He insisted on hiring more servants. As if I did not have my hands full with the staff I already had. I assumed he wanted to increase the household in preparation for his bride. The Honourable Miss Ingram, the daughter of a baron, would expect to live on a grand scale. So we acquired two new footmen — one of them very handsome — an extra housemaid and some kitchen maids to help Mary. I slipped Martha onto the books as a laundry maid.

Then Martha arrived from Ingram Park; her condition was obvious to the most casual glance. I now had two expectant mothers on my hands. The gentry are notorious for turning out servant girls near their time. If a child is born on the premises it is generally thought that the master of the house, or the son, is responsible. It was imperative that I kept Martha away from the grand rooms and confined her to the basement and the back stairs to keep her out of the sight of Mr Rochester. Generous he might be but he would not take kindly to my hiring a girl so close to her time. From the size of her there was scarcely two months' work left in her before she would be delivered. And then what would I do with her? I racked my brains but could come up with no solution.

Not only did I have to keep Martha secret from Mr Rochester, I also had to keep the third floor a secret from Martha. This left me with very few places where she could work. I tried her with Mary in the kitchen but even the kind and endlessly patient Mary could not bear her. "It's not just that she's slapdash and lets the milk boil over," Mary explained. "She keeps talking about Ingram Park. 'At Ingram Park they have three choices at lunch. The baroness likes her beef well done. At Ingram Park they have strawberries in December.'"

Mary imitated Martha's bossy voice. "You'd think she'd like to forget about the place, considering what's happened to her there. Wait till her pains are on her. She'll be calling down curses on Ingram Hall and all its inhabitants."

The third arrival was Miss Eyre. I welcomed her back as I would a daughter. Adele too was pleased to see her. On the first evening of her return Mr Rochester came to my room and found us grouped together by the fire in a ring of golden peace. He bestowed upon us the rare favour of a smile as he gazed at us. It made me hopeful that he might keep Adele on at Thornfield Hall after his marriage.

In the weeks that followed he summoned Adele and Jane frequently to keep him company. He would insist on my presence to act as chaperone and to entertain Adele, which was always a pleasure for me. Miss Eyre seemed sad in her spirits and would ask me nearly every day if there was news of his marriage. She was as anxious on the subject as I was. And with good reason; both our futures hung in the balance. We both feared that Adele would be shipped off to school when Miss Blanche arrived; that haughty madam seemed unlikely to tolerate even such a small rival.

If Adele left there would be no occupation for Jane; she had already considered putting another advertisement in the newspaper but Mr Rochester had persuaded her in the fiercest terms against it. He had made her promise not to advertise, insisting that he would find her another place when the time came. So Jane lived in a kind of limbo, waiting for the axe to fall and powerless to choose her own future. Adele and I were glad of her presence. She kept Mr Rochester occupied of an evening and diverted his attention from the failings of the servants and the less-than-perfect household arrangements.

Thornfield Hall was not a smooth-running well-oiled machine anymore. We had been hard put to find suitable staff. "Scrapings from the bottom of the barrel," Old John called our new recruits. The factories were paying higher wages for those adventurous souls prepared to move to town and we were left with a rag-bag of untrained beginners. Some of them had scarcely managed to wash themselves since they were summoned from herding sheep and milking cows. This made much work for my loyal staff, who had to teach the newcomers how to lay a fire or make a bed or explain what a saucer was for. We were divided into two camps — the knowledgeable and the ignorant. On the one hand there were those who had taken the oath, who were privy to the fact that Bertha was indeed Mrs Rochester. On the other hand there were those in a state of complete ignorance of service in general and of Thornfield Hall in particular. They were not likely to show much curiosity about Bertha just yet. And there was Martha, who fitted into neither of these categories. It was a house jangling with nerves, secrets and subterfuges.

John was upset by the arrival of the new footmen; he feared he was to be replaced. I found him with his head in his hands and all the troubles of the world on his shoulders: Leah, the wedding, the baby and most of all money. "I know it's wicked," he confessed, "but I do envy my brother. He will have the farm. His own house, his own fields and his own animals! It must be wonderful. I don't think Leah and I will ever have so much as a cottage to call our own. What if the new missus takes against me and gives me my notice? I'm that bothered with all this I'm all fingers and thumbs and keep dropping things and forgetting what errand master's sent me on."

I patted his shoulder and made reassuring noises. My diagnosis was a bad case of bridegroom's nerves for both him and Mr Rochester. "Don't forget, John," I told him, "that you have been trusted with Mr Rochester's secret and a key to the third floor. The new footmen have not."

When Mary banished her from the kitchen, Martha had to work in the laundry. I was not happy about this as it is heavy work for someone in her condition. I consoled myself by remembering how clever Martha was at avoiding work. She would contrive to wash nothing more substantial than a collar and cuffs or a chemise. Although it was June the weather was wet and Martha had to take what little washing she had done to dry on the racks in the attic. This brought her dangerously close to Grace and Bertha.

As my plan matured in my mind and began to take definite shape I scented the clear air of freedom from all these oaths and secrets and I grew less careful. I made Martha swear on her soon-to-be-born baby's head not to breathe a word of the existence of the strange lady on the third floor. Naturally I kept the

214

lady's real identity concealed from her. I told her some cock and bull story about a distant connection of old Mr Rochester, the widow of one of his clerks who used to work in the West Indies. The shock of her husband's recent death had overcome her and the master had asked us to look after her for a short time. "Much as we are looking after you," I told her, putting heavy stress on each word to remind her she owed us a debt of gratitude.

I explained away the fact that the door to the stairs was locked by staying as close to the truth as possible; I blamed the temporarily distraught aunt for starting a fire. Martha asked for a key but I refused it. Grace or John or Leah or myself would unlock the door for her when she needed to hang up the washing and would let her out when she had finished. Grace and I had many important matters to discuss; we did not want Martha free to come at will and loiter about the third storey, eavesdropping.

Grace was much more comfortable with Martha than I was; my guilt made me prickly and short-tempered with her. By the time she had climbed the stairs with a basket of washing the girl gave a good impression of being exhausted. Grace would invite her in to rest on the big four-poster bed while Bertha sewed. They tried getting her to read aloud but it was not a success. They tried her with sewing but Bertha soon took the needle from her hand. In spite of the clumsiness Bertha took a fancy to Martha and would sit close and quiet by her as if the strange feeling of contentment that comes from carrying a child had spread into her. She abandoned doll's clothes and started making baby clothes. Between them the madwoman and the reluctant mother-to-be created an oasis of peace in a house of swirling secrets and bitter passions.

Throughout all these changes and adjustments Grace and I stayed doggedly with our plan. Some might call it a plot. Although Bertha and her welfare were the intended goal, we proceeded in our arrangements without her knowledge or agreement. We justified our high-handed treatment by telling ourselves she could not keep a topic in her head for long and that decisions upset her. "Nearer the time," Grace would say. "We'll tell her nearer the time." We were waiting for an important document and that final necessary ingredient for any enterprise — luck. Then we would be ready to strike.

Grace's son brought us the vital document, delivering it himself to ensure it came safely into our hands. He told us that he had a new position near Reading and he had found a suitable property nearby. Did he have our permission to rent it? Grace and I dithered. We decided to delay; our hand would be so much stronger once Mr Rochester had announced publicly that he was to marry Miss Ingram.

Martha had been our sole source of information about what was happening at Ingram Park and she was neither reliable nor up to date. According to Martha, Miss Ingram herself counted the wedding as a certainty. "Has she begun buying wedding clothes?" I asked her, although I had no confidence in the silly baggage's opinion on anything. Martha claimed that new underclothes had been ordered. I was not convinced. I thought the new young baron would be reluctant to spend money on anything that he could not put on show to the whole world. I needed more proof than a few new chemises.

As the month progressed the weather changed and we enjoyed day after day of fine warm weather. The hay, always a tricky crop that makes farmers chew their nails with indecision, was safely brought in. Grace and I were anxious to find the right moment to bring our own harvest in. On Midsummer Eve we met in my room late at night and debated how much longer to wait for Mr Rochester to announce his wedding.

Grace favoured immediate action. "It is a good plan. Bertha living away from here. Whether he wants to marry or not. We are not trying to blackmail him, by threatening to expose him as a bigamist."

"It feels as if we are."

"Stuff and nonsense! We are simply putting forward a fair and reasonable solution to what is for him a difficult problem — his wife. She is his problem, not ours. He should be grateful for our help." Grace gave a smug smile; she thought her logic unimpeachable.

I was not so sure. Our solution was a costly one — for Mr Rochester. Old Mr Rochester would spin in his grave at the thought of parting with a penny of the Rochester fortune. My own motive for wanting more certainty was a selfish one. If the plan went wrong there would be no escape route for me. I would be shown the door and would face a chilling future. I would be neither gentry nor servant. I would be a miserable wretch without family or friends.

"You'd have me. I'd still be your friend."

"Thank you, Grace."

At this moment lightning flashed and we heard a great roll of thunder nearby. The rain rattled down and the air cooled and freshened. The sudden alteration in the weather felt like a sign. I made my mind up to accept this herald of change. I would cease delaying. It was time to put our plan into action. I was about to tell Grace my decision when, in spite of the uproar produced by the elements, some sixth sense alerted me to an unseen presence nearby in the corridor or the hall; the great door to the outside was not yet locked. I put my finger to my lips to warn Grace to keep silent, opened the door to my room and ventured cautiously into the corridor.

The clock was striking twelve as I left my room. On the threshold was Mr Rochester. He was removing Miss Eyre's wet shawl and tenderly shaking it out. I stood transfixed as he went on to kiss her several times and murmur sweet nothings in her ear. They parted with reluctance. As Jane turned away she saw me. A smile of immense and tranquil joy illuminated her face. Without a word she glided up the stairs. Mr Rochester went back to bolt the great door and I slipped back into my room.

The scales fell from my eyes. It was Miss Eyre that Mr Rochester wanted. The fragile little governess was his choice, not the haughty Miss Ingram. The passion I had felt pulsing in the drawing room was mutual. My mistake had been in thinking that it was Jane alone who loved and that the gap between her and Mr Rochester was too wide and deep to be bridged. I had earnestly urged her to strangle her love at birth; instead she had hidden her love, sent it underground. Mr Rochester had used the facade of the house party to disguise his real desire. The lavish attention to Miss Ingram, the coach and the new servants were all a charade. He had been playing the oldest game in the book: making the object of his affections jealous!

When I told her, Grace found it hard to believe me. She lacked the evidence of the embrace that I had seen with my own eyes. Once she was convinced she exploded with anger.

"I knew we should have tackled him earlier. This blows our plan apart." She pounded her fists on the back of a chair.

"Why? What difference does it make?"

"Because it no longer matters that he already has a wife. He will just make her his mistress. Who cares about the reputation of some measly governess? Now the Ingrams are a different matter. They have standing in society. The lofty Blanche has to have the vicar say the words in church and have the ring put on her finger." Grace waved her left hand in my face to show me the wedding ring she wore. I knew it was completely bogus; she had already let slip that she had not been married to her son's father.

"You think he will just make Jane his mistress?"

Grace gave me a look of pity mixed with a large dollop of contempt. "You said it yourself. Gentlemen don't marry governesses. Why not just bed her?"

"Because she won't let him. He must have proposed. Jane Eyre would never have let him put his arm round her and kiss her so many times unless he had proposed. The gentry have rules about these things. A lady who allows a man such liberties is committed to him. The conventions are very strict. And Jane is ferociously virtuous. Besides, that's not what he wants. He wants a wife who will be mistress of Thornfield Hall and who will give him an heir. A legitimate one."

"Let us hope so. Or we have wasted our time and spent our money on lawyers to no avail. We need to think about this." I was pleased that this time it was Grace who wanted to delay. I too needed time to examine our plan from this new angle.

The storm raged that night, but I cannot blame the weather for my disturbed sleep. I had much to think about. The lowly governess was the chosen one. If Miss Eyre consented to be Mr Rochester's mistress our plan would be in serious jeopardy. Jane was virtuous but also strong-minded. I had seen that in the way she teased and vexed Mr Rochester and disagreed with his opinions on occasion. Would her independence of spirit enable her to defy convention and to live with him? Or would she refuse to accept the thankless role of mistress, the position that Adele's mother must have briefly filled? Or had he really defied the conventions of society and the law of the church by proposing marriage to her? Did he intend to lead her to the altar in defiance of God and the courts?

As I pondered these questions I heard over the turbulence of the weather a gentle tap at the door of the bedroom next door. Mr Rochester had come to enquire after his beloved during the thunderstorm. I heard her reassure him, but nothing else. There was no sound of the door being opened, no scampering of feet, no creak of the bedstead or moans of passion. Three times he came and three times the door remained closed and he went away. These were hopeful signs from my point of view.

In the morning I had breakfast with Miss Eyre as usual and my little hopes were dashed. A girl who is newly engaged does not usually keep the news to herself. Jane was radiantly happy, but she said nothing of the events of the previous night, although she knew I had seen Mr Rochester kiss her. I was quiet and cool with her as I waited and hoped for her to announce a formal betrothal rather than an illicit liaison.

Later that morning Mr Rochester came to tell me that he did indeed plan to marry Miss Eyre in four weeks' time at the church in Hay where my late husband had been parson. He waited for me to congratulate him; he was so confident his secret was safe. I managed a few mumbled words before he whirled off to order the carriage to take Miss Eyre shopping.

I should have been filled with delight. It was true. Mr Rochester planned to marry Jane. His words confirmed it. The last detail for my plan had fallen into place.

Mention of my late husband and the church at Hay had startled me and thrown me into confusion. What would my dear husband think of me? I intended to stand by and let his successor perform a bigamous marriage that one word from me could prevent. And Jane! I felt for Jane like a mother to a daughter. How could I let her walk innocently into a marriage that was nothing more than a fraud?

My resolution momentarily failed me. I was tempted to run after Mr Rochester and shout out in the corridor before the whole household, "Stop. Stop this farce. There already is a Mrs Rochester. Bertha who has lived on the third floor these ten years is Mr Edward Fairfax Rochester's legally married wife." The truth would be out but I would have broken my most solemn bible oath and brought unhappiness to three people I held dear.

I was still thinking about my husband when Miss Eyre came seeking my reaction to the news. She was in bliss. Mr Rochester returned her love and against all the expectations of society he had proposed to her in an honourable way. My tepid response must have disappointed her. I had been sitting with my bible open, looking in vain for a verse that told me it was perfectly acceptable to allow bigamy to take place as long as people were happier as a result. There did not seem to be a proverb to that effect. The general feeling of the good book was that human beings flourish best by being honest — especially with God.

Though I could not give her my heartfelt congratulations I did manage not to blurt out the dreadful truth that Mr Rochester was already married. Instead of my felicitations I gave Jane that little talk that older women feel it is their right to inflict on younger ones. I warned her about not anticipating matrimony. It was the little homily I should have given Martha but had failed to do. I worded it as delicately as I could. "Keep your distance," I told her but she grew impatient with me and hurried off. Mr Rochester was taking her to Millcote to buy wedding goods.

"That's good news," said Grace. The minute I was free I had rushed up to the third floor to bring her up to date. "Buying wedding clothes. He must be serious."

"What do you think he bought his French mistresses?"

"True. A few yards of silk do not tie the knot."

"He says they'll be married in four weeks at the church by the gate. It was my husband's church. I feel bad about that."

Grace grabbed my arm and looked fiercely into my face. "Did your husband's church keep you when you were widowed? Did they pay your rent? Didn't they turn you out of your home so that Mr Wood could live there?"

I nodded miserably. It was all true.

Grace cupped her hands round my face and shook me gently. "Do you want to keep working thirteen hours a day? Do you want to spend your life cooking and cleaning until your whole body aches? We women must look out for ourselves. And we have very few ways of doing so. We must fight with the weapons that we find to hand."

"You are right. We will play them at their own game."
I thought for a moment. "We will wait till the first
banns are called. It'll be this Sunday if they want to
marry next month. There'll be no going back after
that."

Grace was enthusiastic. "We will take Bertha. It will
add a certain bite to the occasion and will cut the last
bond that ties her to him. It is time to talk to her about
her future. I will start rehearsing her in her part. Trust
me, she will be ready."

News of the engagement spread quickly round the
household. Those of us who knew the identity of Mr
Rochester's resident lunatic had to hide our very
different reactions beneath expressions of surprise at
his choice of bride. Old John placidly whistled as he
groomed his horses; as long as they had hay in their
mangers and a warm stable, he was happy. Mr
Rochester could have a whole harem as far as he was
concerned. Young John the footman was particularly
affected by news of the betrothal. The banns for his
own wedding had twice been called and the date was
fixed. He took Mr Rochester's intended bigamy as a
personal insult. I told him sternly that Leah's welfare
and the coming baby were more important and that he
should keep his disapproval to himself. A hint that I
would put in a good word for him temporarily sealed
his lips.

As Leah grew rounder poor John grew more nervous
and agitated. He spilled the wine and dropped the
trays. I feared he would start spilling secrets soon and I

224

asked Sam to keep an eye on him. Sam used the occasion to have a quiet word of his own with me. He was growing restless. He had spent too many years at sea to live much longer in the country. He wanted to live on the coast. A place with a little harbour. A bit of fishing and a few odd jobs would keep him going if he had a bit of capital, enough to buy a cottage, you understand. He said no more but gave me a significant look, not so much as a nod or a wink but I felt he had worked out more about my plan with Grace than I thought wise.

Martha, who was under the illusion that Mr Rochester was free to marry, was the most outraged at the news. She was furious when she heard that the master of the house was marrying one of the servant class. If Mr Rochester could marry a governess, why could not young Lord Ingram do the decent thing by her? She was carrying his child, wasn't she? It was no use explaining to her that not only was Mr Rochester a man of courage and independent mind, happy to cock a snook at society, he was also a man of considerable wealth. On the other hand the new Baron Ingram was a feeble specimen, who was afraid of his mother and deep in debt. Reason had no effect on the girl. Jealousy and envy raged through her blood clouding what little judgement she ever had.

In spite of railing at her fate at the hands of the Ingrams, Martha showed a curious loyalty to the family. She took the slighting of the Honourable Blanche as a deep personal insult. The bruises on her arms and the threats over her reference were forgotten. According to

Martha, Mr Rochester had treated Blanche badly. His attentions had been interpreted by the whole neighbourhood as a serious prelude to matrimony. Blanche would be a laughing stock. I will confess that I amused myself by picturing the rage of Blanche and her formidable mother when they heard of the engagement. I told Martha she should be glad she was not in striking distance of either of those bad-tempered harpies when they heard the announcement.

Calling the Banns

1832

Word of the unlikely match spread like wildfire round the servants of the neighbourhood. The groom passed the word to the housemaid, who promptly told the cook. Cook told the butler who might — or might not — pass it on. A valet might whisper the news confidentially into the ears of his master, who would wisely keep the information from his womenfolk. No one wanted to be first to break the news to the Ingram family; shooting the messenger counted as a field sport in that household. We knew the family was in residence and the women usually attended church of a Sunday. The sight of the Honourable Blanche being jilted was one we all wanted to see from a safe distance.

Mr Wood must have wondered at the size of his congregation that Sunday. John and Leah volunteered to stay at Thornfield Hall; the last of their banns was being called and they wanted to avoid all the coarse jokes it would provoke. This enabled the rest of us to attend church, all in our best Sunday clothes.

Much to my annoyance Martha insisted on coming with us. Grace and I were still deciding how much money to ask of Mr Rochester for Bertha's trust fund. It was a delicate question. Ask too much and he would turn us out on our ear. Too little was equally dangerous. There would be no opportunity to come back for more.

We never reached a decision. The silly girl blundered about among us interrupting every conversation and robbing us of any opportunity for the private exchange of information. By this time her condition was evident for all to see. Even Mr Wood might notice. In his nosy parson's manner he would be sure to ask about the father. I feared Martha still harboured hopes that young Lord Ingram would ride up to church on his white horse, get down on his knee and propose to her.

Bertha came in her disguise of widowed great aunt. Black crepe covered her from head to foot. "And a very appropriate costume for this day's work it is too," Grace told her as we clustered protectively round our charge. Sam and Sophie brought up the rear as we climbed up to the gallery at the west end of the church. We had come early to be sure of sitting in the front row and enjoying a bird's eye view of the gentry in the pews below.

Mr Rochester did not attend. He seldom put himself through the tedium of one of Mr Wood's sermons. Most unusually Miss Eyre was absent; he must have warned her to stay away. She was a modest creature and would not enjoy the fuss and attention that would follow the revelation of her engagement. All the knowing eyes were fixed on the Ingrams' pew. Would Miss Blanche be making an appearance today?

The baroness, tall and stately in black, swept in during the first hymn with her two daughters in tow. They bowed to selected acquaintances, sank gracefully into their seats and settled their rustling skirts around them while the rest of us finished singing the verses. I shut my ears to Mr Wood's sermon. I feared he might have chosen a theme that would make my conscience squirm — the importance of honesty, the sanctity of marriage or the necessity for obedience to God's law or some such relevant topic.

As he drew to his conclusion a tremor of excitement flickered round the servants in the gallery; they knew what was coming next. The banns. Mr Wood rushed through the third time of asking for John and Leah. He was keen to reach the main course of the feast. When he arrived there he made the most of it, rolling his tongue round the words as he announced the name of Edward Fairfax Rochester of Thornfield Hall, bachelor of this parish. As Mr Wood spoke, all eyes swivelled to focus on the Ingrams' pew. Most of the gentry among the congregation were under the illusion that the Honourable Blanche's name would follow. It did not. Mr Wood paused for effect before he pronounced the next name: "Jane Eyre, spinster of this parish." A great gasp of surprise barrelled its way through the nave.

In the Ingram pew the feathers on two hats quivered and shook in the windless air as the baroness and her elder daughter reeled from the shock. The younger sister raised her hand to her mouth. Whether it was to conceal a smile or suppress a squeal of pain I could not tell. All I could see were two pairs of white knuckles gripping the pew rail. Next to me the woman in widow's weed bent her head and said nothing. I patted her gloved hand and prayed she would not fall into one of her paroxysms of insane rage. From the far side of her I heard Grace murmuring how well she was doing and how we were going to transform her life.

To give the baroness and her elder daughter their due, they bore their disappointment well. There was no wailing or tears, just stony stares, clenched jaws and a lot of glowering at the congregation as they stalked out of church. They swept past the fawning vicar in the porch and ignored their neighbours' greetings. The baroness signalled for their carriage to be brought up. Without a word they climbed in. The last we saw were three straight backs as the coachman whipped the horses to a trot.

"There'll be tears before bedtime," said Grace.

"And tantrums, and smashing things. And beatings with hairbrushes and nasty painful pinches." Martha added some details from her own experience of life at Ingram Park.

"There'll be none of that kind of behaviour at Thornfield Hall," I told her, hoping that she'd give up all her fantasies of a happy-ever-after before the pangs of childbirth squeezed all the illusions out of her.

We formed a bodyguard round Bertha as we walked back to Thornfield Hall. Sam drew level with me, clapped his gloved hands together like a trap closing and whispered, "You've got him now."

I'll say this for Miss Eyre. Although she was formally recognized as Mr Rochester's betrothed she continued to carry out her duties as an employee. Morning school with Adele went on as before. She frequently accompanied Adele and Sophie on their afternoon walks, insisting that Adele needed the extra practice in speaking English as she would soon have to leave Thornfield Hall and go to school; Mr Rochester was determined to travel abroad with his new wife after the wedding. What I was supposed to do with all the extra servants he had employed he did not deign to explain to me.

The news that I would have to part with Adele was a great sadness to me; I had been captivated by her conscious childish charm and I suspected that an English school would be severe on her continental ways. I was powerless to intervene. I had no right to a say in Adele's future; that was in the hands of Mr Rochester.

Until the wedding day Jane continued to be Adele's governess. She made Mr Rochester wait until after dinner before she joined him. In this way he was left free during the day to go about his business. One of the first matters he dealt with was to go out to the stables and talk with Old John. I found the venerable groom later, sitting with Mary in the kitchen, his face a picture of misery with a suspicion of dampness round his eyes.

It was Mary who enlightened me. "Mr Rochester has told Old John to sell all the hunters."

"Except Mesrour." Old John found his voice in defence of his favourite. "He'll not sell Mesrour."

"The master is giving up hunting," Mary explained. "He doesn't want to break his neck and leave his new wife a widow. Stands to reason. All the horses to be sold and John and I are to go to Ferndean. A sort of semi-retirement. Master wants the house kept up as he might use it for business every now and then. No house parties though. It's much too small." Mary flexed her fingers. Each joint stood out, swollen and red. "And I for one am ready for it," she announced and glared at Old John, daring him to contradict her.

"It's a gloomy place, surrounded by trees. It might not suit Mesrour. He's to go and live there."

"I don't care about the forest. As far as I know a horse doesn't go in for soup or roast pheasant or ice-cream. A bit of hay. That's all a horse wants. The occasional hot mash."

Old John glowered. He glowered for days. He was a master of the art of glowering. But he did not go to Mr Rochester to protest.

Grace chuckled when she heard about Mr Rochester giving up hunting. "That's a good sign," she said. "He hunted so much it was clear he really wanted to kill himself. That's all stopped now he's got Miss Eyre." Grace had always regarded hunting as a polite form of suicide for the gentry. "We'll let him stew for a couple of days. Now that the banns have been called for the first time, the dye is cast and he will think the worst is over. Let him relax and enjoy the prospect of wedded bliss. Then we'll strike." I have never known anyone so well supplied with sheer animal cunning as Grace.

We waited for the third day. Then we set our plan in action. Miss Eyre was busy in the schoolroom with Adele. Mr Rochester was sitting in the library. With Pilot at his feet, a book lying casually on his knee and his head in the clouds he looked supremely happy.

"Ah, Mrs Fairfax," he said. "To what do I owe this pleasure?"

"I have serious matters to discuss with you, sir. Have you time now? It would be best if we were not interrupted." I tried to speak naturally though my heart was banging about like the lid on a boiling kettle.

"Is cook having a tantrum? Has crockery been smashed? Is there fighting among the footmen? Blood on the carpet?" He smiled at his own jest. His black eyes sparkled with amusement. He thought nothing could ruffle his contentment or blemish his joy.

"It is indeed a matter that concerns other people, sir. Two other people to be precise. It would be best if they were present. May I bring them in?" He gave a lazy nod of his head. I felt a moment of joyous anticipation as I went to the door and gestured for Grace and Bertha to come in and burst his bubble of nuptial bliss.

Grace looked as she always did: neat, tidy and unremarkable. Her red hair was hidden under her cap and her plain, strong face was calm. She led in Bertha, who was dressed in a dark dress that she had styled herself. It fitted perfectly. Her hair was brushed back and tied in a chignon. Round her neck was the gold locket with the lock of crinkly baby hair from the child that was certainly hers and possibly Mr Rochester's.

She looked like any society lady accompanied by her maid.

Mr Rochester was glancing at his book as they entered the room. He rose up and started when he saw Grace. Alarm passed over his face; Grace belonged on the third floor — she was not supposed to venture into his library. He pulled himself together. No one could say he was not a brave man. "It's Mrs Poole, I believe. And?" He peered enquiringly at the figure behind Grace.

"Your wife, sir. The lady is your wife." I experienced an exquisite pang of pure joy in saying those words. I had not realized that power could be so invigorating.

That I knew her identity staggered him. That she was in his presence pole-axed him. He sank back into his chair. His book clattered to the floor. Pilot must have sensed his master was in peril of some kind for he growled and bared his teeth at us as if we were all strangers to him.

"Shall I pour you a brandy, Mr Rochester?" I did not wait for a reply but quickly delivered a glass I'd filled from the decanter. I wanted him functioning and decisive, not shocked and wandering in his wits. When I spoke I used the voice of command, the voice I knew so well that was so often directed at me by the gentry. I felt liberated when I heard it issue so confidently from my lips. "Perhaps you could reassure Pilot that we mean you no harm, sir, and then invite the lady to sit down."

He obeyed me. Then he swigged back the brandy and waved to a chair. Bertha sat and Grace stood by her chair. Colour had returned to Mr Rochester's face and he laid his hand lightly on Pilot's collar. Now that I had the participants arranged to my satisfaction I began. "We have come to you with a suggestion, Mr Rochester. To be precise, a list of suggestions. Could we deal with those that involve your wife first, so that she may return to her room? It is very painful for her to be here. We should not test her composure for too long. I have your permission to speak for you, have I not, Bertha?"

Bertha nodded obligingly.

"To put it bluntly, now that your intention to be united with Miss Eyre — I can scarcely call it married — is a matter of public knowledge, the lady wishes no longer to be Mrs Rochester." The very name made him flinch. "She wishes to move away from here and to live under the protection of Mrs Poole and myself. Is that not so, Bertha?"

"I want to be Bertha Mason again." As she spoke her fingers picked at the stuff of her gown, squeezing and kneading the fabric. Always a sign that she was growing disturbed. "I am not always well. These ladies look after me when I sick." She looked up at Grace and then me and received reassuring smiles in return. She turned to Mr Rochester, her husband, who was supposed to be of one flesh with her. "Best I not see you. Or my brother. You make me mad."

Mr Rochester put his head in his hands. I hoped this meant that he acknowledged that our case was unanswerable. If he agreed with her, we could deal with the details without tormenting poor Bertha any further.

"Have you heard enough? Can your wife go back to her room now?"

He groaned. "That word. Wife. Please don't use that word."

I signalled to Grace to take Bertha out. Mr Rochester, my master, as I had thought of him until recently, slumped in his chair; he was a beaten man. All the shine and gloss of his happiness had left him. His face was drawn and grey. I did not wait to be invited to sit, but pulled up a chair and sat opposite him.

"How long have you known?" he asked.

"Grace and I have suspected for some time. We only found out for sure when Mr Mason was here."

He went white and raised his hands in silent appeal. I hastened to explain. "Mrs Poole was present when Mr Mason talked with his sister and afterwards when he talked to you. He called Bertha "your wife" and you did not deny it. It is true, isn't it?"

He nodded and turned away. It was some time before he could look at me. His eyes held a question that his lips could not frame.

I guessed what he feared too much to put into words. "Mr Mason said nothing to Miss Eyre. She is in ignorance and is innocent in all this."

He leant back in the chair and gazed up at the ceiling, giving God thanks for this small mercy.

"I have not come here to destroy your happiness. But I am a parson's widow. My belief in the sanctity of marriage struggles with my desire to see my fellow human beings living good and happy lives. The oath I swore along with my fellow servants still binds me from revealing Bertha's true identity. How long the others will hold their tongues I cannot say. Some may find the idea of bigamy so repellent that they will reveal what they know to Miss Eyre, if not to the world. I believe you have already made plans for Old John and his wife, Mary."

"I have indeed. My plan was to leave Thornfield Hall, to cease being a gentleman of the county. To sell the horses and close the stables. It is time Old John retired. I have asked him and his wife to live at my house, Ferndean. To look after it and treat it as their own home. It breaks his heart to sell the hunters, but it is time."

"Old John has looked out for you since you were a boy. He follows no church so it is easy for him. There are others who took the oath. They too need to be looked after. I am thinking of John, the footman. He is about to marry Leah. And he is taking it very seriously. There is a baby on its way and he is young and idealistic. He is not cut out to be a footman. He is a farmer at heart."

I fell silent and gave him time to work it out for himself. While he did so I went over in my mind the shopping list I had brought with me. John and Leah first, because Leah was dear to my heart and there was a child to be provided for. I hoped to persuade Mr Rochester to grant them a farm under very advantageous terms. The Rochesters do not like to part with land but a generous lease and a good tenant are a different matter. I filled his brandy glass again to help him think.

"Well, Mrs Fairfax, there is an estate about thirty miles from here where I have two or three farms. I was planning to do something about them before I went abroad. Would John make a good farmer, do you think?"

"Most assuredly, sir. Perhaps if you were to approach him, discuss terms. It would make a good wedding present for the pair of them. Leah is a treasure and has been for many a long year and a good friend to the lady." Out of delicacy I reverted to calling Bertha "the lady" in his presence. The term "wife" was a red rag to the bullish Mr Rochester.

"Now Sam is not a farmer, sir. As you know he was a navy man. He is restless and wants to live near the sea." I had now arrived at one of the more difficult subjects on my list. In all his years at Thornfield Hall Sam had appeared cheerily content with very little until Sophie came onto the scene. Now he wanted a cottage by the sea. I tried to picture Sophie gutting fish — and failed. I was sure her ambitions lay in a different direction.

Naturally I kept these thoughts to myself. I suggested to Mr Rochester that he offer the purchase price of a cottage — when Sam found one. A generous tip in the meantime should keep Sam sweet. Mr Rochester nodded his agreement and put a limit of three hundred pounds on the price of the property. I thought four hundred would be nearer the mark. He remained silent. I decided to waste no more time on Sam. I had bigger fish to fry. I took a deep breath.

"And the lady, sir." He gave me a blank look. "Your wife, sir." The word set his teeth on edge and he shivered uncontrollably. "I do not come here to torture you, sir. I have spent many hours with Mrs Poole thinking what is best for everyone. We think we have found a solution. More brandy, sir?"

I took him through it step by step, the way I would have explained it to a child. The great improvement in his wife's . . . er . . . the lady's mental state when she led a quiet, orderly life and was not reminded of her past. Thornfield Hall was a prison and the presence of its owner was a constant provocation to her. The best thing would be for the lady to move away. Returning to the island of her birth was out of the question. Her parents, I understood, were dead and her brother, Richard, was an abomination to her. She expressed no interest in any family members who might still live in Jamaica; on their part they had shown complete indifference to her welfare. A house in a quiet market town in a distant part of the country, somewhere Grace and I could look after her, seemed an ideal solution to the problem. We would pass her off as a widow.

So far Mr Rochester found nothing objectionable. I feared the next part would provoke an explosion.

"The lady, although no longer mad, is not really capable of running her own affairs. Grace and I would have to take all those decisions for her."

Mr Rochester gave a bark of laughter at that. "You have proved yourselves more than capable of doing that," he scoffed.

"The problem is more one of means than of ways, sir."

"Money. I might have known. It always comes down to money."

His words hurt me to the quick; they hurt me more than the sneer on his face. I sprang to my feet and I bellowed at him. "As I understand it, money was the cause of this problem in the first place. Thirty thousand pounds, wasn't it? Thirty pieces of silver might have been a more appropriate amount." I was on my way to the door when he called me back.

"Please, Mrs Fairfax. Come back. Sit down. I am sorry to have spoken to you in that way. You are right. Money, or rather the lack of it, caused the whole unholy mess. I was a weak and foolish young man. I saw only the good side of the lady, the side that you, to your eternal credit, and Mrs Poole have restored to her. My father arranged everything. The dowry was indeed thirty thousand pounds. She shall have it back. All of it."

I sat down abruptly. My little fit of temper had brought me more than I had dreamt of. How strange! I had planned, calculated and rehearsed with Grace. We had agonized over the actual amount of money, estimating how much we could hope for and how little we could manage on. All our heart searching had brought us to no final decision. We had hoped for ten thousand and thought we could manage on five. Who can put a price on justice? In the end my impromptu fit of pique had returned to Bertha more than we would

240

dare to ask for. It was offered me on a platter like the head of John the Baptist.

"Trust," I told Mr Rochester. "A trust. That's the way to do it. Grace and I will be trustees for Bertha Mason. We will run her home for her, nurse her if necessary and help her make decisions. As a woman of property she will no doubt be attractive to many gentlemen in need of an income but her special circumstances make it impossible for her to consider matrimony. I am sure you understand that, sir. As trustees we could prevent her fortune falling into the wrong hands. We have cared for her these ten years. You know we can be trusted. Those with fragile minds are easy prey for the unscrupulous. You didn't see what that Mrs Morgan did to her."

He shook his head. "I was not thinking properly. I was mad with shame and despair."

"You are not the only one to blame. Bertha's family should have ensured that her fortune was better protected."

"They were putty in my father's hands. They did what he advised. And to my eternal shame, I did too. I was young, naive and foolish."

It was good to hear him admit his part in the proceedings. Youth, greed and a tyrannical father make a powerful combination. There was one more important ingredient in the mix that he refrained from mentioning. Lust. How many unhappy marriages is it responsible for? It is the most forgivable of sins. Young blood runs hot.

I returned to the task in hand. "A trust," I reminded him. "It is a job for a lawyer but it is easily done." I admitted then that Grace and I had a draft document already drawn up. There were no names or figures, just gaps to be filled in. The lawyer lived at a distance and we had been anonymous clients. I would bring him the document and he could consult his own lawyer.

As I rose to leave, this time for real, he came and shook my hand and thanked me. He hoped that our talk would result in an increase in happiness for all involved. I could not help but agree with him.

As I opened the door to the corridor I encountered my failure — the one person I felt responsible for who had not featured in my talk with Mr Rochester. Martha. I had not managed to increase her happiness, her income or her security; she did not even exist as far as Mr Rochester was concerned. She was — or should be — an anonymous and invisible laundry maid. I scolded her for being near the library; she was supposed to keep to the back stairs. She had some excuse of course — she always had a pocketful of those. I took the time to move mentally some of the guilt I felt about her and place it squarely onto her own shoulders. I would do my best for her but at that moment I had not an inkling of an idea how to help her.

My most urgent need was to go to Grace and Bertha and tell them of the success of our mission. As I headed to the locked door at the foot of the stairs Martha dogged my footsteps. I did not listen as she rambled on, justifying herself. She had been trying to get up the attic to fetch the washing. It was very inconvenient not having a key. Could she have one? Definitely not.

I watched to make sure that Martha did indeed go up to the attic before I gave Grace and Bertha the good news. Bertha was tearful; seeing Mr Rochester always had a bad effect on her. We were full of praise for how well she had conducted herself at the meeting. Grace's eyes popped out like a frog when she heard how much money Mr Rochester had offered. The amount meant nothing to Bertha. Thirty thousand pounds or thirty pence — they were the same to her.

As a result of having very little and having to work for it Grace and I knew the value of money. The income from thirty thousand pounds would keep all three of us in considerable comfort. We would live like queens alongside Bertha, not as her servants, but as her guardians. I would become gentry again. I need not fear so acutely sickness and old age and we could forget about the workhouse. We agreed that I should write to tell Grace's son immediately to put our plan in motion.

We told Grace's son to take up the lease on the house near Reading. It meant I would be living many miles from my native Yorkshire, which made me sad. It was the price I had to pay for a comfortable future for me and for Bertha leaving her past as far behind as possible. Grace was looking forward to being near her son. It was our intention to keep our destination secret and to say only that we would be living "to the south of Grimsby". Bertha said she would live anywhere but hoped to find a place that was warmer than Yorkshire.

"That won't be difficult," Grace assured her.

When I left Grace and Bertha I hesitated at the foot of the stairs. I was not sure if Martha had come down from the attic; collecting the washing was a job she could spin out for hours. Serve her right, I thought as I locked the door. Later I found out that I had locked her in. As usual she turned my error into an excuse to avoid work. She spent the afternoon taking her ease on the four-poster bed and reading to Bertha.

A Country Wedding

1832

Mr Rochester was in an agony of impatience to be married. We saw him cross off the days on the calendar with mounting glee. First we servants had our own red-letter day on the calendar: the wedding of John and Leah. They chose to be married on a Wednesday as that was their half day. They asked me and Old John to be witnesses.

Unlike the general run of bridegrooms John grew calmer and happier the closer the wedding day came. Mr Rochester's agent had offered him the tenancy of a small farm about thirty miles away. If he made a success of it there were two more farms close by that might become available to him. I'd given a show of delighted surprise when Leah told me and said I thought she would make an excellent farmer's wife. They were keen to move to their new home as soon as possible so that their baby could be born there.

I wore my best black silk frock for the wedding and tried to spruce up Old John for the occasion — with limited success. Mr Wood made a point of briskly wafting the sleeves of his surplice to disperse the smell of horse that emanated from the old coachman and pervaded the sanctity of the holy place. Once Old John had fulfilled his role of giving the bride away he was directed to sit in a distant pew. I felt my dislike of Mr Wood grow faster than bread dough as he gabbled impatiently through the wedding service, scarcely giving John time to make his vows.

The words "till death us do part" gave me pause for thought. I had said those words when I'd married my husband and I meant them at the time. Our years together had been too few to test my resolution. How would I have felt after twenty, thirty, forty years? How would I have felt if he had gone mad, or flogged me, or beaten our children? On reflection I decided that the terms of the marriage contract were spectacularly ferocious.

When Mr Wood warned that those whom God had joined no man should put asunder he failed to convince me. The promptness with which he let go of John's and Leah's hands, and the speed with which he turned on his heels and raced from the church, left me feeling that a bureaucratic procedure had been performed, not some miraculous transformation. The clerk, John Green, took over the congratulating of the happy couple and the completion of the marriage certificate. Mr Wood had left a blank one already signed for the purpose.

I watched as John and Leah kissed shyly in public for the first time. There was ample evidence as John leaned forward over Leah's stomach so as to reach her lips, that this was not their first contact; they had been busy in private. The words parroted by Mr Wood were no more than official recognition of an accomplished fact. John and Leah had made themselves one flesh months ago; the world was just catching up with them. This thought cheered me considerably. I felt much better about letting Mr Wood perform a bigamous marriage.

The wedding breakfast was to take place in the evening, when we could entrust Mr Rochester to the capable hands of Miss Eyre. Before then I had to take tea with Miss Eyre and Adele. These were not always happy occasions. Jane was making enquiries about schools and Adele was fretting about her future. Miss Eyre could do little to reassure her; she did not think that dolls would be allowed, it was unlikely that pink frocks would conform to the regulations and as for taking your maid with you . . . That was unheard of!

I could find no words of comfort for Adele. Neither the presence of Sophie nor visits to Thornfield Hall could be promised as future compensation for her immediate suffering. Mr Rochester intended to leave the Hall immediately after his wedding, never to return. He planned to depart in his new coach with the last of the carriage horses. Old John and Mary would then retire with Mesrour to the manor house at Ferndean. John and Leah would take up the tenancy of their farm. Sam was keeping very quiet and Sophie was staying close to him. Knowing Sam I guessed he'd already got his hands on his sweetener, probably paid in bank notes by the agent with a nudge and wink. They would pretend it was for some disreputable bit of male high spirits that Mr Rochester was paying Sam to keep concealed from the bride.

Meanwhile Grace, Bertha and I waited for the papers to be signed and the thirty thousand pounds to be transferred to the trust. I could not think of leaving Thornfield Hall until I was happy about the arrangements for Adele. I suspected that I would be left to handle that painful procedure. Also I would have to close down the Hall. Perhaps even arrange for it to be sold.

Then there was the staff to be dealt with. Mary had taken to her bed with the rheumatics and I'd had to hire a temporary replacement. There were other new members of staff whom Mr Rochester had hired as part of his pretence of being enamoured of Blanche. Sometimes I would go into the servants' hall at mealtimes and I would not recognize many of them. They would all have to be given notice and paid off and they would want references. I felt tired just thinking about the work ahead of me. Those were just my official duties. There was also my unofficial one to poor Martha.

The evening of John and Leah's marriage I put away all these worries and made merry in the servants' hall. Mary had struggled out of her bed to make desserts for the happy couple. The new cook had done them proud with a huge ham. I made sure there was enough ale for the men but not too much. We still had a secret to keep. I would have been more liberal if the trust papers had been signed and the money handed over. I lived in dread of the secret of Bertha's identity slipping out at the last moment. Drink loosens the tongue, especially the tongue of a bridegroom when his friends ply him with ale.

I never really looked at Martha, just as I never really listened to her. She contrived to irritate me so much that the less attention I paid her the better. That night at Leah's wedding feast I sat across the table from Martha. I saw only her head and shoulders and not her distracting bump of a belly. What I saw gave me a turn. Her face was swollen and discoloured; her whole head seemed to have grown several sizes larger. I thought she must have been drinking. I could scarcely blame her if she drank until she fell unconscious under the table; she must so wish to forget her circumstances. Perhaps her time was nearer than we thought. I knew the daft moppet had no dates to help her work out her probable time.

Old friends and new faces united to send Leah and John to their first shared room that night, with much coarse laughter and many rude jokes about shutting stable doors and all their troubles being little ones. This was the only part of the celebrations that I kept aloof from; after all, I would be giving notice to most of them in the near future.

The atmosphere at the servants' early breakfast next day was very far from jolly. Leah's face was flushed and angry and Martha was in tears. A weeping Martha was nothing new but an angry Leah was something else. It transpired that Martha had burst in on the couple in the course of their wedding night. John and Leah had shooed her out and sent her back to her own room.

Martha insisted she had no memory of the event. She had woken in her own bed and claimed to have stayed there. She was unaware of her nocturnal wanderings.

I took these night-time ramblings seriously. I could not risk her straying onto the second floor, perhaps even into Mr Rochester's or Miss Eyre's bedroom. So I persuaded Grace to let her sleep on the third storey in the room beyond hers. There we could keep her confined at night by locking the door at the foot of the stairs. It seemed to be fated that the third floor of Thornfield Hall was always to have an inhabitant with wild and uncontrolled ways. Now that Bertha was so well-behaved, Martha had taken on that role.

Grace reminded me to arrange for a midwife. She thought Martha might be due any time. The livid colour of the girl's face was not a good sign. Grace had seen swollen purple faces before and sometimes the ending was not happy. "Often the baby comes early but dies. Sometimes the mother dies. Sometimes she recovers afterwards. It is as though there is a battle between mother and baby —" Abruptly she stopped talking.

Martha had appeared with her empty clothes basket; she had been hanging clothes to dry in the attic. For a noisy galumphing creature she could slide quietly into earshot when you didn't want her.

I told her that I would send word to the midwife the next day. Grace tapped her forehead. She had just remembered something. "When you do, ask her if she knows of anyone who is looking for a wet nurse."

Martha squealed in protest at the words "wet nurse", her face twisted in a grimace of disgust. "You mean me! Me be a wet nurse! What a horrible idea. I'm not going to do that. Never, never, never."

Grace squared up to the shrieking girl. "It is good work. You have a roof over your head. You are well-fed. The other mother wants good milk for her child. You get to keep your own baby. One child on each side." Grace demonstrated with her hands. "No problem."

Horror distorted Martha's swollen face even further. "I feel sick just thinking about it. It's like being a cow."

Grace leant over Martha and wagged her finger in her face. "Cattle have a good life. They are housed and fed. You will find that a girl with a baby has very few choices about the way she makes her living. You can have a sweet, clean, lovable little creature suck your breast with his toothless gums or you can have a smelly, hairy creature with a belly hanging down to his knees lift your skirts and poke his grubby manhood in your fanny or in any other hole he fancies sticking it." I had never heard Grace so passionate. When she had finished she straightened her cap, smoothed her apron and recovered her habitual calm. "I don't mean to be unkind, Martha. You have to think about your future — and your baby's."

"I'll be all right." Martha tossed her head. "I'll think of something."

"So that's all right then. As long as you don't plan to go to Baroness Ingram and tell her she has a grandchild. Oootchy coootchy coo. Isn't he lovely?

Won't he make a nice little baronet? And wouldn't it be lovely if your son married me?"

Martha said nothing. Her face said it all.

Two days before his wedding Mr Rochester summoned me, Grace and Bertha to the library. At his side stood a distinguished-looking gentleman with silver hair and a neatly trimmed beard; he was everyone's picture of a family lawyer. But he was not the usual Rochester family lawyer. By his accent he had been specially imported from across the Pennines to carry out this task. There was no risk of his being indiscreet with a local colleague. The Wars of the Roses only finished yesterday to many people round here.

He took us through the documents very carefully, explaining that Grace and I were to be trustees for one Bertha Mason. Bertha bowed to him very civilly at the sound of her name. She sat quietly through the whole proceedings, her eyes fixed on the floor or the lawyer or the view through the window — anywhere, in short, where Mr Rochester was not.

The lawyer explained that Grace and I were to administer the money with care and diligence and provide a home for Bertha. In time we could appoint further suitable people as trustees depending on where we decided to live, so that the future of the said Bertha Mason could be secure. The funds for the trust were on deposit at the Bank of Knaresborough. They would be available for withdrawal in two days' time.

We signed the deed of trust. I have to give Mr Rochester credit for behaving frankly and fairly once we

252

had screwed him to the sticking post but I noted the familiar Rochester caution with money. The thirty thousand pounds would not be ours until the day of the wedding. We gave a respectful curtsy and withdrew.

Dignity and restraint stayed with us in the corridor. We behaved as three middle-aged and respectable ladies normally behave. When we reached the third floor matters took a very different turn. We kissed the legal papers, we laughed and fell into our chairs; we loosened our stays and unpinned our hair. Grace poured out the porter. We were free, independent and soon would be wealthy. We would have sufficient means to live very comfortable lives. We need call no man master again.

The only blight on our happiness was the arrival of Martha, breathless and panting from climbing the stairs with her basket of washing, her face swollen and purple and her belly heaving with a child she did not want. She was a poignant reminder of how unequal fate could be to women. Grace gave her a glass of porter and told her it would help her sleep.

Perhaps we put too much reliance on the soporific effects of porter; it certainly made me sleep like a baby. I was so content and carefree that I forgot to lock the door to the stairs to the third floor. I was growing careless as my plan came into fruition. Only one full day lay between me and the day of the wedding, when Bertha's dowry and her life would be returned to her. The day passed without incident except that Miss Eyre, normally so calm and composed, must have had an attack of wedding nerves. She did not want to spend the night before her wedding alone and went to sleep with Adele and Sophie in the nursery. No doubt there were many jokes in the servants' hall and warnings to Sam to curtail his night-time wanderings.

An Eventful Day in July

1832

Grace woke me before six on the morning of Mr Rochester's wedding day with some unexpected news: Martha had gone into labour. Trust her to choose such an inconvenient moment. "No need to send for the midwife just yet," Grace assured me. "First babies take a long time. She is fussing and groaning already but Bertha is with her. Martha would try the patience of a saint but Bertha is very kind to her. I think poor Bertha has suffered so much it makes her very tender to other people's pain."

"If only Martha had waited a day. Our funds would be secure and we could do something for the silly creature and her unfortunate baby. I dread Mr Rochester or Miss Eyre finding out that we have been keeping her here. It feels so underhand."

"Serves him right. He kept Bertha locked away for years. That's what I call underhand." Grace took hold of my hands and stared me in the face. She spoke forcefully to me. "Four hours from now the happy couple will be gone. They'll be bowling along in their new coach and Martha will be able to scream as loud as she likes. They will not hear her."

Invigorated by her words and her confidence I made a quick visit to the third floor, where I found Bertha sitting calmly next to Martha. She was bathing her face and hands and singing one of the strange soothing songs she must have learnt as a child in Jamaica. Bertha was still in her white nightgown but her black hair was smoothed back into a neat plait. Martha writhed on the bed, her dark hair wild and tangled about her swollen face. In her pain she cursed and swore; she used words that would have made a stable hand blush. If someone had asked you to point at the madwoman in the room you would undoubtedly have chosen the one in the bed.

My regular household duties soon called me away. In honour of the occasion I put on the black silk dress I had worn for John and Leah's wedding. How strange life is. You do not go to a wedding for years and then two come along in quick succession. Breakfast was served in the dining room but the groom had no appetite. He paced about like a caged lion and kept sending to see if Miss Eyre was dressed.

Sophie was to carry out the task of preparing the bride, although I doubted the wedding clothes Miss Eyre had chosen would meet the French maid's exacting standards. Miss Eyre's dress was very plain, though the colour was flattering and the veil was exquisite. Sophie must have lamented the modesty of Miss Eyre's ambition in the matter of dress. What a beauty the French girl would have made of her if she had been given a free hand.

When he wasn't sending messages to chivvy his bride Mr Rochester was sending one of his new footmen to the church to check that Mr Wood was there. The footman soon returned and reported that the parson was putting his surplice on in the vestry. I could not help noticing that on this occasion the clergyman was treating the bridal couple with more respect than he had given to John and Leah. A troublesome thought niggled at the back of my mind. I did not know the name of this new — and remarkably handsome — footman. Was he to be the next John? It annoyed me that I could not recall his given name. I dismissed the matter from my mind. I had more important concerns that day and soon the handsome footman would be away from Thornfield Hall, bouncing about behind Mr Rochester's new carriage.

I waited in the hall hoping to have a word with Miss Eyre before she left for church. It was not to be. Mr Rochester held her by the wrist and positively dragged her past me. There was no opportunity to wish her joy or tell her how well she looked. As she passed I noticed that she was not wearing the handsome veil that Mr Rochester had bought for her but a plain simple square of fine lawn.

As soon as possible I went back upstairs to check on Martha. The scene that met my eyes was a copy of the one I had witnessed earlier. The only change was that Martha's groans were louder. The midwife had sent word that she would come in the afternoon; her services were unlikely to be needed earlier. "Should we send for Carter, the surgeon?" I asked Grace.

She gave me one of her withering looks. "Only if she is having a foal."

A glance at my watch told me that the wedding party would soon be returning. Again I descended the stairs and from force of habit I locked the door at the foot of the staircase. I cannot tell you how glad I was later that I had remembered to carry out that small routine task. I collected Adele, who had spent much longer dressing than Miss Eyre did, and Sophie. We trooped down to the hall to greet the happy couple on their return. Leah joined us there. "What became of that lovely veil?" she wondered. Leah had been watching from behind a door when Jane came down. She tried to mime her question to Sophie. The only response she received was a shrug of Sophie's shoulders. Sam's English lessons had not proved very successful.

My first inkling that something was wrong came when I saw three gentlemen struggling to keep up with Mr Rochester as he raced up the drive with Miss Eyre, or Mrs Rochester as I should call her, dragged along in his grasp. One was Mr Wood in his surplice, the other two gentlemen were formally dressed. I guessed that Mr Rochester had called them to be witnesses. At the door he dismissed the carriage that had been waiting to take him and his bride on their wedding journey. Automatically we advanced to greet the wedding party to congratulate them in the conventional way. I saw then his face was thunderous and livid with rage. He shouted at us, "To the right about — every soul!" And told us our wedding congratulations were fifteen years too late. My heart dropped like a stone. The secret of his marriage to Bertha must be out.

He charged through the hall and bundled his bride up the stairs whilst urging the other gentlemen to follow him. As they passed me I recognized Mr Wood and Mr Mason, Bertha's unwelcome brother. The third man was a stranger to me. I realized that Mr Rochester's destination was the third storey. Mason must have stopped the wedding. Mr Rochester was going to show them his so-called mad wife to justify his deception. What a disappointment was in store for him! They would never believe him. Miss Eyre would think him no better than a miserable failed bigamist if she saw Bertha as I had seen her that morning, calm, clean, self-possessed and most definitely in her right mind. It was not a strong mind but it was not currently disordered. The frustrated bridegroom might find his "wife" disappointed his companions. The discovery of an illicit laundry maid giving birth would more than compensate them. It would be a catastrophe for me.

I shadowed their footsteps as they raced along the gallery. Mr Rochester unlocked the door to the stairs with his key. How pleased I was that I had remembered to lock that door! For some reason I was immensely comforted by this small detail; it was evidence that I did not completely neglect my housekeeper's duties. It would not weigh much in the scales against my misdeeds in harbouring a pregnant servant girl or being responsible by some slip or accident for revealing the existence of his first wife.

Someone must have told Mr Mason that the banns had been called. My mind raced over a list of suspects as I waited for the chance to climb the stairs unobserved. It could not be Leah, not my favourite Leah. She was as stunned as I was by their return from church. John's mind was too full of breeds of sheep and choosing chickens. Old John and Mary were too loyal to the family to risk injuring them. Could it be Sam? His sweetener had probably already been spent bringing Sophie to his bed. I tried to picture Sam sidling off to warn the parson. It was not a convincing vision; Sam never had a civil word for Mr Wood.

The most likely culprits were me and Grace. We had tried to be discreet but servants, as we well know, have sharp ears. Secrets cannot be kept from them. Martha was my first suspect. I had her in the dock, tried and found guilty before my feet had finished climbing the stairs. There had been many opportunities for her to eavesdrop and she liked causing trouble. Even when there was no advantage in it for her.

By this time the wedding party was through the first room. I peeped in. The hangings had been parted and the door to Bertha's room was unlocked. Quiet as a ghost I glided down the corridor past them and gently tried the handle of the room at the end, Martha's room. To my relief it was unlocked.

I found Martha on the bed, struggling with her pain. She was alone in the room but someone, Grace no doubt, had taken the precaution of giving her a towel to bite to stifle her screams. The fabric was clenched between her teeth. A great spasm of pain hit her. Her

260

hands flailed in the air and she pulled desperately at the improvised gag, tearing it free from her mouth. Her back arched in an attempt to escape the agony that nature was inflicting on her. I saw the scream as it travelled up her throat and faster than thought I covered her mouth with my hands to deaden the sound. Her eyes popped wide open; she was so shocked by the force I'd used she forgot to finish her scream.

The pain diminished and her body relaxed. I took my hand away and whispered to her that something had gone wrong with the wedding, that Mr Rochester and Miss Eyre were here on the third floor and that we risked being discovered.

"Miss Eyre is she still? Not Mrs Rochester?"

I nodded and she gave a hoarse laugh that was interrupted by another pang. Again I clamped my hand across her mouth. As the pain receded she looked slyly at me. "Was she wearing her veil?"

"No. How did you know?"

"That'd be telling." She smirked at me. Martha loved to feel superior to others, to know something they did not. Her smugness even protected her from her pains for a moment. Then the pains returned and she made so much noise I feared discovery and covered her mouth. In between screams I struggled with her for possession of the towel. I would hold it over her mouth and she would try to tear it from my hands.

From Bertha's room along the corridor came muffled wails and much female shouting. The baritone voices of the men blended together to provide a background to the shrill screams that I recognized as

Bertha's on a bad day. Whoever had alerted Mr Wood to her existence had done her a bad turn. The arrival of both Mr Rochester and her hated brother had proved too much for her frail mind.

Distracted by this gloomy thought my attention slipped from the task at hand. Martha with a sudden lunge pulled the towel from my grasp and as I tried to suppress her scream she bit my hand, sinking her teeth into the flesh at the root of my left thumb. Blood spurted out. My rage was such that I could not help myself. My right arm found it had a mind of its own. It swung backwards and then forwards to land a stinging slap on Martha's cheek. Her jaw snapped open and I retrieved my other hand.

I was immediately ashamed of myself. Slapping her while in the pangs of labour must count as the very worst crime in my list of offences against Martha. I could not help noticing that her piercing shrieks were now more subdued; groans rather than screams. I held the towel ready but did not feel the need to use it. Her complaints did not seem loud enough to penetrate through Grace's bedroom next door and along the corridor to Bertha's room where bedlam still reigned.

My imprisonment in that room seemed to last for hours before the door opened and Grace appeared. Never have I been so pleased to see her. Her strong face and her calm manner reassured me before she even spoke a word. She held a bowl of gruel out to Martha and suggested she try to eat something. The girl struggled to sit up and for a brief time seemed to forget her pains as Grace spooned the unappetizing stuff into her mouth. I surreptitiously inspected Martha's left cheek for my handprint but failed to find evidence of my crime. The whole of the girl's face was swollen and livid.

"Bertha is getting dressed," Grace told me. "She was quite wonderful in our bit of play acting. This was part of the charade as well." Grace waved the sticky spoon of white gruel at me. "I pretended I was cooking it for our lunatic. You might as well have it, Martha."

If Grace thought to quell my anxiety she was not doing a very good job of it. Bertha crept quietly into the room. She was dressed and her hair was smoothed back under her cap. She took up the seat next to Martha and returned to bathing her face and hands with cool water as if there had been no interruption to her self-imposed task. She began to sing one of her strange melodic songs whose words we could not understand.

"Explain," I commanded Grace.

"Like the battle of Waterloo it was a close-run thing. I was keeping lookout while Bertha kept an eye on Martha. We both wanted to see the new Mrs Rochester return from church. When I saw the way Mr Rochester sped up the path and the three men chasing behind him I realized something was wrong. Bertha recognized her brother; she hates him worse than poison. She did not want him to know of the new life we have planned.

"We realized the brother must have stopped the wedding. He brought a lawyer with him, a Mr Biggs or something. Rochester wanted to show Jane — and the parson and Mr Biggs — that his wife is wildly deranged. His justification for attempting to marry Jane is that his wife is mad. Quick as a flash Bertha works it out. 'He needs mad wife. I act mad.' She pulls her hair out of its plait and shreds her fingers through it. She's still in her white nightgown, not properly dressed, so it is easy to look wild. She throws the remains of the tea over it. Makes a nice brown stain. I fling some old medicine on the fire to make a bad smell and pretend to be cooking gruel. We can just hear Martha screaming so Bertha shrieks and gibbers to cover the sounds."

Bertha stopped singing. "I have to keep them away from here. No baby safe near my brother. Not Mr Rochester either." Her voice was icy. She turned back to Martha and took up her sweet song again. It was as if a curtain had come down in her mind.

Grace looked at her charge with a fond eye. "She has convinced them all that she is still raving mad. She went for Mr Rochester's throat and provoked him into tying her up. Miss Eyre was horrified. The brother was terrified. It was fiendishly clever. Miss Eyre may feel so sorry for Mr Rochester that she will agree to something less than marriage. He will look like a man more to be pitied than condemned. The brother will go away never to return now that he has done such damage. Better to be pitied for being tied to a madwoman than despised for being a common or garden bigamist."

A sudden shriek from the bed startled us. Bertha stopped singing. Grace pulled back the bedclothes. "Go for more towels," she ordered Bertha, "and some hot water. Here. Take this." She handed her the key that opened all the doors. "Make sure the door is unlocked

264

so the midwife can get here. Where is that dratted woman?"

Bertha looked down at the key in the palm of her hand. Never before had she been entrusted with it. Then she set about the task she had been given.

There followed several minutes that I never want to live through again. All I can say is that my best black silk dress that I put on especially for the wedding was ruined. There was much noise and a great deal of confusion. None of us really knew what we were doing. The end result was that a very small bloodstained baby boy lay in the bed between Martha's legs with a grisly purple tube sprouting from his navel.

"That's what I like. All the dirty work done before I arrive." The midwife breezed in followed by Bertha. The midwife took a quick look at the situation and produced a pair of scissors to cut the cord. When the baby was free she handed him to me. "Put him over there." She waved a casual hand at the washstand in the corner and turned her attention to Martha, who was no longer purple but pale and unusually quiet.

I turned away with the little body in my bare hands and found Bertha holding out a towel to wrap the poor creature in. He was a strange blue colour and his folded limbs reminded me of nothing so much as a skinned rabbit. Between us Bertha and I wrapped him in the towel but I could not bear to set him on the cold and unforgiving marble top of the washstand. I held him in my arms and Bertha stretched out one of her gentle giant's fingers to smooth his wrinkled face. The midwife bent over Martha and spoke quietly to her.

Her voice was reassuring but her words were not — though Martha may have found them so. They made my blood run cold. With a casual, "I don't think he will last very long," the midwife condemned the tiny scrap of life in my hands.

A huge sob burst up through my chest and forced itself out of my mouth. I had lost my beautiful little girl; now we were to lose this poor wizened little boy. Tears streamed down my face as I passed the child to Bertha. She held him in one of her strong and capable hands. With the first two fingers of her other hand she massaged him firmly but gently along his tiny spine. I watched, helpless. He was small but perfectly formed, yet the midwife had condemned him without a second glance. There must be something very wrong with this baby. It dawned on me then what was wrong. It was the silence. A new person had arrived in the room without making a sound. The baby had not cried.

I am a parson's widow and I was raised as a churchgoer. We cannot escape the habits of a lifetime. I looked round for some clean, warm water. I dipped my fingers in and sprinkled the tiny head with its thin strands of dark hair plastered to its skull. I spoke the words of baptism or as near as I could get them from memory. "I baptize you in the name of the Lord." I could not remember any more; I hoped that would be enough.

"A name. He must have a name."

"You are right, Bertha. He must have a name." I floundered, unable to think of a single boy's name.

"James. Call him James."

At the sound of his name a thin wail rose from the little body that lay in Bertha's hands and our tears flowed even more strongly.

I suppose I should not blame the midwife. In her trade she must grow hardened to the misfortunes of others. When she came to claim her fee, which she did remarkably quickly, I did not think she deserved it; she had done very little work and had caused me much distress. I took her down to my room and handed over the money and wished her good riddance. It was tea time so I went to the servants' hall to check that the routine of mealtimes was carried out as normally as possible under the strange circumstances that ruled that day.

Leah was my most reliable informant and I found her sewing baby clothes for her own baby. She was pleased to hear that Martha was delivered of a boy. I played down the perilous nature of the birth. I did not like to think of Leah enduring the pain that I had just witnessed tear through Martha. Leah would not make such a performance of it, I was sure. She would bite her lip and perhaps groan softly. There would be none of the high-pitched screams, the self-pitying wails of anguish and the dreadful curses that Martha produced. But then Leah wanted her baby. Martha did not want hers.

The great news of the day was of course the abandoned wedding and the revelation of the existence of Mr Rochester's first wife. The new servants were agog. The handsome new footman was cooling his heels in the kitchen instead of riding behind the carriage to the continent. The two horses were back in the stable and Old John was whistling as he went about his business. Leah had made sure that food was set out in the dining room at lunch time but no one had touched it. Miss Eyre had shut herself in her room and Mr Rochester was sitting outside her door like a faithful hound.

The clerk, John Green, had called in the afternoon to set the record straight on certain matters. Leah had taken the liberty of offering Mr Green tea in my room. Did I mind? I assured her she had done the right thing. He had completed her marriage certificate and it had formed a bond between them. The result was that he confided to Leah more than he might otherwise. He had been present in the church in the morning and revealed all that had happened.

It had been very dramatic. A solicitor, a Mr Briggs, had stepped forward just after Mr Wood had asked if there were any impediment to the marriage. The clergyman did not anticipate any objections and had started on the words of the wedding vows when the solicitor stopped the proceedings. Mr Wood was always keen to curry favour with the gentry but even he could not ignore the objection. Mr Mason had then reluctantly and in apparent fear of Mr Rochester borne witness to the effect that his sister had married Mr Rochester fifteen years ago and he had seen her alive and living at Thornfield Hall three months ago.

The unwitting cause of these revelations was Miss Eyre herself. John Green had wormed the full story out of Mr Wood. It appeared that Miss Eyre had written to an uncle in Madeira and by some evil fortune Mr Mason had been on the island and with that same uncle at the very moment the news arrived. An ill wind had blown him back to England in time to prevent the match. It was agreed by all that Miss Eyre was a completely innocent party. John Green was most anxious that we should be made aware of this.

As if I was not most painfully aware of Miss Eyre's innocence. She was the only one of us with clean hands. We had all colluded and connived, balancing our bible oaths against the legality of a marriage and the happiness of others. Poor girl! My heart went out to her, alone in her room while the man she loved sat outside separated from her by something more substantial than a wooden door. The great powers of church and state divided them irrevocably.

I resolved to go to Jane and offer what I could in the way of assistance though I feared she would blame me for keeping her in ignorance. When I arrived the chair was outside her door in the corridor but Mr Rochester had gone. I tapped at the door but there was no answer. I tried the door, which opened at my touch. The room was empty. I tiptoed to the library and peeped in.

Miss Eyre and Mr Rochester sat at the far end deep in heartfelt conversation. Mr Rochester was passionate and energetic in his speech and Jane was tearful and shaking with emotion. There was no point in my blundering into this intimate dialogue. I left them in their agony and made my way up to the third floor. I might be of use there.

As I climbed the stairs I took the little bible from my pocket and kissed its black leather cover to give me courage. I feared little James had already grown cold as my daughter did all those years ago. Dread filled my heart. I did not think I could endure the piercing pain of another lost little one.

In the first room Bertha lay stretched out on the four-poster bed. In her arms lay Martha's son. What a difference a few hours can make to one so young. His face was not so wrinkled and his eyes were unscrewing as if his next move was to open them. Someone had cleaned him and he was mewling and squirming. Bertha gazed down on him with that besotted look that comes over women's faces when they see a new-born child — not just their own new-born but anybody's.

"He's hungry," she announced, as if hunger in babies were a novelty.

"How is his mother? Martha, I mean." It was taking me some time to adjust to this unexpectedly warm and living baby. Bertha jerked her head in the direction of the adjoining rooms and said nothing. I made my way through Grace's room to find out.

Martha was lying in bed with her face to the wall. Grace was haranguing her in a low urgent voice. "You must try. Unless you do, you are condemning that innocent little creature to starve. He didn't ask to be born." She saw me at the door. "Look. Here's Mrs Fairfax. She'll tell you the same." Grace looked at me in appeal. "She says she won't feed the baby."

Martha whipped round and sat up in bed. The transformation in her appearance was as marked as the change in her son's. The livid swollen look to her face had gone and her skin was now pale again. Her eyes flashed with sudden energy. "Let's get this straight. I did not want a baby. I tried to get rid of it but nothing worked. I will not feed him. If I do that the next thing I know I'll be a wet nurse in some awful farmhouse. I'll be stuck in pig shit for ever. As soon as I can walk there he's going to the orphanage. There's a place you can leave them. Sort of swivel thing. They don't see you. You just pop the baby on it, give it a shove and it's gone."

Grace said nothing. She turned on her heel and strode out through the door. I followed her. She went straight to Bertha. Her face and voice were calm as she spoke to her. "We are going to have to spoon feed him."

"Good," said Bertha. "Show me."

Spoon feeding a baby is a slow and tiresome business. It demands inexhaustible patience and neatness of hand. These are two qualities that Bertha possesses to a fault. The hands that made doll's clothes and fashioned flowers from silk were soon occupied in giving the gift of life to Martha's abandoned baby.

It was late when I climbed into my bed that night and I was very tired. It had been an eventful day. Since the morning I had witnessed a birth, seen a marriage abandoned and a death narrowly averted. Mr Rochester, my respected employer of long standing, had been exposed to the world as a fraud and a potential bigamist. His ancient and noble house would be the subject of scandal for years to come. At the same time he had unwittingly provided a refuge to an abandoned servant girl while she brought a new life into the world.

I will not, as some unkind people do, refer to the child by that vile term "bastard". However it would be a violence to the truth to call him a love child. There may have been love, on Martha's part, at the time of his conception. I prefer not to speculate about the feelings of the Honourable Theodore Ingram on that occasion. Martha's small store of love was all used up before the time came to welcome her son into the world. She had nothing to offer the unfortunate child so she had turned her back on him and refused him her breast. With this thought the tears started to flow. The strong and conflicting emotions that I had controlled all day burst out like a river breaking its banks and I sobbed into my pillow like a green girl.

Morning brought no relief from the tide of disaster that was sweeping through Thornfield Hall. I knocked at Miss Eyre's door but there was no answer. When I ventured to look in I saw on the table a jeweller's box. When I opened it I saw that it contained the pearl necklace that Mr Rochester had given her. Further investigation revealed the wedding clothes hanging in the wardrobe. Strangest of all, the beautiful veil she had not worn on what was supposed to be her wedding day lay in a drawer ripped into two separate pieces. Now there was a puzzle. Jane was not malicious; she would not destroy what she could not have.

What was clear to me was that Miss Eyre had left. She had gone out into the world with little more than the clothes she stood up in. I regretted bitterly that I had not managed to exchange a few words with her, to let her know that I was still her friend and to ask her pardon for concealing Mr Rochester's strange situation from her. I was in debt to her, a situation that makes me uncomfortable; I owed her wages and a character. How would she manage without money and a character reference?

If I was upset that Miss Eyre had gone, Mr Rochester was distraught. He spent the day in the library gnashing his teeth and tearing his hair. We sent up his favourite meals to tempt him to eat. The beef, the apple tart, the crusty rolls came back untouched. I asked him about sending for Mr Carter, the surgeon, and was treated to a basilisk glare that would have stopped a running stag in its tracks.

The new footmen earned their keep, not sitting behind his carriage on the way to the continent but running up and down stairs for instructions and then haring off round the neighbourhood in quest of sightings of Miss Eyre. He sent them to enquire at the coaching inns to see if she had boarded a stagecoach. They were ordered to ask at the turnpikes and at the churches and the vicarages. They knocked at the doors of cottages and at the back doors of the gentry's houses; the front doors were closed now to the name of Rochester. Miss Blanche must be congratulating herself on her narrow escape.

My one consolation was to hear that baby James had survived the night. Grace and Bertha had taken turns to watch over him and to spoon feed him. Grace looked with approval at Bertha as she patiently slipped the precious drops of life-saving milk into the tiny pink mouth. As I watched I wondered which of the residents of Thornfield Hall was mad. Was it this woman with a child at her breast or the pacing red-eyed parody of a man raging about in the library?

I looked in at Martha, my last and least-favourite charge. She was asleep. Her chest rose and fell rhythmically, her breathing deep and slow. She had bound her breasts tightly to stop the milk coming in. I thought of Bertha, locked in a ship's cabin, believing her child to be dead. I thought of Grace, who knew from bitter experience the hardships a woman with no husband has to endure in order for her child to survive. And here lay Martha comfortable in her bed, her face smoothed free of care and restored to its normal size and colour. She slept the sleep of the just while in the next room two women battled to keep her child alive. A moment of malicious joy swept through me; I was glad I had slapped her yesterday. I only wished I had done it harder.

My Mad Mr Rochester

1832

Two letters arrived at Thornfield Hall: one for me, which was not unusual, and one for Grace, which was. They were both written in the same hand. I took Grace's up to her as I was confident she would enjoy the news it contained.

"You read it." Grace shook the paper at me; it was the first time I saw her show a small sign of weakness.

"I don't need to read it. It is the same as mine. It tells us that thirty thousand pounds is deposited in our names in the Bank of Knaresborough." Grace did a jig of joy. We had feared that Mr Rochester might find a way to cancel our agreement now that the secret of his first marriage was out. I had misjudged him; as a man of honour he had kept his word. "You must write to your son," I told Grace, "to let him know the money is safely in our hands. Then he can pay the rent on a house for us. We could be away from here in three weeks. We none of us have much to pack."

I turned to Bertha. "You have your dowry back."

She ignored me. "Bertha happy. Bertha has baby." She beamed down at the infant on her breast.

Sometimes I envied her; she lived like a lily of the field, careless of all the practical details that fretted and worried the rest of us.

As bad luck would have it, Martha arrived at that moment. That girl had a way of appearing when there was anything to her advantage and disappearing when there was work to be done. I was fearful that she had overheard how much money we had received. The combination of Bertha's devotion to the baby and the arrival of sudden wealth created a situation that Martha could easily twist to her advantage. I could feel my mouth set in a grim line as I determined to prevent her exploiting Bertha and her newly recovered dowry. It was, I told myself virtuously, one of my duties as a trustee.

Martha draped herself round the door frame and examined the three of us in a detached way. You could see her thinking that she was glad to be young; her skin was smooth and soon she would have her waist back. She looked with a critical eye at Bertha, who continued to spoon feed the baby. "Watch what you're doing," she told Bertha. "You're spilling that milk all down your dress. Don't make washing. There's enough of it as it is."

I thought the remark very cheeky. Officially Martha was back at work in the laundry though I doubted she washed anything more than a handkerchief. Tomorrow, I decided, she is going to tackle the sheets. While I was busy devising ways to punish Martha, Grace had been inspecting the front of Bertha's bodice.

"Look," she said and pointed at Bertha. Circles of dampness showed up on each breast. We all gazed fixedly at Bertha's bosom.

Grace looked up with wonderment in her eyes. "It doesn't seem possible. I don't think it is milk you have spilt, Bertha. I think it is milk that is leaking out of you. You've started to produce milk again."

I found it difficult to understand the full meaning of what Grace was saying. Martha was even slower. Suddenly she grasped what had happened. She squealed in disgust, made retching sounds and fled to her bedroom. Although she slammed the door shut behind her, it did little to muffle her squeals of distaste. Grace scratched her head and came up with an explanation that sounded both persuasive and reasonable — indeed quite scientific. "It must be holding the baby so much. It's the nursing him that's brought the milk in. Try feeding him and see what happens."

Bertha put the baby to her breast. The baby grabbed the nipple, sucked and seemed satisfied with the results. By this time I had remembered a biblical precedent; being a parson's widow does sometimes have its uses. "There's a story in the Bible about a grandmother or a mother-in-law who did the same. Breastfed a grandson. I think it was a Ruth or a Naomi." The comparison with a grandmother was reassuring; Bertha was near forty. It was ten years since she had fed her own child.

We watched as the child fed. Bertha's face radiated contentment. I remembered how she had been bundled aboard a ship and locked in a cabin while her breasts leaked milk for the baby that had been torn from her. I

277

felt I was witnessing a minor miracle, like a scene from a stained-glass window of the Nativity. There was a strange sense of justice, of an unexpected bounty. Bertha, who had lost her own child, was now able to feed a neglected baby. I assumed some other woman, somewhere in Jamaica, had done the same for Bertha's baby, the boy who was snatched from his crib at night and carried off into the dark. There was no other way for him to survive.

The rooms on the third storey of Thornfield Hall had served in their turn as a torture chamber, a prison, a sewing room and a place of healing: they now became a nursery. A cradle held centre place in the sitting room and little James basked there, bathed in the attention of all the female members of staff and some of the male ones too. John regularly came with Leah so he might see what the future held in store for him when Leah's time came. Old John came to pay his respects to his late friend's grandchild. He pronounced him a fine boy and did his inarticulate best to make Martha proud of her son and serious about his future. To no avail. Sam and Sophie stayed away; they probably thought that fertility was catching.

By some magical chemistry that was beyond our comprehension Bertha continued to breastfeed James. Grace topped him up with spoonfuls and the little chap flourished like the proverbial green bay tree. The only blot on the landscape was, as usual, Martha. She did everything she could to avoid her baby; she did not hold him, talk to him or feed him. She went to work

278

with a smile on her face, happy to put three flights of stairs between her and her duties as a mother.

I let this neglect continue. I was sure without consulting them that Bertha and Grace were keen to co-operate in the raising of this child; we had the means to provide for him handsomely. Bertha would fight like a tiger to keep him, an eventuality I was anxious to avoid. I knew from past experience that Bertha fought with tooth and claw, not to mention scissors. Every day that we cared for James gave us a tighter hold on him.

The awkward fact, however, was that Martha was the mother of this child that we all wanted to mother. Martha, whom I had dismissed as incurably stupid, was nevertheless sharp enough to spot an advantage and would play her cards when the time was ripe. I was at a loss what to do about her. I had clear plans for the future for the rest of us but there was nothing for Martha. When I looked into her future all I saw was a blur.

On the floor beneath what was now a nursery suite Mr Rochester suffered in perfect ignorance of the new life that had arrived at Thornfield Hall. He continued to behave in a wild and uncontrolled manner. Where once we had doubted his wife's sanity, now it was his reason that was in question. His distress and despair at the loss of Jane had not diminished in the weeks that had passed. He received no callers and he made no visits. He stayed locked up in the house all day and would venture no further than the garden or the orchard at night. I think he hoped for Jane to return. The thought that she might appear when he was absent terrified him. Most disturbing of all he started to sleep in Miss Eyre's room. He slept in her bed and he would not let us change the sheets. He did not seem to find much comfort there; at night I heard him pacing the floor or groaning in his sleep.

I began to grow impatient with his grief; there were decisions to be made about the household and he would not listen to my concerns or say Yes or No to any of the questions I asked. In the end I used my best judgement and made the decisions for him. I placed the necessary bills or letters in front of him, pointed where he should write, put a pen in his hand and watched as he obediently signed his name.

My first move was to get John and Leah into their new home so they would have time to settle before their baby was born. It was easily accomplished. The last night before the eve of his planned wedding Mr Rochester had ridden over to the estate to make the final arrangements. The documents had all been signed before Jane's sudden flight so John and Leah were able to take possession of their new farm. I was sorry to part with them. Leah had been a good and reliable friend and ally. We promised to keep in touch, though I warned Leah that I would leave Thornfield Hall when Mr Rochester had recovered the use of his wits.

Sam came one evening to say he had found a property in Harrogate. "That's a long way from the sea," I teased him. He had the grace to look a little sheepish. He told me there was a lease available on a shop there. It seemed that it would be a good place for Sophie to start up as a dressmaker. She needed to live where there would be customers for high-class gowns. He would like his capital sum now, please.

I squealed at the amount he asked for. "It's an expensive place," he told me.

"I know." I tried to picture Sam with his rough out-spoken ways in Harrogate at a high-class business for ladies and failed. It was clear that Sophie had made all the choices. I beat him down to three hundred and fifty pounds. He did not seem too unhappy. Mr Rochester signed a cheque for the three hundred pounds and I made up the difference in cash. The two of them slipped off very quietly one Sunday, without benefit of clergy, as they say. They would have to keep quiet about the informality of their living arrangements in Harrogate; the good people there are notoriously strict about such matters.

Now that John and Sam had gone I was left with two unfamiliar footmen to carry out a multitude of tasks. Even in his state of confusion, Mr Rochester found many errands he wanted running. He had placed advertisements in all the newspapers and continued to have enquiries made about the whereabouts of Miss Eyre. I never did master the footmen's names, even that of the handsome one. I continued to use the names John or Sam for them interchangeably. They did not seem to mind — or notice.

These new servants were very disgruntled about their employment. They had come in expectation of improving their lot in life and had been bitterly disappointed. The prospect of settled employment with steady promotion in a house with a good reputation had been dangled before them, only to be whisked away one July morning. I did not think that Mr Rochester had played fair with them. Now they were all on notice from Thornfield Hall, a house whose name was anathema to many in Yorkshire. Our servants' hall was not a happy place. I did my best for them, sending notes to every housekeeper in the neighbourhood asking about openings.

I kept the grooms and stable lads on while they looked for new work, although there were very few horses in the stables. I took my courage in both hands and offered for sale the carriage that Mr Rochester had bought for his wedding journey while he was still pretending he wanted to marry Miss Ingram. I did not think he would want to be reminded of that time.

Young Lord Ingram, tasteless and reckless as ever, made an offer for the luxurious purple carriage and the two horses that many thought had been destined for his sister. Old John was keen to sell to him at a very high price. The more cash the young baron wasted the better as far as Old John was concerned. Then there would be less for the gangly peer to offer his creditors and the carriage would be sent to auction for a knock-down price. Old John had been as good as his word and had spread a panic among the new baron's creditors.

In the end the carriage and horses went to a factory owner who drove a hard bargain. Old John shrugged his shoulders. His heart wasn't in carriage horses; he liked hunters. Now that only Mesrour was left in the stables he packed his bags and left for Ferndean Manor. Old John thought it would be good for the old horse to have a change of scene. He reckoned the animal was pining away in his stable, while his master sulked in the house and never took him out for exercise. I thought the change would be good for the grouchy old coachman too, though Ferndean had a reputation for being damp. I feared Mary's rheumatics would grow worse in the unhealthy atmosphere but she refused to be downhearted; she was looking forward to a life with less work.

The hardest parting of all was from Adele. With no sign of Jane Eyre and Sophie gone there was no escape for the poor child; she had to go to school. I followed up the enquiries Jane had made but none of the schools seemed really suitable. English schools thought reading and writing and bible study more important than hairdressing, clothes, charm and deportment. Jane had told me a little about her old school, Lowood, and it had not filled me with confidence. In the end I chose the most expensive school I could find, on the principle that you get what you pay for. I hoped that one day Mr Rochester would begin to take real care of the girl we all thought was his daughter rather than paying other people to do so. The large bills each term would serve to remind him regularly of the child's existence.

We cried a lot in the days before she left. On the day of her departure Adele behaved gallantly and strode off with her little chin in the air. She wore a new outfit that Bertha, in intervals between breastfeeding, had made especially for her. Solemnly Adele showed me the grey dress with its white collar. Her hair was tied back severely with a black ribbon. "Do I not look the part?"

she asked as slowly she turned to show me the back view. "Even Miss Eyre would approve."

I promised to write as I handed her over to the servant the school had sent to accompany her. Although she looked a sensible sort of woman with a kind face, at that moment I wished Jane Eyre was still governess at Thornfield Hall, that Mr Rochester had never fallen in love with her and that Adele was in the nursery upstairs, playing with her dolls and fussing with her hair. Then I watched as Adele pointed at her luggage and the school servant obediently followed instructions. I had underestimated the child. By Christmas Adele would have won many hearts among her fellow pupils. The chances were she would be spending the holiday with one of them, the daughter of someone with a fine house and most probably a title.

All this time letters were passing backwards and forwards between us, the lawyer in Grimsby and Grace's son. He had taken the lease on a house for us, a good substantial merchant's house in a quiet market town. There was a fine drawing room, we were told, with bay windows, four good bedrooms and ample accommodation for servants. It was exciting to think that I would employ servants on my own account and I vowed I would be a firm but fair mistress to them. Behind the house was a large garden with apple and pear trees and even a coach house. We had decided we would have our own coach. No more begging a grumpy coachman if he could spare a horse for a trip out of an afternoon!

284

There was a sad irony in the fact that I would live the life of a woman with a comfortable income and her own carriage. Mr Rochester, in the meantime, would be left to the mercy of disgruntled servants who did not know his preferences or lacked the skills to provide them. His stables were empty and through neglect and extravagance his bank balance would soon be in the same condition. He was spending money like water on his search for Miss Eyre. Every wayside beggar who claimed to have caught a glimpse of her was handsomely rewarded and promised more gold for keeping his eyes open. The footmen were sent hither and thither, hiring horses to chase false trails. I had no doubt that most of the so-called sightings of Miss Eyre would be at inns where the landlord would have to be interrogated at length.

When Mr Rochester's agent came to bring him reports or ask for decisions he was sent brusquely away. I took him to my room and there we consulted earnestly. The agent shrugged his shoulders and held up his hands in horror at my tales of Mr Rochester's reckless distribution of money on the search for Miss Eyre and the complete lack of supervision of how it was spent. He could not help me. In his opinion, although I might have some control over the household expenditure, Mr Rochester was entitled to spend his money as he wished. If he wished to spend it on fools and rogues that was up to him. His verdict was no surprise to me. I nodded miserably.

The agent had his own problems. Collecting the rents was proving more troublesome than it had been for years. "They're full of excuses. The cow died, the corn failed. The usual sort of thing. Truth is, they know summat is badly wrong with master and they're taking advantage." He stared thoughtfully into the fire before he picked up his hat. "Ah! Well. We mun just soldier on."

Another gentleman came to call on me at Thornfield Hall. This time it was a much more cheerful occasion than my meeting with the agent had proved. One of the new maids brought a well-dressed man to my room. She could not announce him as she had neglected to enquire his name and ran off before I had a chance to scold her.

"Don't you recognize me, Mrs Fairfax?" The man stepped forward so I could see him in the light. He was a well-built man of fifty or sixty with very little hair and a broad smiling countenance. He wore the clothes of a prosperous country man and carried his cap in his hand. Even after this inspection I was none the wiser. "I'm Merryman. I used to be butler here. For old Mr Rochester."

I was disbelieving. This could not be the solemn butler who had introduced me to the formalities I had to follow in the realm of the servants. Some great change had come over him. "Your pug face! You've lost your pug face!"

He beamed at me. "I don't need it now. I am my own master. I can smile as much as I like. In fact it's almost obligatory. I'm a landlord now. At the Rochester Arms.

Just two miles across the fields from here. It is longer by road."

"Sit down, sit down and tell me all that has happened." Few people can resist that particular invitation so I rang the bell to order tea. No one came. I rang again.

"I take it Leah has gone. I can just about remember her. A good girl. You would not have to ring twice for her."

Briefly I explained that Leah was now a farmer's wife and was soon to give birth to her first child. Then I went to the kitchen to snap at the maid. I used my absence from the room to work through in my mind how much I could tell Merryman. The mad wife and the interrupted wedding were public knowledge. Martha's baby and Bertha's trust fund were not.

Once we were settled with our tea Mr Merryman told me about the rich wool merchant he had worked for in Bradford. Life had been very comfortable there and Merryman's knowledge of the ways of the landed classes had been much appreciated. So successful had he been in teaching refinement and table manners that the daughter of the house was now married to an impoverished nobleman. Mr Merryman had been generously rewarded for his part in bringing this about. "A good employer," he concluded about his Bradford wool merchant, "but not a gentleman."

"That word means less and less to me these days," I told him. Mr Merryman, like the rest of the county, knew all about the present Mr Rochester's misfortunes.

We spent a few moments lamenting the decay of the house of Rochester.

"Old Mr Rochester would be turning in his grave at the waste of money," said the old butler when we went out to the drive where his pony and trap waited for him. He gave a penny to the boy who held his horse's head. "Don't forget, Mrs Fairfax, a warm welcome awaits you at The Rochester Arms."

I laughed at the thought of my walking two miles across the fields to drink with the labourers at his inn. Grace and I had plenty of porter. Mr Rochester did not concern himself with counting bottles. Meanwhile I had plans of my own to pursue.

It took some weeks to deal with all the arrangements before the date could be set for Grace and Bertha to leave Thornfield Hall. The post chaise was booked to arrive in the afternoon to take them to the turnpike road. There they would pick up the stage in the early evening. It was agreed that I should stay behind for a few more weeks in the hope that Mr Rochester's condition improved. I thought the departure of his wife might help his recovery; he blamed her for all his troubles. Many times in the past he had threatened to close down Thornfield Hall. Now he clung to the place; it was his sole link with his beloved Jane.

Mr Rochester no longer made any pretence of dealing with his business affairs and I was left to struggle with his correspondence. One day a letter arrived that enquired after the whereabouts of Miss Eyre. Mr Briggs, the solicitor who had interrupted the wedding, wished to contact her. With much trepidation

I brought the letter to Mr Rochester's attention. His rage was explosive. I might just as well have thrown gunpowder on the fire.

No one wanted to know the whereabouts of Miss Eyre more earnestly than he did. If that snivelling lackey of the law had not put his nose into business that was no concern of his and if the wind had obliged him by dashing the ship that carried that lickspittle of a brother against the rocks then Miss Eyre's whereabouts would not be a mystery that woke him wailing at his loss in the small hours of the morning. She would be reigning as queen of his heart and the world would acknowledge her as the rightful Mrs Rochester.

I wrote to Mr Briggs myself, regretting that I was unable to help him. If he did manage to trace Miss Eyre I would be pleased if he would write to Thornfield Hall so that I could contact her.

You will see from his reaction to Mr Briggs's letter that Mr Rochester was still in a state of despair about Jane. In spite of his frantic efforts there had been no news of her. I had employed the servants' unofficial — and probably more efficient — grapevine but to no effect. We knew she had gone north on the stagecoach but after that we had lost all track of her. The few big houses in that part of the country were so widely scattered that there was little traffic between the servants. At the farms and cottages our enquiries had met with sullen silence and suspicion.

I hoped that Mr Rochester would gather his wits and begin to take charge of his affairs again. Already in my head I was rehearsing the conversation I would have to hold with him before I could leave; I was not looking forward to it. I decided I would begin by reminding him that his beloved Jane did not tolerate self-pity; she regarded it as an indulgence. She believed in hard work and discipline. If I was allowed to continue — which I doubted — I would insist that he get help from some other reliable person. He had been a good employer in many ways; his unfortunate marriage was the source of all his flaws. Incidentally I was pleased to note I no longer thought of him as "my master". That particular bad habit had been cured.

The problem of Martha still nagged at me. I fretted about it so much to Grace that in the end she sat me down and wagged her finger at me. She gave me a very stern talking to. "Forget about her. I will deal with Martha. You feel guilty about her and so you are too kind to her. You pussyfoot about. I don't feel guilty about her. She's had more luck than I had in a similar situation. Leave her to me. Not long now before we go."

I asked Mr Rochester if he wanted to say farewell to "the lady", the unwitting cause of so much distress in his life. The mere mention of her brought a snarl to his lips and made his black eyes flash with fire. This brief sign of ferocious life was preferable to his usual gloomy silence. "Tell me the day of her departure," he ordered me, thumping his desk for emphasis. "Tell me the day and I will make it my business to be out of sight and earshot of Thornfield Hall."

The momentous day of Bertha's departure dawned. It was more than ten years since she'd arrived, a wild stranger driven demented by grief and ill-treatment. Grace had packed their few belongings. There was little they wanted to take to their new life. There was only one important item of luggage — baby James. It was taken for granted that he would go with them; they had fed the baby when Martha had refused to do so. The feeling was that in saving his life they had acquired the rights of a parent. No one asked Martha if she was accompanying them. It was assumed she would. Where else could she go?

Once she had recovered from childbirth I had kept her on the books as a laundry maid. It had not been difficult given the chaotic nature of the household. I had not moved her to the servants' sleeping quarters; the new maids were unhappy enough without having to endure Martha's bragging. I had let her continue to sleep in her room on the third storey. There Bertha fed the baby both night and day while Martha enjoyed long hours of untroubled sleep.

During the day she swanned around the house, pretending to work and making eyes at the handsome footman. My suspicions of her were not confined to flirtation. I had fears of a darker and more sinister plan brewing in her twisted mind. Somehow she had sniffed out that we now had money, though I do not think she realized how much. We were women of substance and any fool could see that James would prove a powerful lever to use on us.

In the event when the post chaise arrived Martha followed Grace and Bertha out. Bertha carried the baby and Martha carried the suitcases. Martha's eyes were very red. It was a subdued departure; I was alone in seeing them off. Gone were the familiar faces of those who had taken the bible oath; they were all launched on new and better lives. Mr Rochester had been as good as his word. He'd walked to Mr Carter's house in the morning.

Grace embraced me to say goodbye, or rather *au revoir*, we would be reunited soon in our new home. She whispered in my ear that Martha had agreed to be employed as a nursery maid on a generous salary. As Grace said, we could afford it.

To my surprise Martha came to embrace me. "I will so miss Thornfield Hall, Mrs Fairfax. You have all been so kind to me. I don't know how I'll get on. I've never been out of Yorkshire before." Tears streamed down her face. She seemed genuinely distressed at parting. She took a long look round the courtyard before she climbed into the chaise. I think she'd been hoping for a farewell kiss from the handsome footman, but she was disappointed. He did not appear. Once she was settled on board she sobbed and hiccupped into her hanky.

I heard Grace telling her to pull herself together and to listen to instructions. "In future, Martha, at the new house I am Mrs Poole to you and this lady is to be addressed as Mrs Mason. Every time you speak to us, remember Mrs Mason and Mrs Poole. You should start now and get into practice. And this young man will be Master James. You understand me. I warn you, Martha, old servants make bad masters."

My room felt very empty when they had gone. I did not venture up the back stairs to the third floor, their territory. It was too sad. It was no use seeking solace in the servants' hall. All the faces there were new and I regarded them with suspicion. Long years of keeping secrets had left their mark on me. For distraction I set about chivvying them. I found dirt in obscure places, stains in teacups, fireplaces without coal. I felt much better after that.

At six o'clock there was a commotion at the front door. It was Mr Carter's servant with a dog cart. In the back was Mr Rochester's dog Pilot, and Mr Rochester himself. He was very much the worse for drink. Pilot slunk off into his kennel in the yard as if he was the culprit. Mr Carter's man stood, twisting his cap in his hands, and surveyed the figure slumped in the back of the dog cart. "He's not that bad," he consoled me. "Mr Carter can't understand how your master got rid of all his horses. Might as well be dead as not have a horse, he says. Wouldn't hear of Mr Rochester walking home."

I summoned the two new footmen to help Mr Rochester up the stairs. Mr Carter's man unscrewed his cap, popped it on his head, and was off. No one enjoys seeing the mighty fallen.

I spent a sad evening alone in the housekeeper's room. No Adele or Miss Eyre to keep me company. No Grace with her glass of porter and her pipe or Bertha with her sewing and her swift and accurate arithmetic. Even Pilot would not come in from the yard to keep me company but stayed in his kennel with his head on his paws. I spent my time calculating how soon I could leave Thornfield Hall and prayed I would not be long delayed.

When darkness fell I checked on Pilot outside in his kennel, locked the big front door behind me and made sure the windows downstairs were all closed and fastened. They had been open all day; it was harvest time and the weather was wonderfully warm. I climbed the stairs with my candle and looked in on the library where Mr Rochester was sprawled in a chair, pretending to read his unopened book and drinking yet more brandy.

For old time's sake I climbed up to the third floor. I checked the big sitting room with its elaborate hangings and four-poster bed where we had sat and sewed in the afternoon while Leah read to us. I went through to Bertha's room where I had first seen my unusual house guest chained to the bed, a poor starved deranged creature at the mercy of the frightful Mrs Morgan. That name evoked the memory of the foul stench that had pervaded the chamber, which was now clean and fresh. I went no further. Beyond was Grace's neat and nun-like bedroom which I knew would be stripped bare. The next room had been Martha's. I did not want to torment myself by seeing the chaos, disarray and dirt in which I was sure she had left it. That could keep till the morning. I'd heard Grace taking her in hand, outlining her future duties to her. If anyone could teach Martha discipline and order it was Grace.

I retraced my steps and descended the stairs to the floor below. Out of habit I locked the door that closed off the staircase. I smiled as I remembered how pleased I was that I had done so on that fateful wedding day. Tonight there was a harvest moon. The great disc hung low and glowed in the evening sky. There was enough light for the labourers to work late to bring in the last of the corn. Soon the farmers would start burning the stubble and the air would be full of foul black smoke.

As I lay down to sleep I counted my blessings, as has been my habit for many years. Sometimes I've struggled to find a single one but that night I had to use my fingers to count them all. Bertha and Grace. Leah and John. Old John and Mary. Sam with his Sophie. They were all launched on new lives that were more suited to them and more comfortable than their previous ones. Adele, I was not so sure about. School would not be to her taste. I had every confidence that in a few years she would quickly arrange matters to her satisfaction. She would charm her way into having a fine house and an extensive wardrobe. Mr Rochester might improve now that Thornfield Hall was free of the incubus of his wife. He could not live for ever in his state of morose gloom. I was looking forward to my new life as a woman of independent means.

The Harvest

1832

In the small hours of the morning I was woken by shouting in the corridor outside and banging on my door. Mr Rochester erupted into my room. I sat up in bed, dazed and startled. He grabbed me by the shoulders and shouted his orders straight into my face. "Get up. Put shoes on. The library is on fire." I thought it was one of his mad drunken fantasies. I smelt no smoke. He reeked of brandy but his speech was clear and his movements were brisk.

"You must help me get the servants out. I will turn my back for thirty seconds. Then you must be ready. If not, I swear I will dress you myself." I pulled my dressing gown over my nightgown and had the sense to pick up my little bible and thrust it into my pocket. I climbed into the first pair of shoes I could find. Mr Rochester lit a candle and handed it to me.

"You will need that." Outside the corridor was dark but at the library end there was an ominous scarlet glow. "You take the women's side. I will rouse the men."

I had to run to keep up with him as he raced down the corridor. All the time I was racking my brain trying to remember how many live-in servants we had. There had been so many comings and goings that I had quite lost track of them. I found the new cook first. A phlegmatic woman, she insisted on getting properly dressed while I went to wake the two kitchen maids and the housemaid who had replaced Leah. Cook assured me that four was the full complement of female staff. They had all managed to scrabble into their clothes. How I envied them as I flapped about in my dressing gown. Cook even had her stays on.

I led my little flock out into the main corridor where we rendezvoused with the menservants. The two new footmen were there. They too had managed to dress, but then men's clothes are so much more convenient than women's with their endless hooks and loops and buttons. Mr Rochester appeared, herding the boys who worked in the stables, the garden and the kitchen. They assured me they were all there. As they preferred to travel in a pack I believed them.

We could hear the fire now. The flames roared and crackled and we could smell the smoke. Mr Rochester held his candle aloft as he led us down the main staircase. Calm, confident and positive, he was in full command of the situation. It will be worth a fire if it returns him to his senses, was the foolish thought that ran through my head. Like a Moses, he led us through danger into safety. I thought all peril was over. I did not understand the full power of fire, that ferocious and greedy element that devours everything in its path.

Once outside the house Mr Rochester went straight to release Pilot from his kennel. The animal greeted his master and attached himself firmly to his heels. Mr Rochester sent the handsome footman to Millcote for the fire engines. The footman would have to run as there was not a horse in the stable for him to ride. Mr Rochester then asked the rest of us if we'd be willing to help carry out of the house some items of furniture. The ground floor was so far untouched. It was in the upper storeys that the flames roared and flickered like a coronet of fire.

I took the opportunity to race into my housekeeper's room and scoop up all the spare cash I could find in the bureau drawer. I would have liked to rescue the bureau where I had worked so many hours but it was too heavy for me to carry. The money went into the pocket of my dressing gown where it joined my bible. Then I quickly retreated to the safety of the lawn.

When Mr Rochester decided it was too dangerous to risk bringing out more furniture he collected all the servants together on the lawn and addressed us. He assured us that we would be looked after and compensated for the loss of our belongings. We all murmured our gratitude. My eye was caught by the presence on the lawn of a chair that someone had had the good sense to rescue. I sank into it with relief and surveyed the scene in front of me.

Thornfield Hall was ablaze. The flames leapt upwards into the sky. The conflagration had roused the village people in Hay. They were coming down the drive and straggling across the lawns to offer their help. I could not imagine what they could possibly do against the fiery diadem that crowned Thornfield Hall. Among the orange flashes and sparks that lit the night sky I saw something move on the roof, a solid mass among the flickering and shifting tongues of fire. The smoke billowed round, obscuring my view. A gust of wind gave me a brief glimpse of a pale shape flitting among the chimneys. As it approached the battlements I saw it was a figure in white with a great mane of dark hair. A concerted gasp from those around me told me I was not dreaming. The others had seen the apparition too.

Frantically I went through my mental list of servants. Their names eluded me, so I pictured their faces and then looked around me to match my image against a real person. I was not alone in doing this. The servants themselves were clutching at each other to check they were really there. There was a brief panic about the absence of the handsome footman until they remembered he had gone to Millcote to fetch the fire engines.

Mr Rochester groaned aloud as he looked up to the roof. He shook his fists at the sky and gave a wail that sent Pilot cowering to the ground. "She has come back to haunt me! She has come back to haunt me." He pointed dramatically at the skyline. "Will I never be free of my cursed wife?" He held up his hands to heaven in supplication and then on an impulse dashed inside the burning building. Afterwards people claimed that he went to rescue her. I fear I have a different interpretation. He thought her spirit had returned to haunt him.

The flames writhed and flickered on the roof and the figure, desperate to escape the heat and the scorching fire, climbed the battlements in a fruitless attempt to cheat death. With arms outstretched and her white robe billowing about her she launched herself from the parapet. She fell like Lucifer, crashing down upon the paving stones. All around me the servants and the villagers shivered with horror. The mad wife, the mad wife, they muttered. Few of them had seen her but her story was well known in the neighbourhood. After the interrupted wedding it had passed, with embellishments, through the servants' halls, the drawing rooms and the parsonages. The entire population of Hay would know some version of the scandalous events.

I sat helpless in my chair and watched the tragedy in front of me. I had waved Bertha off scarcely eight hours ago. She had been with Grace. Grace would not have let her return alone. Was it indeed a ghost? An apparition, as Mr Rochester thought. Had we all dreamt it? Such thoughts buzzed about in my head, distracting me from the simple fact that whatever it was, it had summoned Mr Rochester from safety into danger; he had gone back into the burning building. My first duty was to get him out.

I roused myself and approached the inferno. I called to Mr Rochester to return. It was too late to save her. A footman — the not handsome one — gallantly plunged into the building. He had to drag Mr Rochester from under a beam that had fallen on him as he tried to climb up the great staircase. The footman returned unscathed but Mr Rochester looked terribly injured.

By now help was arriving from more distant neighbours. I went to the crumpled figure in white that

300

lay sprawled on the ground. Her nightgown had flown upwards as she jumped. I pulled it down to cover her for decency's sake, for she was naked underneath; she must have been sleeping in her bed when the fire started.

Her body lay face down on the stones and the hair covered her face as it had done when I first saw Bertha chained to the bed. I drew back the hair to reveal the face, blackened by smoke and with a great wound on the forehead. There was little blood; she had died instantly. My heart stopped with a great spasm and then started to beat again. It was not Bertha who lay dead on the ground. It was Martha.

"So the mad bitch is dead." The voice came from behind me; it was Carter, the surgeon who spoke. He leaned over and felt at the neck of the body. He straightened up. "I don't know why I bothered. No one could survive a fall like that. I'll tell Rochester he is a free man at last." He strode off, satisfied that his duty was done. I stayed silent, my throat paralysed by shock.

I did not move from the body, keeping a sort of vigil by her. The other servants came to gawk from a safe distance at the famous madwoman from the attic. They knew she existed but had had very little contact with her. They all remarked on the swarthiness of her skin. They could not see that their own faces were blackened by the smoke. This simple explanation for the dark complexion of the corpse did not occur to them.

First my mind and then my body began to work again. I found myself sifting through various shreds of information, trying to weave them into a satisfactory

301

fabric. Martha had no family to make enquiries after her. Old John had accepted that she would leave Thornfield Hall to live with me and Grace. Her silence would not concern him. Bertha was Bertha Mason now. As far as she was concerned Bertha Rochester was already dead. What would happen if I let everyone continue to believe the body was Bertha's? It would make no difference to Bertha. Mr Rochester would be free of a burden that had blighted his life. If — or when — he found his beloved Jane he would be able to take her to church and marry her in good conscience and in the eyes of the Lord.

Those were the advantages in letting the corpse be identified as Bertha's. The next important question was, "Could I get away with it?" The new servants knew Martha a little but did not know Bertha. Although her existence was no longer a secret she had clung to her familiar territory of the third storey and the back stairs. Most of her time had been spent in private feeding baby James.

As these thoughts ran round my head I watched the people from the village of Hay as they gawped at the body and whispered behind their hands about the lunatic wife of Mr Rochester. They stood well back for fear the contagion of madness might leap from the dead woman in search of a new body to inhabit. Everyone believed the madwoman to be dead. It would be uphill work to convince the assembled locals of their error. I decided to let Bertha stay dead.

At last the fire engines from Millcote arrived. As they set about their work Carter returned to me, wiping a bloody knife on his handkerchief. "Bad business. Just had to amputate Rochester's hand. He is dreadfully damaged. Poor chap. One eye's definitely gone. Taking him to my house. Look after him there." I said nothing. I was so glad I had found the chair. This latest news would have felled me to the ground.

Mr Carter's gaze wandered round the scene of devastation and he shook his head in disbelief at the horror of it all. His attention fell upon the dead woman at his feet. He poked gently at her with the toe of his boot, stirring the fabric of her nightgown. "Not the first time is it that she's played with fire? Nearly burnt Rochester in his bed one night. Mad bitch. Good riddance." He put his knife in his pocket and surveyed the crumbling wreck that had once been Thornfield Hall.

Carter turned towards the still blazing building. "One good thing. Rochester got rid of all his horses. Mesrour is safe up at Ferndean. Stables here are empty. Fire is a terrible thing for horses." The thought of horses trapped in blazing stables unmanned him for a moment. His normally dogmatic manner deserted him as he asked pathetically, "Don't suppose you managed to rescue any brandy? I could do with a nice big tumbler full with a splash of hot water." I shook my head. He knew the question was hopeless even as he asked it. Away he loped, to see to his surviving patient.

Cook and the maids came to tell me they had found shelter for the night. The villagers were making room for them and for the stable lads in their cottages. The footmen had gone with Mr Carter to help look after Mr

Rochester. I promised I would be in touch with them all to settle any outstanding business and gave them some coins from the cash in my pocket.

Mr Wood came to inspect the corpse. I thought he might have a care for the living but his mind was on theological matters. As I sat by the still-warm body he pontificated about the manner of her death. "She jumped from the roof I am told. I fear the unfortunate wretch may have committed the sin of suicide. They say she was mad. So often madness is the punishment for sin. I do not think in all conscience she can be buried in holy ground."

"Perhaps she jumped to escape the heat of the flames?"

"Such little faith. The fire might have abated." He went on to lament that the deceased Mrs Rochester had not sought the consolation of religion in his church while she was alive. He thought that to be a grave mistake for one so disturbed in her mind. Little did he know that Bertha, shrouded in widow's weeds, had sat in the gallery many a Sunday; she was one of his best attenders.

He chuntered on about the disgrace. The Rochesters had been buried at his church since Damer de Rochester, slain at Marston Moor in the civil wars. There was much to object to in what he said but I let it pass. I hoped he might offer me a bed for the night. It would be a comfort to sleep in my old home, even though the present incumbent was not to my taste. It was not to be. He wafted away without a thought to my situation. I was not fully a servant so the villagers did not invite me; I was not gentry so the parson ignored me. I began to think I should have to spend the night beside the burning ruin of my former home.

A horse and cart pulled up a safe distance from the flames. The driver dismounted and came over to me and my silent companion. He doffed his hat. "Mrs Fairfax, I am glad I find you safe." It was Mr Merryman. I was very pleased to see him.

"I'm glad you thought to bring your cart," I said and offered my hand, for all the world as if we were meeting in a parlour of an afternoon, not sitting outside a smouldering house in the small hours of the night.

"I did say you would be very welcome at the Rochester Arms. Very unfortunate circumstances though."

"Could you supply me with a room in your inn? And perhaps an outhouse where I can store the body of this poor soul. There is no one else to look after her." Mr Merryman was happy to oblige.

Men were still lingering round the smouldering mass, watching the drama as the ceilings caved in and the rafters fell. They all wanted to say they had been there the night Thornfield Hall burnt down. They came to help carry the corpse to Mr Merryman's cart with murmurs of mingled pity and horror.

"Poor mad soul. At peace now. I saw her. She were on the roof. Squire went in to rescue her. I saw him up there myself. He got all the servants out. He tried to stop her jumping. Fought with her on the roof." They exchanged these and similar snippets of fact and fiction as they gently carried the body and exclaimed at how dark the lady's skin was and how tall she was for a madwoman.

I wanted to ask why madness stunted your growth but I restrained myself. I did not want to interrupt the process that was taking place around me. They were all conspiring to create a story, to build a myth. According to this version of events, Thornfield Hall had been set on fire by Mr Rochester's mad wife whom he kept confined in the attic. Like a noble master he had made sure all the servants were evacuated and then had gone on the roof to rescue his lunatic wife. In spite of his efforts she managed to jump from there to her death. I noted how well Mr Rochester came out of this version. From being his wife's gaoler and a failed bigamist he had become the hero of the hour. All I had to do was to stay quiet and let the process of mythmaking run its course.

The errors of fact were many and various. The fire had been started in the library by Mr Rochester himself. He had been drinking brandy and had a candle to read by; it was not the first time he had been careless with candles. His wife was no longer mad, though her abilities were somewhat limited. To the best of my knowledge she was a woman with a trust fund on her way to live somewhere south, very far south of Grimsby.

Martha had left Thornfield Hall in the same coach as her baby son. For some reason or other she had abandoned the journey. I prayed to God that she had also abandoned her son. I knew Martha's first thought in a burning building would be to save herself and not her son. I pictured the child left to the mercy of the flames, his little limbs unable to move him from danger, his tiny mouth sucking in the deadly smoke. I shuddered so at this dreadful vision that I rattled the whole cart and startled the horse.

"Steady now, steady," Merryman urged the horse and put a hand on my arm.

I gathered my wits. Reason asserted itself. Would Bertha let Martha take the baby from her arms? Even though Martha was the child's mother, it would not happen. Bertha would hang on to the child. She would not let a second child be taken from her in the night. She would resist and Bertha was a woman who knew how to fight; she had gouged and bitten her own brother.

Martha must have returned secretly to Thornfield Hall. There she must have hidden herself on the third floor. The door at the foot of the stairs had been left unlocked after Grace, Bertha, Martha and the baby had left. She could have sneaked in, up the back stairs, along the gallery and up to the third floor. There she had hidden herself. Late that night I had made a final tour of the rooms. I had stopped short of going into Martha's bedroom. I had descended the stairs and locked the door behind me.

I must have locked Martha in.

The thought screamed in my ears and vibrated in my brain. I had not checked the room Martha used. I had never let her have a key to the staircase door. When she had discovered the fire, she must have run down the stairs. Her way out would be blocked by the locked door. As the flames and smoke and heat battered at the door she must have climbed up into the attic, opened the trap door and climbed out onto the roof. There she would have found temporary relief, until the fire found its way inexorably upwards. In the end the heat drove her to take that final fatal leap.

Disturbed though I was I said nothing to my rescuer; silence has often been my friend. I let Mr Merryman talk as he drove me and the body to his inn. As he guided his horse through the darkness I listened as he worked on his account of the fire at Thornfield Hall. He seemed to be unaware that I had been present for the whole time and that he had arrived after all the main events had taken place.

Mr Merryman was not going to let a few inconvenient facts interfere with a good story. It became clear that he had assigned himself a leading role in the drama. By the time I saw the sign outside the Rochester Arms he had been first to arrive at the fire, well before the fire engines. Soon he would be claiming that he had seen Mr Rochester on the roof struggling to save his mad wife from the flames.

It was all very satisfactory from my point of view.

The Rochester Arms welcomed me with a bed and a bowl of water. The mirror provided me with a view of my smoke-blackened face and hair. Washing turned the water black and yet my face and hands were still several shades darker than normal. I left word with the landlord that I was keen to acquire some respectable clothes first thing in the morning. If the local ladies had

Martha and I Join the Gentry

1832

My account books were destroyed in the fire but I did my best to calculate the wages owed to the servants and to advance them some small sums to see them over the next few days. Then I made a start on writing their references. I planned to distribute them after the funeral. My intention was that the servants would be obliged to attend the service. I was determined that Bertha/Martha should not go to her grave alone and unlamented. I felt I owed her what is called a good send-off. There should be mourners, mourners who could act as witnesses, if questions were ever asked.

I sent Mr Rochester a list of what was owed to the servants in wages and compensation. They would need replacements for the uniforms they had lost in the fire; these were valuable items. In the testimonials I explained how they were put out of work through no fault of their own but as a result of the destruction caused by a fire. I stressed that they were not responsible in any way for the fire and had behaved with admirable calm. The unhandsome footman received full credit for his courageous rescue of Mr Rochester. As they say, handsome is as handsome does.

Mr Rochester's agent arrived with sufficient funds for me to pay the servants and for my own expenses. He also brought news of his employer. Mr Rochester was still at Mr Carter's where he was recovering slowly. The agent described his injuries and shook his head in sorrow at how Mr Rochester had been mutilated by the fire. I was sorry that Mr Rochester had lost his sight, but I could not help thinking that here was an advantage for me. A blind man can hardly challenge the identity of the corpse.

"Back to being the same old master in his mind though." The agent called me back to the present. "Added the money all up in his head and worked out how many notes, how many half crowns and how many shillings you'd need to give everyone his due. Generous, too. Dress lengths for the ladies and — begging your pardon Mrs Fairfax — new underthings too. He says to tell them he'll speak for them. Anyone as wants a character can ask new master to send word. He'll speak up for them."

And much good his words will do them in this neighbourhood, I thought. The Cliffords and the Dents had not taken kindly to his attempt at bigamy and the Ingrams spat at the mention of his name. Emboldened by the knowledge of Mr Rochester's loss of sight I asked the agent, "Will he be coming to the funeral? I expect most of the household to attend."

"Now that's another story. That's when I see another side of master. He snarls and rages and claws at his collar like it's choking him. His one eye that's left looks like it's going to pop out his head he's that angry. Just bury her deep, he says. With a stake through her heart. Put stones on top of coffin. Make sure she stays there."

We were silent for a moment as we contemplated such hatred in a man so generous and large-minded in other ways.

"He's had a falling out with Mr Wood too," the agent offered.

Good, I thought, but did not say. I do not like Mr Wood; he has taken my husband's place but he does not fill it with distinction. Mr Rochester is not the only one who can harbour irrational hatreds. The agent went on to explain.

"Parson says she's not to go in consecrated ground. Claims she committed suicide."

"What did Mr Rochester think to that?"

"He was very angry. He don't take lightly to being thwarted. Especially by parson. Blames him for stopping his wedding to Miss Eyre. He summoned Mr Wood and gave him a dressing down from his sick bed. You could hear him all over Carter's house. Threatened to put parson on roof and light a fire under him. See whether he waited for a miracle or whether he jumped."

"I guess he won that argument."

"Aye. Parson wasn't happy at being bested. So he came on a new tack. Said she couldn't go in the family vault. Claimed he had the power to decide. As it's inside the church itself. Master goes mad. Rochesters been buried there for hundreds of years. Wives too. Parson says not this one. She's lucky to be going in churchyard in consecrated ground."

"I guess Mr Rochester reminded Mr Wood where the butter on his bread comes from."

"He did indeed. Pointed out it's his family's church, his family's burial place and his family's living to dispose of. Parson soon saw the error of his ways. It's decided. She's to go in the family vault and have 'Bertha, wife of Edward Fairfax Rochester' inscribed on the side. With the date of her death."

"Not 'dearly beloved wife'. That would be too much. The servants will be coming to the service. I'm paying them what's due afterwards."

The agent laughed. "Not the kind of mourners you expect at a Rochester funeral. Parson's going to be disappointed. Gentry'll not come. Bigamy and a mad wife. Probably nothing much to talk about in London but here in Yorkshire . . ." He rolled his eyes to heaven and sucked his cheeks in to mimic the gentry's disapproval. "I'll not see you at the funeral, Mrs Fairfax."

"You are mistaken. I'll be there."

"But I won't. Special commission from master. Auction of Ingram Park. I'm to bid for master."

"Auction! That's quick. The old baron's not been dead a year."

"Aye. The young'un has set a record in how quick you can lose an estate. It's to be sold over the new baron's head. And his mother's and sisters' too."

314

"And Mr Rochester wants to buy it. Of course the land adjoins his. No doubt this is how the Rochesters got their hands on so much land in the first place."

He nodded. "True. But it is not the land this time. Not enough cash in the coffers to buy the whole lot. Money has been flowing out like water."

I restrained a smile. Thirty thousand had flowed in my direction.

The agent went on. "I am commissioned to bid for the dower house. If I succeed I'm to tell the Ingram ladies they can have it as their home. Peppercorn rent. Master seems to think he owes them."

"Certainly, Blanche. He is in debt to Blanche. He wasted her good name in pursuit of Jane. I like a man who pays his debts."

"Unlike the new Baron Ingram."

The agent set off on his next errand.

I was pleased to hear that the battering of Mr Rochester's body seemed to have restored the working of his mind. Not only was he taking charge of his affairs, he was also busy remedying some of the wrongs he had done. I guessed he still lived in hope of having Jane restored to him. Better for him to be able to claim her with a clear conscience; she would examine him over his misdeeds as severely as a confessor. She would not forgive his sins easily.

By contrast I wondered what poor Martha would think about the fate of the object of her affections — the bankrupt baronet. She would probably weep at his misfortune and claim it wasn't his fault. She would blame the bookies, the horses or the colour of the jockeys' silks for the effete nobleman's ruin. What she did not know was that Old John had a hand in his downfall. She would not have taken kindly to such interference from her grandfather's old friend.

Mr Merryman brought me word that the coffin was ready. I took it upon myself to prepare the body. I wanted Martha to be in gentle hands. That was what I told myself. To be strictly honest it was a practical rather than a pious decision; I couldn't risk anyone else identifying her. I suppose, too, like Pontius Pilate I wanted to wash some of my guilt away. Sending her to Lord Ingram's had been my doing, though her seduction there was not part of my plan. I should have warned her against the Ingram men — and the women, come to that! As I worked I reminded the unresponsive Martha that I had given her shelter and a place to give birth when the rest of the world turned its face against her.

When I took the pennies from her eyes her gaze seemed to pursue me with accusation. "That's all very well," it said, "but you turned the key that locked me in." There was no answer to that. As I washed her face I saw there was little risk of her being identified. The wound on her forehead helped to disguise her features. Her poor face and hands were scorched by the fire. Black smoke had settled in the cracks and fissures scorched into her flesh. I worked very gently for fear of pulling off the fragile flaking skin and, to be honest, it suited my purposes that there should be a certain duskiness in her colouring. The word in the neighbourhood was that the real Mrs Rochester was positively black.

When I had dressed her in a clean white gown Mr Merryman came to help me put the body in the coffin. I used the time we were together to feed him some snippets of information about the fire, details he could weave into the story he was making to entertain his customers for years to come. Mr Rochester was far from perfect but he had many good qualities. I did not want him to go down in history as a drunken sot who burned his own house down.

"You remember the third-floor rooms at the front, don't you Mr Merryman?" Indeed he did. "That was where the fire started. The lady lived up there. We had some nice hangings up there. She must have set fire to them. And the bed in the governess's room next to me. That was set on fire too. I expect she did that for sheer wickedness. I'd have burnt in my own bed if Mr Rochester had not been so prompt to save me." Between us we lifted the body of Martha. "Gently now. There. Poor girl. She is at peace now."

Girl! I called her a girl! I should have said "lady". Mr Merryman appeared not to have noticed the slip of my tongue. My fingers trembled as I arranged her hands. I was in a panic that he would notice there was no wedding ring on her finger. He was peering closely into the coffin. I felt his breath on my neck as he leant over to examine her face. Would he see beneath the scars and the crust of grime the features of Martha, the Martha he had known briefly all those years ago when he was butler to my first Mr Rochester?

317

I need not have worried; he saw what he wanted to see.

"She is very dark is she not? You can see the wickedness in her face even in death. Mr Rochester is more to be pitied than blamed."

I breathed a sigh of relief. Like a lamb to slaughter he had obligingly come to the right conclusion from the evidence I had placed before his eyes. I hoped the rest of the neighbourhood would follow his example. "Fasten down the lid, Mr Merryman. There is no one else who will come to pay their respects to this poor creature."

With every turn of the screws I felt a weight fall from my shoulders. My last and greatest fear still remained like a ball of ice where my heart should be. I feared that as the ruins of Thornfield Hall cooled a search party would find among the debris a tiny blackened corpse, a little life cruelly destroyed. If baby James really had perished in the fire, by the laws of nature I should place him in this very coffin so he could rest on his mother's heart.

The next day the coffin was loaded onto Mr Merryman's cart, the same one that had carried us away from the fire. As I sat on the board next to Mr Merryman I used the time to rehearse the story of the great fire at Thornfield Hall until he was word perfect. How he had arrived first, long before the fire engines, how he had seen the madwoman on the roof. Indeed he had seen Mr Rochester climb to the roof and struggle

318

with the huge dark woman with the great mane of hair. He had seen her fall and smash upon the paving stones.

He startled me by asking about Mrs Poole, the madwoman's keeper; he had learned his lesson too well. I had no role prepared for Grace in the story. I could not let her be trapped in the building to be consumed by the flames. The search of the ruins would reveal no body. I racked my brains for a plausible answer. I was sure I was the only one to see both Grace and Bertha depart. The new servants were too busy with each other and their complaints about their treatment to concern themselves with the comings and goings of the residents of the top floor. They had not noticed the absence of Grace or Bertha when we counted heads before we fled the burning Thornfield Hall. How could I remove Grace from the scene without setting off a hue and cry in search for her? Inspiration came.

"Gin," I explained promptly. "She had a weakness for gin. I expect she over-indulged and fell asleep. Woke to find the house in flames. Knew she should have watched the madwoman better. Fled in shame at the dereliction of her duty." I crossed my fingers as I spoke and asked for Grace to forgive me for the calumny.

Mr Merryman nodded wisely and a great smile of satisfaction spread across his face. He had the perfect story for his customers now. It had drama, a hero — himself — death and fire engines. Best of all, the whole catastrophe was the fault of some women, one mad and one drunk. How they would enjoy that in the snug bar! The men would puff on their pipes, nod knowingly and

319

order another pint of the landlord's best. After a happy evening basking in masculine superiority they would go home and regale their wives with the story. The wives, isolated in their cottages and farmhouses, would lap up this dramatic tale of fire, death and bigamy. This authorized version would soon spread round the whole neighbourhood.

It was a motley group of servants who collected in the church for the funeral service. The poor souls were dressed in the clothes they had scrambled into on the night of the fire, supplemented by a few garments borrowed from the villagers' scant wardrobes. I cannot say that my well-worn and shabby clothing was what I would have chosen for the occasion. It was bitter cold in the church and we shivered in our raggedy outfits. Many of the servants wore black armbands to show respect for the mad mistress they had not met but thought they were burying.

Considering the circumstances we made a respectable show of mourning. Sometimes appearances are more important than motive. It did not matter that it was the promise of their wages and compensation for their losses that had brought them to the funeral service. Or that I had misled them as to the identity of the body. A Rochester, even such an unsatisfactory one, was entitled to a certain amount of pomp.

We all stood with bowed heads as the coffin was carried in. Mr Wood set a cracking pace as he strode down the aisle in front of it. It was clear that he wanted this service to be over as quickly as possible. I was surprised to see Mr Carter walking behind the coffin in the position usually taken by the chief mourner. He carried his black top hat pressed against his chest and for once he was wearing dark trousers, not his riding breeches. As he reached the front pew where I sat he did a swift left turn and came to join me.

Under cover of all the rustling and coughing as we took our seats I asked him if he had come to represent Mr Rochester.

"You could say that," he told me out of the side of his mouth.

"I will say exactly that," I told him. "It is what the world wants to hear. Mr Rochester was too ill to attend his wife's funeral so he sent his friend to take his place." The conventions would be satisfied.

"Course, you could say he wants to be very sure that she is securely boxed up and buried very deep."

"You could say that, but we won't."

Meanwhile Mr Wood gabbled his way through the beautiful prose of the funeral service. Was he taking his revenge on Mr Rochester by deliberately mangling the words? I wondered if it was any consolation to poor, silly, dead Martha that at last she was joining the gentry. Her body was to be interred in the Rochesters' tomb and would decay in the company of the bones of the local aristocracy. She had nursed an ambition to move up in the world and in death she had at last achieved it.

When the service was over Mr Carter said farewell to me and hurried after Mr Wood, who was speeding out of church with his surplice flapping about him. Before

321

the cleric reached the church door I heard Carter's great voice braying out how pleased he was that the vicar had seen reason and that he could give a good report on him to Mr Rochester. He made sure that none of us was left in doubt that the vicar took his orders from Mr Rochester rather than God.

Afterwards at the back of the chilly church I used a pew to spread out my calculations and the coins and notes that the staff were due. Most were grateful for the generosity of their payments. A surprising number already had offers of work or were happy to return to their parents' home until they had replaced their uniforms. The handsome footman was on his way to work for the mighty Clifford family. He was an exact match in height for one of their existing footmen. The not-so-handsome footman received a generous bonus for saving Mr Rochester from the flames. It seemed only fair. He was certainly not going to get any credit for his bravery in Mr Merryman's version of the story; that heroic action was sure to be undertaken by the landlord himself.

John Green came after I had finished handing out the money. I was glad Mr Wood had left the clerk to deal with the paperwork; he had been so kind to Leah and behaved so well after the notoriously interrupted wedding.

"Strange to see business done in a church. A little like the money changers in the temple," he remarked.

"Yes. You have no objection to my paying these people what is their due? They have lost all their clothes and belongings."

322

He shook his head. "There is no better place than a church for such a deed." When I had finished saying farewell to the servants it was time to deal with the paperwork of death. Mr Green had his pen and his book ready. "I must fill in the details of the lady's death in the Parish Register. Can you give me her full name?"

That was a nasty moment. I could not avoid giving Bertha's name. What a storm it would cause if I suddenly decided to say it was Martha in the coffin! There was no going back. I took a breath. "She is Bertha Antoinette Rochester. She was born in Spanish Town, Jamaica."

The pen scratched as he wrote the words. "She was the wife of Edward Fairfax Rochester?"

If only she had not been! What a deal of misery would have been saved. I nodded and he wrote in the date of the fire as the date of her death. I had to do some calculations to work out a year for her birth. I guessed she was between thirty five and forty. I knew she was a little older than Mr Rochester. In the end we settled on 1794. I could not give a month. Bertha did not concern herself with birthdays.

I checked that the clerk knew the exact wording to be inscribed on the vault. He allowed himself a brief smile. "Just wife. No beloveds or dearly missed. And the date of her death. We do not want there to be a repeat of the unfortunate events in this church when Mr Rochester tried to marry Miss Eyre."

I pictured Mr Rochester if he found his beloved Jane. He would bring her to inspect the vault and point to the inscription. There engraved in stone for all to see would be the incontestable record of the demise of Bertha Rochester. I asked the efficient clerk if he would make a copy of the entry in the register of deaths, so I could send one to Mr Rochester. He made one so quickly and so easily I was emboldened to ask, "Will you make one for me? I will keep it safe in case the other one is lost. Mr Rochester has lost his sight and is very ill at the moment. He may not appreciate the importance of the document." How glibly the small untruths slipped from my tongue once that first great falsehood had passed my lips!

Mr Green obliged me, as people so often do if asked politely. I folded the piece of paper and slotted it between the pages of my bible. It made a fitting companion to the flimsy first letter I received from Mr Rochester where he announced he was bringing a mad lady to live at Thornfield Hall. For some reason I had kept that letter. The two documents lay side by side, the beginning and the end, the alpha and the omega of Mr Rochester's mad wife.

Mr Merryman drove me back to the Rochester Arms. I fed him a further detail to add to his story. Terribly injured though he was, Mr Rochester had sent the surgeon to represent him at the funeral of his poor mad wife. I was anxious that Mr Merryman include this fact in his account. The rehabilitation of my former employer's reputation in the neighbourhood was the final service I could undertake for him. By the time we reached The Rochester Arms Mr Merryman had his lines by heart.

I may have led Mr Merryman by the nose over the events of the fire but when it came to travelling by stagecoach he had the advantage of me; he was an expert on the subject. The coaches regularly stopped at The Rochester Arms to water the horses. Passengers could be picked up or dropped off there. "You must pay four pounds for an inside ticket if you possibly can," the landlord urged me. "It's only two pounds for an outside ticket, but it is fearsome cold up there on the top. And they put the livestock up there once they've filled the boot."

I thanked him for his concern for my purse. Money was the least of my worries, but I wasn't going to tell Mr Merryman that. It was difficult enough concealing my destination from him. Just south of Grimsby was not precise enough for the knowledgeable landlord. I claimed some relatives in a village nearby and said I would send word to them when I was nearer my destination. In my desperation to end his inquisition I invented a name for this imaginary place. True to form he thought he might have a connection who lived in the vicinity. I promised to look up his acquaintance when I arrived. It was a relief to board the coach in the morning and to say farewell to the invaluable Mr Merryman.

My relief did not last long. There were only two other passengers, respectably dressed businessmen or clerks, when I climbed into the coach optimistically named Meteor. We soon acquired the full complement of six passengers crammed inside and heaven only knows what was piled on the top. Much of the life up there squawked or squealed while those inside talked, and talked and talked. My sole consolation was that I no longer had to conceal who I was or where I was going. Nobody was interested in the shabby old lady in the corner. Each new passenger who climbed aboard was much too busy with his or her own affairs to be concerned with a nondescript widow woman.

As I listened to my fellow passengers' talk of their journeys, their destinations and their purposes I detected new and unfamiliar accents. When the realization came to me that I had left Yorkshire, the county of my birth, I felt the tears rise in my eyes. I had never travelled beyond its boundary before and now I would never set foot there again. The occupants of Thornfield Hall were lost to me and the house was ruined. I closed my mind to the past as I would pull down a blind on a window and made myself look to the future. I tried to picture the house I was going to live in. I saw Grace and Bertha there, I dressed them in fine silk, I saw them waited on by servants. Suddenly the image crumbled. There was a gap in the very centre, the heart of it. Where was the baby? Where was James in this image of the future? Had I locked him in with his mother?

When night fell I clambered stiffly out of the coach and made enquiries about a bed at the inn. The landlord looked me up and down and proceeded to offer me a place in a room with six others. "There's two other females," he assured me. "There isn't another spare bed in the house." How I longed for my black silk dress and my starched white cap and my fur-lined cape.

What was the point of my new-found wealth if I had to pile into a bed with so many other bodies? I offered the landlord money. He took it and showed me to the garret where the maid normally slept. She scowled at him — and at me — as she was forced to move out but I was past caring. In the morning I examined the damage to my person. My legs were covered in tiny red lumps. The bed bugs had been busy in the night. In this manner my journey continued. Tiresome, uncomfortable and lacking in privacy.

I had received many warnings from Mr Merryman about the dangers of travel. My purse was to be kept close at all times and I should be wary of the entire population of the parts of England that were not Yorkshire. Everybody was in a conspiracy to trick the unwary traveller out of her money. I need not have feared. I looked too poor to tempt even the most desperate thief. Indeed I received much kindness from strangers who took pity on a poor elderly female travelling without the assistance of a man. Their advice about the best route, though well-meant, was often contradictory. I fear I may not have taken the most direct route but eventually I arrived at my destination.

When the coach stopped at The Coach and Horses on the High Street I dismounted and looked about me with wonder at the town that was to be my home. The long vista of the turnpike road stretched to my left and my right. A handsome bridge spanned the river. A church spire pierced the air. I felt a thrill of excitement; I had never lived in a town! I had always lived in the countryside, surrounded by woods and green fields.

Here houses lined the road without interruption. The street was thronged with people, carts and carriages; all was noise and bustle.

"If you please, ma'am, would you be Mrs Fairfax?" A young boy stood before me. He was dressed in the haphazard way of poor boys who grow out of their clothes with astonishing speed or ruin them with rough play. I assured him I was indeed Mrs Fairfax. "In that case, ma'am, if you will take a seat here at The Coach and Horses I will go to tell Mrs Poole you have arrived. She has bid me to look out for you." Wondrous polite he was!

He set off with all the speed his young legs were capable of. No sooner had he disappeared round the corner into some alley than I heard shouts and scuffles and a long wail of defeat. I guessed he had been waylaid by some bigger boy who would now claim his reward. I sat in the inn and waited.

I did not have to wait long. Grace appeared in the doorway, followed by a tall lad. He raised his hand to point at me and then held it out for his reward. I could see Grace was taken aback by my appearance. She stared at me for several seconds; she found it hard to reconcile the worn and shabby woman in front of her with the Mrs Fairfax of Thornfield Hall she had left behind. By contrast, Grace was looking sleekly groomed and polished. Her dress was of a fine lustrous fabric; her white cap, trimmed with lace, was freshly starched. She was every inch the genteel lady.

I was glad of her hand to help me rise from my seat; my legs had gone weak and started to tremble. "It is not far," she murmured. "Just round the corner." She looked round the room, crowded with travellers and their belongings. "Your luggage?"

I pointed to the small bundle at my feet. "That is it. Everything went. In the fire."

Grace's jaw dropped briefly. "Fire!" she repeated.

"This is no place for explanations," I warned her.

"Let us get you home. Your new home. I think you will approve."

In the doorway the boy waited with his hand out for his reward. "Not him," I told Grace. "This one's a bully. It was a much smaller boy. There he is." I'd spotted the wondrous polite boy, his face streaked with tears. As she passed the large boy in the doorway Grace elbowed him sharply in the ribs. He gasped and would have protested loudly if he'd had the breath. No one would believe him. Grace was obviously every inch the respectable lady.

"I feel better after that." Grace spoke with satisfaction. "I can't abide bullies. If there weren't so many witnesses I'd have boxed his ears. Now I am a lady I have to be careful about appearances." She beckoned to the tear-stained boy and put a shilling in his hand. "Now carry Mrs Fairfax's bag to my house and you can have a bit of dinner in the kitchen. By the time you've finished the big lad will have found someone else to bother. With luck you'll get your shilling home."

Grace led me into what I afterwards learned was called the Market Place and to a fine double-fronted house. A neat little maid opened the door to us and led the boy off to the kitchen. In the handsome drawing room was Bertha, dressed in grey silk. She sat by the window and was busy with some embroidery. The scene was tranquil, ordered, a picture of domestic bliss. There was one thing missing. There was no sign of the baby.

"James!" The name came out as a croak. Fear strangled the voice in my throat. "Where is James?"

"Why? Bless you!" said Grace. "He's asleep in the nursery. He always has a nap at this time."

What a fool I was! I thought that once I arrived at my new home and found the baby had survived, my life would be plain sailing. I would live in a calm upland without the storms and dramas that had plagued my life recently. When I discovered that baby James was safe, I don't mind admitting, I fell into hysterics. All my carefully guarded strength deserted me. I cried for several days and just couldn't stop. My mind, normally so clear and decisive, ran out of my control. It felt as if it had melted into a great river that was so choked with water that it overflowed its banks.

Between them Grace and Bertha nursed me. I was in a great fever and alternately cried by day and raged by night, convinced that the heat that consumed me came from the flames sweeping through Thornfield Hall. I had not sent Grace and Bertha word of the fire. They had no clear account of the disaster, so they found many of my ravings difficult to understand. One thing

330

was clear to them; I feared baby James was no longer with us.

Every day, Bertha brought the baby to the doorway of my room to show me that he lived and thrived. They would not bring him closer for fear of contagion. Bertha would list his small achievements to me: he had tasted porridge, he had smiled, he had slept for six hours. At night she would take his chubby arm and wave it at me to say goodnight.

Every night in my sleep I would forget. In my dreams I would scour the third floor of Thornfield Hall. As the flames licked at my ankles, I hoped desperately to hear his feeble cry above the roar of the inferno. Sometimes I would stand outside in the grounds, a helpless spectator, while Martha in her nightgown, with her baby in her arms, sought escape from the roof. In despair she would come to the edge and hurl the tiny body into the air. I would strain my outstretched arms to catch the flying baby — and fail. He would crash onto the paving stones at my feet and I would wake wailing. Grace would come to comfort me.

Two weeks passed before I woke to find myself in a bright and pleasant room. And in more or less my right mind. There was a bell on my bedside table. I rang it. A smartly dressed maid appeared. She would tell Mrs Poole and Mrs Mason that I was awake and would bring me tea. She drew the curtains and made to leave the room. I heard my voice speak as if of its own volition. My words floated across the room. "And Master James. Where is he?"

"Why, bless you, ma'am. His nurse is giving him his breakfast. Up on the third floor."

And this time I believed her.

That afternoon Grace arrived at my bedside with two glasses of porter. "I've prescribed it for you," she announced. "And for myself." She raised her glass to her lips and drank with obvious satisfaction. "Now we are such grand ladies we have to keep our coarse habits secret."

"I thought we'd done with secrets."

"Not entirely. We are doing very nicely at inventing our past lives here. We are both widows, of course. My late husband was a medical man, like his son. Bertha's was a merchant in Spanish Town, Jamaica. No one here is very interested in our past. They find the price of land and cattle more important."

"How is Bertha managing?"

"Very well. The baby is a great distraction to people. How he's grown. Has he teeth? That sort of thing. She can cope with that; she was never one for complicated conversations."

"How have you explained James?" I asked Grace.

"He is Bertha's nephew. Child of a wayward niece. We try to look embarrassed when we say that and so far no one has pursued it further."

I smiled. How often have I seen it happen? News of the impending arrival of an illegitimate child sours faces, screwing them up with disapproval. The physical presence of such a child brings a softening smile to the pursed lips of respectability.

"Tell me about Martha," I commanded Grace. "I want the authorized version from you."

Grace, as usual, was brisk. "I told you I would deal with Martha. When we left Thornfield Hall, all the way to the turnpike road she was crying and sobbing fit to burst. Then she banged on the roof to get the coachman to stop. Claimed she was homesick, frightened to go away from the place she knew. She couldn't leave Yorkshire, never mind go to Grimsby; we had not told her that our real destination was considerably further south. There was a handsome new footman she had hopes of. She was convinced he had a fancy for her.

"In the end I said we would stop the chaise and she could walk back to Thornfield. It was no more than a couple of miles. The moon was very low and bright that night. Out she gets with her bag and her cloak and the driver points out the way for her. She sets off and the driver climbs back on his box and has his whip raised to start the horses. I shout him to stop and call out to Martha. I ask her if she's forgotten something. She looks puzzled for a moment. So I say to her, 'Your baby. You've forgotten your baby.' That stops her in her tracks.

"She doesn't want to take him but she doesn't like to say so. I tell her we'll take him. And we'll take good care of him. She hesitates but I can see she wants to say yes. So I offer her twenty pounds for him and that clinches it. She gets back in the coach and we write a bit of something on a piece of paper and I give her the twenty gold sovereigns. I had taken the precaution of

333

hiding them about my person. I thought I might bribe her into parting with him. I nearly fainted with relief when the deal was done. I don't know what I would have done if she'd wanted to take him back to Thornfield with her. Bertha would have gone for her throat rather than part with him. Murder would have been done that night."

"It was."

That shook Grace. Never one to waste a word, "Explain," she commanded me.

So I told Grace about Martha, and locking the door. I told her about the fire and the leap from the roof. And how everyone thought it was Bertha and that I had not corrected them. And how I'd coached Mr Merryman to spread the story and how Bertha would be blamed for starting the fire — and Grace herself. I even told her about the gin.

"I never thought the silly baggage would creep back into the house like that. I thought she'd go straight to the servants' hall to make eyes at the handsome footman."

"No one knew she was there. I expect she arrived late and went straight up to the third floor. She'd want her beauty sleep to be ready for the handsome footman. And knowing Martha she'd want a nice lie-in the morning."

"Who knows? You just hold on to that thought, Alice Fairfax. You are not the only one to blame. For a start, there's Martha herself, and then there's your beloved Mr Rochester and his careless ways with candles. He started the fire." She wagged her finger at me like a school ma'am pressing a lesson home.

I lay back on the pillows and pondered her advice. "You must show me that piece of paper Martha signed some time." I leant across to pick up my tiny bible. "We have quite an interesting collection of documents now." I passed Grace the copy of Bertha Rochester's death certificate. She whistled through her teeth. "Better not make a sound like that in the drawing room when there are guests," I warned her.

"So Bertha Rochester is officially dead. Long live Bertha Mason." Grace straightened her cap and thought for a moment. "I don't think we need bother Bertha with that piece of information."

"She might turn snappish."

Grace laughed. Not the unearthly ghoulish laughter she had used at Thornfield Hall to warn Bertha of approaching danger. It was a warm full-throated chuckle.

Postscript

1833

By the new year my health had recovered. It was with a mixture of trepidation and delight that I looked forward to life in my new home in Berkshire. For our plan to work our disappearance from Yorkshire had to be both secret and complete. Now that it was thought that Bertha was dead it was imperative that our whereabouts should not be traced. Even here I keep the details hidden; I am still wary of being found.

Neighbours had called and left cards for Grace and Bertha when they first arrived. In their ignorance of the conventions of the gentry they simply ignored them. As soon as I was well enough I remedied this mistake and called on neighbouring families. Bertha and Grace were very puzzled by the fact that what were described as "morning calls" were always made in the afternoon.

Not everyone returned my visit but we were soon acquainted with some very pleasant people; the presence of a baby in a house always speeds up the making of friends. Bertha and I are now generally accepted as gentry. Grace, they are not so sure about. The fact that her son is a medical man provides her with a quick varnish of middle-class respectability. Our sober behaviour and handsome income have added depth to the illusion.

Grace is her usual inscrutable self. Her warning about former servants making bad mistresses has not come true. On the whole she leaves the management of the servants to me. Her greatest pleasure is to have her own newspaper. A small boy brings one of the London papers to the house. As soon as it has cooled after the housemaid has ironed out the creases, it is put at Grace's place on the breakfast table. She loves the cracking sound as she opens out the pages and knows that she is the first to read them. For myself, I miss the good old *Yorkshire Herald*.

When she is not reading her newspaper Grace still spends most of her time with Bertha. They both love to go out to take the air in their own carriage. After years of being confined to the third floor, only venturing out in darkness or behind a black veil, they delight in ordering the horses to be harnessed to the brougham. They sit behind the smartly dressed coachman as they bowl along the country lanes admiring the soft green hills and the fluffy white sheep. Grace insisted on having a handsome and cheerful coachman, such a contrast to grumpy Old John.

Bertha is much improved. Since she suckled James all the rage and anger has left her. It is as if some urgent need of her body has been satisfied and it no longer torments her admittedly limited mind. I fretted that she would not want the baby to be weaned. I need not have worried; the process was accomplished smoothly by both baby and foster mother. Occasionally she takes to her room and cries for a couple of days but the paroxysms of rage are a thing of the past.

She has learnt how to blend in with society. She is regarded as both a handsome widow and a kind aunt to the adorable James. Her Thursday evening entertainments are acquiring a reputation in the town. The food is fine and the wine good. Bertha says very little but nods her agreement with the opinions of the gentlemen. In this way she has won a reputation for good conversation. We have had to forbid her from playing cards in company. Her skill with numbers enabled her to win too often and too thoroughly; success at cards is not regarded as ladylike. Now she sticks to her embroidery when there are guests present. When Grace's son visits, the four of us play cards in front of the drawing-room fire. We send the maids to bed early and secretly drink porter. Bertha wins most of the time and delights in demanding her small winnings. We pay her with what is in truth her own money.

I blame much of her illness on her unfortunate marriage to Mr Rochester. It blighted both their lives. Bertha has survived but I wonder sometimes if all his misfortunes have succeeded in destroying his spirit. Jane is gone, his place in society is lost, his home is a blackened ruin and he has terrible injuries to bear. I am saddened to think that a man of such allure and vivacity has been brought so low.

I have had to turn my back on the past but it still has a hold on me; it gives me bad dreams that wake me in the small hours. Clear as day I will hear my voice cajoling Martha into looking for work away from Thornfield Hall. At other times the palm of my right hand tingles and smarts and I know that I have just delivered a ringing slap to her face to stop her screaming from the pains of labour. Sometimes I think I can smell burning and I feel the heat of the flames on my face and arms. I have to get up and patrol the house to check that all the candles are safely out. The first room I go to is James's nursery on the third floor. I hold up my candle and look at his smooth baby cheek and his little round arms and watch his sweet innocent breathing, and I grow calm and wonder at the good fortune that has befallen me.

My resolve to cut all ties with Yorkshire lasted nine months. It was the thought of Leah's baby that snapped my willpower. I set up an elaborate route through the lawyer in Grimsby to get a letter to Leah and arranged for her to reply through the same intermediary. I gave her some excuse for the procedure, said I was moving about visiting friends and relations. Even to Leah, I could not risk revealing my true address, although I knew she would guard it with vigilance. I was mindful that Jane Eyre's wedding had been prevented by the coincidence of her letter to her uncle arriving in Madeira when Bertha's brother was there.

Leah wrote that her baby had arrived safely — a girl. The child was healthy and her family flourished in the clean air of their farm. Leah had little time for sewing now as she spent many hours in the kitchen cooking the good food that John's farm provided. As for John, he was as happy as a king. He would be even happier if the child due next year turned out to be a boy. Every farmer needs a son — or two.

Leah was sorry to hear about the death of Bertha, who had endured a most unhappy life. I was shocked to realize that I had deceived Leah along with the rest of the neighbourhood. She too now believed that the woman who jumped from the burning roof of Thornfield Hall was Bertha. I felt uncomfortable having deceived my young friend. There was nothing I could do to disabuse Leah of her mistaken belief. In a way it was pleasing to think that the story I had created about the fire at Thornfield Hall had been so successful. The later part of Leah's letter contained some interesting news. There had been developments in the story of Jane and Mr Rochester.

Mr Rochester had gone to live at Ferndean, where Old John and Mary looked after him. His faithful old servants were convinced that he could not bear to move far from the ruin that was Thornfield Hall, in case Jane came looking for him. In the summer Jane did exactly that. She was no longer a poor friendless governess; she arrived as a woman with an independent income inherited from the uncle in Madeira. She found her old master a much changed man, battered in body and subdued in spirit.

What had not changed was the love between them. It sprang into immediate and passionate life like a fire from hot embers. Mr Rochester proved that his spirit had not been entirely crushed by his misfortunes and that he was still capable of bold and decisive action. A special licence was obtained — from the bishop himself. I was pleased that he had managed to arrange his wedding without the offices of the objectionable Mr Wood. In the eyes of God and the necessary witnesses Jane Eyre and Edward Fairfax Rochester were duly united in holy matrimony. And this time there was no officious solicitor in the congregation to say that the groom already had a wife. The bishop himself had declared that Mr Rochester was free to marry.

So, Reader, Jane married him. Well, that's what she thinks. Grace and I are the only people alive to know that the body lying in the Rochester tomb is Martha, an obscure, silly and unfortunate girl. The words "Bertha Rochester, wife of Edward Fairfax Rochester", and the date of her death, now deeply etched in stone, are a complete fiction. Both Jane and Mr Rochester genuinely believe that Bertha died, jumping from the roof of Thornfield Hall as the fire destroyed it. Mr Rochester witnessed it with his own eyes and Jane accepted the official version.

She believes she is married to him; therefore she is married to him. Such a pity she could not have him in the splendour of his prime, when he had his health and vigour! An unkind piece of me thinks that the strait-laced Jane might prefer him now he is humbled and brought low. There is a self-denying streak in her nature that fits her to be the saintly nurse and helpmeet of a damaged sinner.

I sit in my fine drawing room and look out upon the market place. I ring the bell and a maid brings me tea. As I drink from the fine china cup, one of the tea service that I chose and paid for myself, I work my way through the list of people that I care for and I am satisfied with how my plans for them have worked out. John and Leah prosper on their farm. If Sophie's plans work out she and Sam should be in business in Harrogate. I cannot see the old sailor staying there for long, but I cannot be responsible for every detail. Old John and Mary will see out their days in comfort as devoted and faithful servants. I can trust Miss Eyre — or Mrs Rochester as I should call her — to ensure their work load is not too heavy. One blank place on my list belongs to Adele. I wonder how she fares at her expensive school and whether Miss Eyre, that is, the new Mrs Rochester, will welcome her back into the Rochester household.

My list has a new name on it. I seem unable to stop feeling responsible for the welfare of others. The new addition is the small boy who was nearly bullied out of his tip for spotting me when I first alighted from the stagecoach at The Coach and Horses. He delivers Grace's newspaper and is rewarded with a hearty breakfast in our kitchen; he is filling out nicely now. He is much better dressed and much cleaner. His mother makes no objection to our contribution to his upbringing; she has too many children to waste her time looking in the mouth of a gift horse. I have my eye on the lad as a companion for James, a sort of substitute for an older brother. Unless Grace's son gets busy quickly James is condemned to be the solitary male child in a house with three honorary female aunts; it is certain that we shall spoil him.

He will inherit Bertha's trust fund, of course. We have not talked of it but I am sure that it will be the wish of us all. What a strange history he has already had in his brief life! He is supposed to be the son of a baron but has no right to the title. His so-called father offered his foolish mother five guineas before he was born. Grace bid twenty gold sovereigns for him. Now his natural father's estate is in ruins and has fallen under the auctioneer's hammer. Yet one day little James will be worth thirty thousand pounds, money that I picked from the pockets of my third Mr Rochester. The boy's value has grown faster than mushrooms.

I drink my tea and wonder about the fate of that other baby, Bertha's son, who was snatched from his cradle by unkind hands. Does the boy survive in the wild hidden heart of Jamaica? He is the firstborn legitimate son of Edward Fairfax Rochester and so is the true heir to the Rochester fortune. The chances are he is a barefoot and hungry fugitive. At least he will not be cold; I know from Bertha that it is very hot there.

I have done my best to be fair, to even out the injustices of life. I have plotted and planned and tweaked the strings of fate for many people but the boy in Jamaica is beyond my power. All I can do is to include him in my nightly prayers. My nightly prayers! I remember when my so-called prayers consisted of giving God a good ticking off for his unkindness to me. Now they no longer consist of outpourings of rage and despair but occasionally have a flavour of genuine devotion. As an independent woman with a comfortable income I find I am on much better terms with the Almighty.

It was Grace's idea that I should write this account of the events at Thornfield Hall. It would settle my mind, she said, help me let go of the past and stop my nightmares. Her plan worked; it is not so often now that the ghost of Martha appears in my dreams and points an accusing finger at me. I keep these pages locked in a drawer; one day I may feel strong enough to destroy them. If death takes me unexpectedly Grace has promised to burn them. The secrets they contain will go with me to my grave. Keeping secrets is a habit I caught from the Rochesters. You'll not find a Rochester writing about family matters for all the world to read.